Tales

OF THE
WILD WEST

AN ILLUSTRATED COLLECTION OF ADVENTURE STORIES

Tales
OF THE
WILD WEST

Compiled by Lois Brown

Introduction by B. Byron Price

NATIONAL COWBOY HALL OF FAME

WINGS BOOKS
New York • Avenel, New Jersey

This 1995 edition is published by Wings Books,
distributed by Random House Value Publishing, Inc.,
40 Engelhard Avenue, Avenel, New Jersey 07001,
by arrangement with Rizzoli International Publications, Inc.

Random House
New York • Toronto • London • Sydney • Auckland

Printed and bound in the United States of America

Library of Congress Cataloging–in–Publication Data

Tales of the Wild West : an illustrated collection of adventure stories /
compiled by Lois Brown ; introduction by B. Byron Price.
p. cm.
Contents: Up the trail / by B.J. Fletcher — Red and White on the border /
by T. Roosevelt — An outpost of civilization / by F. Remington — Oregon journal /
by V. St. Clair Chapman Mickelson — Top hand / by L. Short — From Missouri / by Z. Grey —
The gift of Cochise / by L. L'Amour — All Gold Canyon / by J. London — The fool's heart /
by E. M. Rhodes — An ingenue of the Sierras / by B. Harte — The Blue Hotel /
by S. Crane — The reformation of Calliope / by O. Henry
ISBN 0-517-14703-3
1. West (U.S.)—Literary collections. 2. Western stories. [1. West (U.S.) — Literary collections 2. Short stories.]
I. Price, B. Byron. II. Brown, Lois. III. National Cowboy Hall of Fame and Western Heritage Center.
PZ5.T267 1995
813' .087408—dc20   95-9766
CIP
AC

8 7 6 5 4 3 2 1

CONTENTS

INTRODUCTION

On a rainy fall afternoon more than fifteen years ago, I descended deep into Palo Duro Canyon in the Texas Panhandle in search of cowboy stories. Bouncing along a primitive red-dirt road more suitable for horses than automobiles, I followed the steep and sometimes difficult incline until it gave way to a level, grassy plain of extraordinary beauty. There, on the Prairie Dog Fork of the Red River, I met a weathered, bowlegged cowpuncher named Tom Blasingame, who had ridden the range for nearly sixty years.

At age seventy-seven, Tom lived alone, save for the *remuda* of horses he used to make his daily rounds over part of the still vast range of the historic JA Ranch. He had first worked for the JA as a teenager in 1916 but, driven by wanderlust and a desire to see what lay beyond the horizon, had not stayed long. Like many cowboys, he drifted from job to job, working for some of the largest and most famous outfits in the Southwest—the Bell Ranch of New Mexico, the Chiricuahua Cattle Company and the Double Circle Ranch of Arizona, and the Matador Ranch of Texas.

After some two decades on the move, Blasingame, now a top hand, returned to the JA Ranch during the 1930s. On large spreads like the JA, horse-drawn chuck wagons still accompanied roundup crews on their annual spring-to-fall circuit to gather, brand, doctor, separate, and ship their herds to market. Tom, who had bossed one such cow outfit on the Matador Ranch, assumed the same duties on the JA during World War II. With most of the men away in the service, old-timers, young boys and adventuresome women took over the range work.

Tom and his fellow cowhands were driving pickups and pulling horse trailers when the JA chuck wagon rolled in for the last time in the early 1950s. By then, electricity and telephones, whose lines often paralleled pasture-enclosing barbed-wire fences, linked remote ranch outposts, while radio and television brought news and entertainment.

When I met him, Tom possessed only two of these modern conveniences: a well-worn Toyota pickup and a radio, used mostly to listen to summer broadcasts of baseball, a game whose leisurely pace seemed perfectly fitted to the pastoral life of a cowboy. The electrical and telephone lines to his camp had played out long before and were never replaced, but Tom did not seem to miss them. Coal oil lanterns provided ample light when evening embraced his tiny frame house, a gas-powered stove cooked his meals, and regular visits to headquarters and to see his wife, who lived in a small town forty miles away, helped relieve any monotony and loneliness he may have felt.

Tom depended on his horses for daily companionship and spent far more time in the saddle than behind the wheel of his truck. After all these years, he still enjoyed the challenge of breaking and training fresh colts to work cattle.

Like most of his aging breed, Tom Blasingame lamented the passing of the chuck wagon and with it an ancient way of life.

If he did not miss the privation and hardship of living in the open for months on end, he still yearned for the fellowship and traditions of an old-time roundup crew.

His memories of the era when "the wagon" was the center of a cowboy's universe warmed him like a blazing campfire on a cold fall evening. A natural storyteller, Tom reminisced without effort, drawing on decades of observation and experience and a wonderful memory for detail. His characters came alive in the rich colors and bold strokes of an artist. For hours he regaled me with anecdotes, often told with sensitivity and humor, but rarely with the sort of exaggeration for which cowboys are notorious. We ran out of time and daylight before Tom ran out of tales.

Tom Blasingame was descended from a long line of gifted cowboy storytellers. Despite their reputation in movies and books as men of few words, many cowpunchers actually were quite gabby, particularly around their own kind. The more talkative among them acquired reputations as "augurs," men never shy of words or wind when it came to spinning yarns. During idle evening hours on the open range, roundup outfits sometimes matched champion augurs in storytelling contests or debates. Participants in such matches came from varied backgrounds and cultures and told their tales in many accents and dialects, from Spanish to African-American.

Whatever their language or level of education, cowboys all seemed to relish a good story, whether told around the campfire or read from a book. Around most early-day ranches, however, libraries were virtually nonexistent and reading material so scarce that cowpunchers sometimes amused each other by reading the labels on canned food. The few magazines and dime novels that eventually found their way into cow camps were eagerly devoured, as were more common publications like the Bible, the plays and poems of William Shakespeare, and illustrated merchandise catalogs, known as "wish books." Newspapers, too, were read and reread with enthusiasm,

long after the events they recorded were no longer news. Bunkhouses sometimes were wallpapered with newsprint, providing literate cowpunchers with time on their hands a whole winter's worth of reading enjoyment.

The stories that cowboys loved best, however, sprang not from what they read but from personal and collective experience and observation. Because cowhands appreciated well-told tales, the spirited performances of accomplished narrators often were accompanied by humorous expressions, gestures, and imitations. Exaggeration of characters and action also played a role in capturing and maintaining audience interest. Known as "stretching the blanket" or "mixing in the red paint," this technique was especially effective when the listener was a gullible "greenhorn" or "tenderfoot."

Over the years, the choicest cowboy yarns passed from camp to camp and generation to generation, their characters and locales altered from time to time to fit new circumstances and surroundings. And while the chuck wagon and campfire of the old-time cowhand have disappeared, those stories are still a vital part of western-range lore and the legend of the Wild West.

B. Byron Price
National Cowboy Hall of Fame
and Western Heritage Center

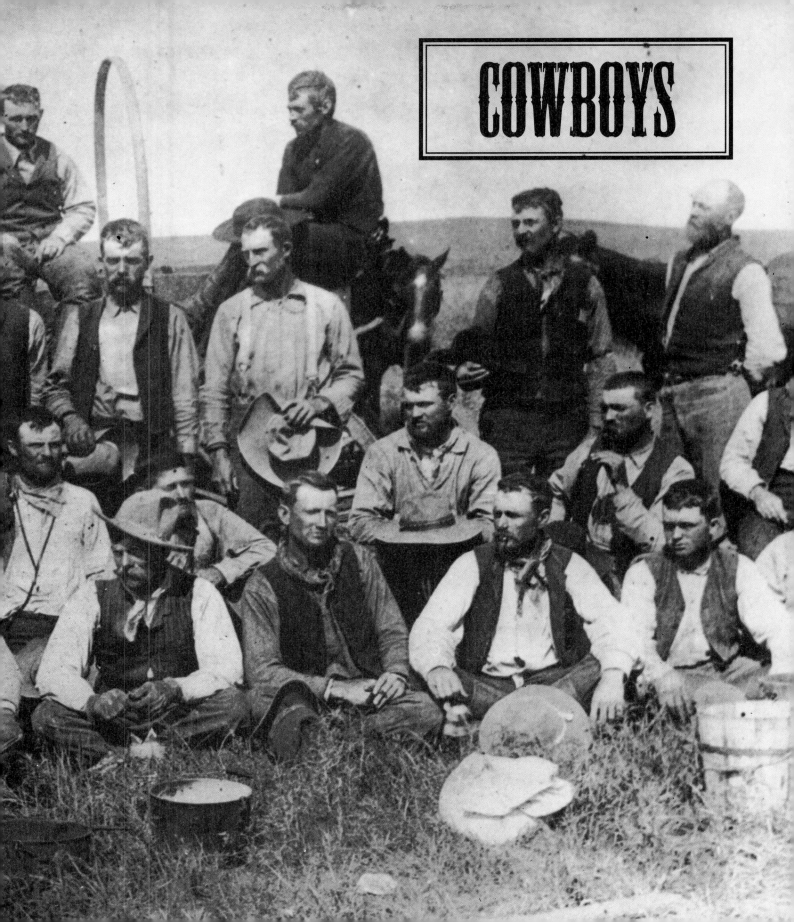

COWBOYS

UP THE TRAIL

BAYLIS JOHN FLETCHER

"Wilderness was a source of great joy to the cowboy."

On the morning of April 11, a supreme moment for us, we started up the trail to Cheyenne, Wyoming. To gather the cattle in the pasture into one great herd took up the forenoon. In the afternoon we made only about five miles, bedding our cattle that night just south of Victoria, near the Guadalupe River. On the following morning we forded the river, which was low.

When we were passing through the streets of Victoria, a lady, fearful that the cattle would break down her fence and ruin her roses, ran out to the pickets and, waving her bonnet frantically at the cattle, stampeded those in front. With a dull roar, they charged back upon the rear of the herd, and but for the discreet management of boss Arnett, heavy damage to city property would have resulted.

"Give way at all street crossings and let the cattle have room," he shouted as he galloped about, giving orders to save the City of Roses from a disaster.

We complied quickly and soon had half a dozen residence blocks surrounded by excited and infuriated cattle. Soon they became so confused that the stampede was ended. We gave their fears time to subside, then drove them quietly out of the city without doing any serious damage.

On the second night, when we were camped near the source of Spring Creek, a real midnight stampede occurred. All hands were called to the saddle, and it was near dawn before we could return to our pallets for rest. We proceeded to the north and, in a few days, reached the mouth of Peach Creek, north of Cuero, where we paid for the privilege of watering in the big Kokernot pasture.

Here water was procured in the Guadalupe River, and we stopped on its banks to rest our cattle and eat dinner. While grazing the cattle along the bank of the river, we discovered a big alligator idly floating on the water's surface. All hands were attracted by the strange sight and began shouting at the big saurian, who protected himself by sinking out of sight in the turbid waters.

After dinner Joe Felder took off his boots and washed his feet in the river. Then he sat on the root of a big tree facing the stream and fell asleep. Manuel Garcia, our cook, with that levity characteristic of the Mexican, conceived a practical joke. Throwing a log so that it fell into the river just in front of the sleeping Joe, he shouted, "Alligator!" In a quick effort to rise, Joe slipped into the river, going entirely under and rising by the side of the floating log, which he mistook for the alligator. He screamed for help, and stake ropes were thrown him, which he seized frantically, to be drawn out, as he thought, from the jaws of death. His disgust was profound when he discovered that he was escaping only from a rotten log.

On the following night we bedded our cattle in a short, wide lane between high rail fences a few miles

Edward Borein, *California Cattle Herd*, 1912.
Mixed media, 20 x 29”

east of Gonzales. This was a thickly settled region, timbered with a variety of oaks, and the surface was covered with gravel. My shift at guard duty was the last in the night, and at about two A.M., Sam Allen, Carteman Garcia, and I were called to go on herd. Allen and I were stationed at the east end of the lane, while the Mexican guarded the other end. The night was frosty, and as the cattle seemed to be sleeping soundly, Sam and I dismounted and built a fire of dry branches by which to warm. At first we would warm by turns and ride time about. But everything was so still that we became careless and both dismounted at the fire, where we began to spin yarns. As the bright fire lit up the scene, it was beautiful to behold. Two thousand cattle rested quietly, lying down and chewing their cuds. Suddenly there was a loud and ominous roar, while a cloud of dust obscured our vision

“Stampede!” shouted Sam as he let loose his bridle reins and I sprang behind an oak, which he hugged with both hands. I did not have time to turn Happy Jack loose but threw my arms around Allen on the side of the tree opposite the herd. We were none too quick, for now the horns of the stampeding bovines were raking the bark from the opposite side of the oak as they rushed madly past us. It was a moment of supreme terror, but only a moment. In less time than it takes to relate it, the cattle had passed us and, mounting Happy Jack, I was in full pursuit.

I soon overtook the cattle, pressed on past them, and turned their leaders back. They now formed a circle, where they milled in one great wheel, revolving with almost lightning velocity. By holding them in this mill, I soon had them confused, and they began to bellow to one another. I had learned that these were welcome sounds in a stampede. As soon as the bellowing becomes general, the run begins to subside. Of course, such a revolving wheel cannot be stopped suddenly. The momentum they have acquired makes it necessary to slow down the cattle gradually, or else the ones that stopped first would be trampled to death.

I now heard a voice shouting, "Stay with them, Fletcher." In a moment I was joined by Mr. Snyder, riding one of the wagon horses bareback and with a blind bridle. "Where is Sam?" he asked. But I did not know.

We soon had the cattle quiet, and as it now was about dawn, we drove them back to the bed ground. I learned from Mr. Snyder that something had frightened the cattle in about the middle of the lane where we had bedded them and that I was holding only a part of the herd, the remainder having run out of the other end of the lane past Garcia. Thinking that the whole herd had gone that way, the cowboys had all gone to the aid of Garcia, but when Allen and I were missed, Mr. Snyder had gone in search of us. When Allen's horse was found loose with the saddle on, it was supposed that the horse had fallen with him as he rode out ahead of the cattle and that he had narrowly escaped being trampled to death.

We did not confess until long afterward that we had been caught off our horses by the stampede and that Allen had let his horse go. Such admissions were not expected on the trail. After getting the fragments of our herd together, we strung them out in a thin line, and as they passed a certain point, the cattle were counted. It was found that we were about one hundred head short. That many evidently had escaped in the stampede.

While we were discussing the feasibility of recovering the lost cattle, four hard-looking citizens rode up and said, "Had a stampede last night, did you?" We answered in the affirmative. Then the strangers offered their services to help put the cattle back in the herd. Their offer was to bring in all they could for one dollar per head. Mr. Snyder then offered them fifty cents per head, to which they readily agreed. It seemed plain to us that these accommodating gentry had stampeded our herd for this revenue.

They were joined by recruits, and during the day they delivered sixty cattle bearing our road brand. We still were forty short, but time was precious. Mr. Snyder said that the missing ones would go back to the range near Victoria and be gathered there for his account and that we must proceed. Later our own scouts brought in about twenty additional renegades, so that we were only about twenty short when we started forward on the following day.

BAYLIS JOHN FLETCHER *in 1879, at twenty years of age, was among the cowboys driving a herd of longhorn cattle up the Chisholm Trail from Texas to Wyoming. This selection is from his true account of what it was like to be on the trail.*

RED AND WHITE ON THE BORDER

THEODORE ROOSEVELT

Up to 1880 the country through which the Little Missouri flows remained as wild and almost as unknown as it was when the old explorers and fur traders crossed it in the early part of the century. It was the last great Indian hunting-ground, across which Grosventres and Mandans, Sioux and Cheyennes, and even Crows and Rees wandered in chase of game, and where they fought one another and plundered the small parties of white trappers and hunters that occasionally ventured into it. Once or twice generals like Sully and Custer had penetrated it in the course of the long, tedious and bloody campaigns that finally broke the strength of the northern Horse Indians; indeed, the trail made by Custer's baggage train is to this day one of the well-known landmarks, for the deep ruts worn by the wheels of the heavy wagons are in many places still as distinctly to be seen as ever.

In 1883, a regular long-range skirmish took place just south of us between some Cheyennes and some cowboys, with bloodshed on both sides, while about the same time a band of Sioux plundered a party of buffalo hunters of everything they owned, and some Crows who attempted the same feat with another party were driven off with the loss of two of their number. Since then there have been in our neighborhood no standup fights or regular raids; but the Indians have at different times proved more or less troublesome, burning the grass and occasionally killing stock or carrying off horses that have wandered some distance away. They have also themselves suffered somewhat at the hands of white horsethieves.

Bands of them, accompanied by their squaws and children, often come into the ranch country, either to trade or to hunt, and are then, of course, perfectly meek and peaceable. If they stay any time they build themselves quite comfortable tepees (wigwams, as they would be styled in the East), and an Indian camp is a rather interesting, though very dirty, place to visit. On our ranch we get along particularly well with them, as it is a rule that they shall be treated as fairly as if they were whites; we neither wrong them ourselves nor allow others to wrong them. We have always, for example, been as keen in putting down horse-stealing from Indians as from whites—which indicates rather an advanced stage of frontier morality, as theft from the "redskins" or the "Government" is usually held to be a very trivial matter compared with the heinous crime of theft from "citizens."

There is always danger in meeting a band of young bucks in lonely, uninhabited country—those that have barely reached manhood being the most truculent, insolent and reckless. A man meeting such a party runs great risk of losing his horse, his rifle and

Overleaf: Charles M. Russell, *Caught in the Circle*, 1903. Oil, 24 x 36"

Frederic Remington, *Standing off Indians*.

all else he has. This has happened quite frequently during the past few years to hunters or cowboys who have wandered into the debatable territory where our country borders on the Indian lands; and in at least one such instance, that took place three years ago, the unfortunate individual lost his life as well as his belongings. But a frontiersman of any experience can generally "stand off" a small number of such assailants, unless he loses his nerve or is taken by surprise.

My only adventure with Indians was of a very mild kind. It was in the course of a solitary trip to the north and east of our range, to what was then practically unknown country, although now containing many herds of cattle. One morning I had been traveling along the edge of the prairie, and about noon I rode Manitou up a slight rise and came out on a plateau that was perhaps half a mile broad when near the middle, four or five Indians suddenly came up over the edge, directly in front of me. The second they saw me they whipped their guns out of their slings, started their horses into a run, and came on at full tilt, whooping and brandishing their weapons. I instantly reined up and dismounted. The level plain where we were was of all places the one on which such an onslaught could best be met. In any broken country, or where there is much cover, a white man is at a great disadvantage if pitted against such adepts in the art of hiding as Indians; while, on the other hand, the latter will rarely rush in on a foe who, even if overpowered in the end, will probably inflict severe loss on his assailants. The fury of an Indian charge, and the whoops by which it is accompanied, often scare horses so as to stampede them; but in Manitou I had perfect trust, and the old fellow stood as steady as a rock, merely cocking his ears and looking round at the noise. I waited until the Indians were a hundred yards off, and then threw up my rifle and drew a bead on the foremost. The effect was like magic. The whole party scattered out as wild pigeons or teal ducks sometimes do when shot at, and doubled back on their tracks, the men bending over alongside their horses. When some distance off they halted and gathered together to consult, and after a minute one came forward alone, ostentatiously dropping his rifle and waving a blanket over his head. When he came within fifty yards I stopped him, and he pulled out a piece of paper—all Indians, when absent from their reservations, are supposed to carry passes—and called out, "How! Me good Indian!" I answered, "How," and assured him most sincerely I was very glad he was a good Indian, but I would not let him come closer, and when his companions began to draw near, I covered him with the rifle and made him move off, which he did with a sudden lapse into the most uncanonical Anglo-Saxon profanity. I then started to lead my horse out to the prairie; and after hovering round a short time they rode off, while I followed suit, but in the opposite direction. It had all passed too quickly for me to have time to get frightened; but during the rest of my ride I was exceedingly uneasy, and pushed tough, speedy old Manitou along at a rapid rate, keeping well out on the level. However, I never saw the Indians again. They may not have intended any mischief beyond giving me a fright, but I did not dare to let them come to close quarters, for they would probably have taken my horse and rifle, and not impossibly my scalp as well. Towards nightfall I fell in with two old trappers who lived near Killdeer Mountains, and they informed me that my assailants were some young Sioux bucks, at whose hands they themselves had just suffered the loss of two horses.

A few cool, resolute whites, well armed, can generally beat back a much larger number of Indians if

attacked in the open. One of the first cattle outfits that came to the Powder River country, at the very end of the last war with the Sioux and Cheyennes, had an experience of this sort. There were six or eight whites, including the foreman, who was part owner, and they had about a thousand head of cattle. These they intended to hold just out of the dangerous district until the end of the war, which was evidently close at hand. They would thus get first choice of the new grazing grounds. But they ventured a little too far, and one day while on the trail were suddenly charged by fifty or sixty Indians. The cattle were scattered in every direction, and many of them slain in wantonness, though most were subsequently recovered. All the loose horses were driven off. But the men themselves instantly ran together and formed a ring, fighting from behind the pack- and saddle-ponies.

One of their number was killed, as well as two or three of the animals composing their living breastwork; but being good riflemen, they drove off their foes. The latter did not charge them directly, but circled round, each rider concealed on the outside of his horse; and though their firing was very rapid, it was, naturally, very wild. The whites killed a good many ponies, and got one scalp, belonging to a young Sioux brave who dashed up too close, and whose body in consequence could not be carried off by his comrades, as happened to two or three others who were seen to fall. Both the men who related the incident to me had been especially struck by the skill and daring shown by the Indians in thus carrying off their dead and wounded the instant they fell.

THEODORE ROOSEVELT *(1858–1919) was born in New York City and, upon graduating from Harvard, traveled West to a ranch in the Dakota Territory in an attempt to improve his delicate health; he suffered from asthma among other ailments. Later he would become president of the United States, but he would never forget the beauty and savagery of the Wild West. This is a selection from a longer piece in* Stories of the Great West.

AN OUTPOST OF CIVILIZATION

FREDERIC REMINGTON

The hacienda of San Jose de Bavicora lies northwest from Chihuahua (in north central Mexico), 225 of the longest miles on the map. The miles run up long hills and dive into rocky canyons; they stretch over never-ending burnt plains and across the beds of tortuous rivers thick with scorching sand. And there are three ways to make this travel. Some go on foot—which is best, if one has time—like the Tahuramaras; others take it ponyback, after the Mexican manner; and persons with no time and a great deal of money go in a coach. At first thought this last would seem to be the best, but the Guerrero stage has never failed to tip over, and the company makes you sign away your natural rights, and almost your immortal soul before it will allow you to embark. So it is not the best way at all, if I may judge from my own experience. We had a coach which seemed to choose the steepest hill on the route, where it then struck a stone, which heaved the coach, pulled out the king-pin, and what I remember of the occurrence is full of sprains and aches and general gloom. Guerrero, too, is only three fourths of the way to Bavicora, and you can only go there if Don Gilberto, the patron of the hacienda—or, if you know him well enough, "Jack"—will take you in the ranch coach.

After bumping over the stones all day for five days, through a blinding dust, we were glad enough when we suddenly came out of the tall timber in the moun-

tain pass and espied the great yellow plain of Bavicora stretching to the blue hills of the Sierra. In an hour's ride more, through a chill wind, we were at the ranch. We pulled up at the entrance, which was garnished by a bunch of cow punchers, who regarded us curiously as we pulled our aching bodies and bandaged limbs from the Concord and limped into the patio.

To us was assigned the room of honor, and after shaking ourselves down on a good bed, with mattress and sheeting, we recovered our cheerfulness. A hot toddy, a roaring fireplace, completed the effect. The floor was strewn with bear- and wolf-skin rugs; it had pictures and draperies on the walls, and in a corner a washbasin and pitcher—so rare in these parts—was set on a stand, grandly suggestive of the refinements of luxury we had attained to. I do not wish to convey the impression that Mexicans do not wash, because there are brooks enough in Mexico if they want to use them, but washbasins are the advance guards of progress, and we had been on the outposts since leaving Chihuahua.

Jack's man William had been ever present and administered to our slightest wish; his cheerful "Good-mo'nin', gemmen," as he lit the fire recalled us to life. After a rubdown I went out to look at the situation.

Opposite: Robert Henri, *La Trinidad*, date unknown. Oil, 76½ x 38"

Jack's ranch is a great straggling square of mud walls enclosing two patios, with adobe corrals and outbuildings, all obviously constructed for the purposes of defense. It was built in 1770 by the Jesuits, and while the English and Dutch were fighting for possession of the Mohawk Valley, Bavicora was an outpost of civilization, as it is today. Locked in a strange language, on parchment stored in vaults in Spain, are the records of this enterprise. In 1840 the good fathers were murdered by the Apaches, the country devastated and deserted, and the cattle and horses hurried to the mountain lairs of the Apache devils. The place lay idle and unreclaimed for years, threatening to crumble back to the dust of which it was made. Nearby are curious mounds on the banks of a dry arroyo. The punchers have dug down into these ruins and found adobe walls, mud plasterings, skeletons, and bits of woven goods. They call them the "Montezumas."

All this was to be changed. In 1882 an American cowboy—which was Jack—accompanied by two companions, penetrated south from Arizona; and as he looked from the mountains over the fair plain of Bavicora, he said, "I will take this." The Apaches were on every hand; the country was terrorized to the gates of Chihuahua. The stout heart of the pioneer was not disturbed, and he made his word good. By purchase, he acquired the plain and so much more that you could not ride round it in two weeks. He moved in with his hardy punchers and fixed up Bavicora so it would be habitable. He chased the Indians off his ranch whenever he "cut their sign." After a while the Mexican *vaqueros* from below overcame their terror when they saw the American hold his own with the Apache devils, and by twos and threes and half-dozens they came up to take service, and now there are two hundred who lean on Jack and call him *patron*. They work for him and they follow him on the Apache trail, knowing he will never run away, believing in his beneficence and trusting to his courage.

I sat on a mudbank and worked away at a sketch of the yellow sunlit walls of the mud ranch, with the

great plain running away like the ocean into a violet streak under the blue line of the Pena Blanca. In the rear rises a curious broken formation of hills, like millions of ruins of Rhine castles. The *lobos* (wolves) howl by night, and the Apache is expected to come at any instant. The old *criada*, or serving woman, who makes the beds saw her husband killed at the front door, and every man who goes out of the patio has a large assortment of the most improved artillery on his person. Old carts with heavy wooden wheels like millstones stand about. Brown people with big straw hats and gay serapes lean lazily against the gray walls. Little pigs carry on the contest with nature, game chickens strut, and clumsy puppies tumble over each other in joyful play; burros stand about sleepily, only indicating life by suggestive movements of their great ears, while at intervals a pony, bearing its lithe rider, steps from the gate, and breaking into an easy and graceful lope, goes away into the waste of land.

I rose to go inside, and while I gazed, I grew exalted in the impression that here, in the year 1893, I had rediscovered a Fort Laramie after Mr. Francis Parkman's well-known description. The foreman, Tom Bailey, was dressed in store clothes, and our room had bedsteads and a washbasin; otherwise it answered very well. One room was piled high with dried meat, and the great stomachs of oxen filled with tallow; another room is a store full of goods— calicoes, buckskin, *reatas*, yellow leather shoes, guns, and other quaint plunder adapted to the needs of a people who sit on the ground and live on meat and corn meal. "Charlie Jim," the Chinese cook, has a big room with a stove in it, and he and the stove are a never-ending wonder to all the folks, and the fame of both has gone across the mountains to Sonora and to the south. Charlie is an autocrat in his curious Chinese way, and by the dignity of his position as Mr. Jack's private cook and his unknown antecedents, he conjures the Mexicans and d___s the Texans, which latter refuse to take him seriously and kill him, as they would a "proper" man. Charlie Jim, in return, entertains ideas of Texans which he secretes, except when they dine with Jack, when he may be heard to mutter, "Cake and pie no good for puncher, make him fat and lazy"; and when he crosses the patio and they fling a rope over his foot, he becomes livid; and breaks out, "Da__ puncher; d___ rope; rope man all same horse; d___ puncher; no good that way."

The *patron* has the state apartment, and no one goes there with his hat on; but his relations with his people are those of a father and children. An old gray man approaches; they touch the left arm with the right—an abbreviated hug—say, "*Buenos dias, patron!*" "*Buenos dias,* Don Sabino!" and they shake hands. A California saddle stand, on a rack by the desk, and the latter is littered with photographs of men in London clothes and women in French dresses, the latter singularly out of character with their surroundings. The old *criada* squats silently by the fireplace, her head enveloped in her blue *rebozo*, and deftly rolls her cigarette. She alone, and one white bulldog, can come and go without restraint.

The administrator, which is Mr. Tom Bailey, of Texas, moves about in the discharge of his responsibilities, and they are universal; anything and everything is his work, from the negotiation for the sale of five thousand head of cattle to the "busting" of a bronco which no one else can "crawl."

The clerk is in the store, with his pink boy's face, a pencil behind his ear, and a big sombrero, trying to look as though he had lived in these wilds longer than at San Francisco, which he finds an impossible part. He has acquired the language and the disregard of time necessary to one who would sell a *real's* worth of cotton cloth to a Mexican. The forge in the blacksmith's shop is going, and one puncher is cutting another puncher's hair in the sunlight; ponies are being lugged in on the end of lariats, and thrown down, tied fast, and left in a convulsive heap, ready to be shod at the disposition of their riders. On the roof of the house are two or three men looking and pointing to the little black specks on the plain far away, which are the cattle going into the *lagunas* to drink.

The second patio, or the larger one, is entered by a narrow passage, and here you find horses and saddle and punchers coming and going, saddling and unsaddling their horses, and being bucked about or dragged on a rope. In the little doorways to the rooms of the men stand women in calico dresses and blue cotton *rebozos*, while the dogs and pigs lie about, and little brown *vaqueros* are ripening in the sun. In the rooms you find pottery, stone *metates* for grinding the corn, a fireplace, a symbol of the Catholic Church, some serapes, some rope, and buckskin. The people sit on a mat on the floor and make cigarettes out of native tobacco and cornhusks, or roll *tortillas*; they laugh and chat in low tones, and altogether occupy the tiniest mental world, hardly larger than the patio, and not venturing beyond the little mud town of Temozachic, forty miles over the hills. Physically the men vacillate between the most intense excitement and a comatose state of idleness, where all is quiet and slothful, in contrast to the mad whirl of the roaring rodeo.

In the haciendas of Old Mexico one will find the law and custom of the feudal days. All the laws of Mexico are in protection of the landowner. The master is without restraint, and the man lives dependent on his caprice. The *patron* of Bavicora, for instance, leases land to a Mexican, and it is one of the arrangements that he shall drive the ranch coach to Chihuahua when it goes. All lessees of land are obliged to follow the *patron* to war, and, indeed, since the common enemy, the Apache, in these parts is as like to harry the little as the great, it is exactly to his interest to wage the war. Then, too, comes the responsibility of the *patron* to his people. He must feed them in the famine, he must arbitrate their disputes, and he must lead them at all times. If, through improvidence, their work cattle die or give out, he must restock them so that they may continue the cultivation of the land, all of which is not . . . profitable in a financial way, as we of the north may think, where all business is done on the "hold you responsible, sir," basis. The *vaqueros* make their own saddles and *reatas*; only the iron saddle rings, the rifles, and the knives come from the *patron*, and where he gets them from, God alone knows, and the puncher never cares. No doctor attends the sick or disabled, old women's nursing standing between life and death. The Creator in His province has arranged it so that simple folks are rarely sick, and a sprained ankle, a bad bruise from a steer's horn or a pitching horse, are soon remedied by rest and a good constitution. At times instant and awful death over-takes the puncher—a horse in a gopher hole, a mad steer, a chill with a knife, a blue hole where the .45 went in, a quicksand closing overhead; and a cross on a hillside are all.

Never is a door closed. Why they were put up, I failed to discover. For days I tried faithfully to keep mine shut, but everyone coming or going left it open, so that I gave it up in despair. There are only two windows in the ranch of San Jose de Bavicora, one in our chamber and one in the blacksmith's shop, both opening into the court. In fact, I found those were the only two windows in the state, outside of the big city. The Mexicans find that their enemies are prone to shoot through these apertures and so they have accustomed themselves to do without them, which is as it should be, since it removes the temptation.

One night the *patron* gave a *baile*. The *vaqueros* all came with their girls, and a string band rendering music with a very dancy swing sat in a corner and observed the man who wears the big hat and who throws the rawhide as he cavorted about with his girl, and the way they dug up the dust out of the dirt floor soon put me to coughing. Candles shed their soft luster—and tallow down the backs of our necks—and the band scraped and thrummed away in a most serious manner. One man had a harp, two had primitive fiddles, and one a guitar. One old fiddler was the leader, and as he bowed his head on his instrument, I could not keep my eyes off him. He had come from Sonora, and was very old; he looked as though he had had his share of a very rough life; he was never handsome as a boy, I am sure, but the weather and starvation and time had blown him and crumbled him into a ruin which resembled the pre-existing ape from which the races sprang. If he had

Olaf Seltzer, *Trouble on the Circle Diamond*, 1908.
Oil, 18¼ x 23"

Frederic Remington, *The Music at the "Baile"*

never committed murder, it was for lack of opportunity; and Sonora is a long travel from Plymouth Rock.

Tom Bailey, the foreman, came round to me, his eyes dancing and his shock of hair standing up like a Circassian beauty's, and pointing, he said, "Thar's a woman who's prettier than a speckled pup; put your twine on her." Then, as master of ceremonies, he straightened up and sang out over the fiddle and noise, "Dance, thar, you fellers, or you'll git the gout."

In an adjoining room there was a very heavy jug of strong-water, and thither the men repaired to pick up, so that as the night wore on their brains began to whirl after their legs, and they whooped at times in a way to put one's nerves on edge. The band scraped the harder and the dance waxed fast, the spurs clinked, and bang bang bang went the Winchester rifles in the patio, while the chorus, "*Viva el patron*," rang around the room—the Old Guard was in action.

We sat in our room one evening when in filed the *vaqueros* and asked to be allowed to sing for the *patron*. They sat on my bed and on the floor while we occupied the other; they had their hats in their hands, and their black dreamy eyes were diverted as though overcome by the magnificence of the apartment. They hemmed and coughed, until finally one man, who was evidently the leader, pulled himself together and began, in a high falsetto, to sing; after two or three words the rest caught on, and they got through the line, when they stopped; thus was one leading and the others following to the end of the line. It was strange, wild music—a sort of general impression of a boys' choir with a wild discordance, each man giving up his soul as he felt moved. The refrain always ended, for want of breath, in a low expiring howl, leaving the audience in suspense; but quickly they get at it again, and the rise of the tenor chorus continues. The songs are largely about love and women and doves and flowers, in all of which nonsense punchers take only a perfunctory interest in real life.

These are the amusements—although the puncher is always roping for practice, and everything is fair game for his skill; hence dogs, pigs, and men have become as expert in dodging the rope as the *vaqueros* are in throwing it. A mounted man, in passing, will always throw his rope at one sitting in a doorway, and then try to get away before he can retaliate by jerking his own rope over his head. I have seen a man repair to the roof and watch a doorway through which he expected some comrade to pass shortly, and watch for an hour to be ready to drop his noose about his shoulders.

The ranch fare is very limited, and at intervals men are sent to bring back a steer from the water holes, which is dragged to the front door and there slaughtered. A day of feasting ensues, and the doorways and the gutter pipes and the corral fences are festooned with the beef left to dry in the sun.

There is the serious side of the life. The Apache is an evil which Mexicans have come to regard as they do the meteoric hail, the lightning, the drought, and any other horror not to be averted. They quarrel between themselves over land and stock, and there are a great many men out in the mountains who are proscribed by the Government. Indeed, while we journeyed on the road and were stopping one night in a little mud town, we were startled by a fusillade of shots, and in the morning were informed that two men had been killed the night before, and various others wounded. At another time a Mexican with his followers had invaded our apartment and expressed a disposition to kill Jack, but he found Jack was willing to play his game, and gave up the enterprise. On the ranch the men had discovered some dead stock which had been killed with a knife. Men were detailed to roam the country in search of fresh trails

of these cattle-killers. I asked the foreman what would happen in case they found a trail which could be followed, and he said, Why, we would follow it until we came up, and then kill them." If a man is to "hold down" a big ranch in northern Mexico, he has got to be "all man," because it is "a man's job," as Mr. Bailey of Los Ojos said—and he knows.

Jack himself is the motive force of the enterprise, and he disturbs the quiet of this waste of sunshine by his presence for about six months in the year. With his strong spirit, the embodiment of generations of pioneers, he faces the Apache, the marauder, the financial risks. He spurs his listless people on to toil, he permeates every detail, he storms, and greater men than he have sworn like troopers under less provocation than he has at times; but he has snatched from the wolf and the Indian the fair land of Bavicora, to make it fruitful for his generation.

There lies the hacienda San Jose de Bavicora, gray and silent on the great plain, with the mountains standing guard against intruders, and over it the great blue dome of the sky, untroubled by clouds, except little flecks of vapor, which stand, lost in immensity, burning bright like opals, as though discouraged from seeking the mountains or the sea from whence they came. The marvelous color of the country beckons to the painter; its simple natural life entrances the blond barbarian, with his fevered brain; and the gaudy *vaquero* and his trappings and his pony are the actors on this noble stage. But one must be appreciative of it all, or he will find a week of rail and a week of stage and a week of horseback all too far for one to travel to see a shadow across the moon.

FREDERIC REMINGTON *(1861–1909) is known for his dramatic paintings, but he was a journalist as well as an artist and documented the Old West in word and picture. After studying two years at Yale, at age nineteen he left for the West and worked as a cowboy until he was able to publish his stories.*

EMIGRANTS

OREGON JOURNAL

Vittwia St. Clair Chapman Mickelson

September 1–3, 1924

No, indeed, I haven't forgotten how to dance. I danced on my 83rd birthday, to celebrate the occasion. "A good many of the young women of today are a pampered self-indulgent lot. For the past eleven years I have lived all alone. I do my own housework, cook, bake, clean house, do my own washing, and work in the garden, so I have no time to sit around and feel sorry for myself and indulge in nerves or tantrums.

"I was never a nagger, a calamity howler, or a complainer. I have always been too grateful for health and the possession of all my faculties to moan over my sad lot. In fact, sunshine has always appealed to me more than gray clouds or weeping skies. I not only work with my flowers, but my garden comes pretty near to supporting me. I sell eggs and chickens and with the money I buy the few things that go on my table that I do not raise.

"Tell you about myself? If you listened and wrote up all the things I could tell you you would have a book instead of a newspaper article, so I will just give you a few highlights of my life.

"My father, Samuel Chapman, was born in England, as was my mother, Sarah Smeed Chapman. I was born August 2, 1841, in Kentucky, and I was christened Vittwia St. Clair Chapman.

"My father's people were wealthy, so he spent his boyhood in travel. My father and mother spent their honeymoon in travel in Europe. They liked it so well that they put in the first year or so of their married life in seeing the sights of Paris and other European capitals and world ports. Their first baby, a little girl, died at the age of three weeks.

"From Paris my parents went to Scotland. They lived for the next eight years at Inverness or Aberdeen. Of their 13 children, 12 lived to maturity, but I am the only one now living. Two of my brothers and three sisters were born in Scotland, my next brother in England, the next brother in New York City, the next four children, including myself, in Kentucky, and the last child at Burlington, Iowa.

"My father studied art in Europe and planned to make painting his life work, but with a family of 13 children it was necessary to turn his hand to other things to bring in money to support his family. Do you remember Captain Barckley, the pedestrian, who made a tour of the world afoot—or at least that part of the world that was dry land? He was a good walker, but poor at writing, so he sent his travel notes to Father, who prepared them for the press. These articles were published in many of the larger papers in Great Britain and Europe and brought in considerable money, so that as long as the captain kept walking my

Previous pages: Albert Bierstadt, *Emigrants Crossing the Plains,* 1867. Oil, 67 x 102"

father could keep writing and the money flowed in.

"After coming to America, Father met the governor of Kentucky, who employed him to go back to England and select a herd of Durham and Devon cattle for his estate in Kentucky. Father executed this commission so well that the governor employed him as his private secretary. We lived for some time at Frankfort and later at Lexington, Kentucky.

"When I was four years old we moved to Burlington, Iowa. That was in 1845. I saw there, for the first time, some Indians. I was so frightened that I ran away and hid in some standing grain and lay as still as a quail or little rabbit. I remember a few years later seeing lots of prairie schooners going westward with mottoes like these on the canvas tops: 'California or Bust,' and 'For Oregon.' That was in 1849, when I was eight years old. We moved back to Kentucky in the early '50s, but just before the Civil War we moved back to Iowa.

"I volunteered for service as a nurse. What I saw as a nurse is as vivid today as if it had happened last week, in place of 60 years or more ago. I was 20 years old when Fort Sumter was fired on, and, like most young women, I was anxious to do all I could for the young men who were fighting for their convictions.

"Scores and hundreds of young medical students, as well as more experienced doctors, became army surgeons, or 'contract doctors.' This last was a great mistake. In the hospitals where I served as nurse I have seen scores of times a contract doctor amputate a young man's leg or arm that could have been saved just as well as not. Frequently they would cut off a young lad's leg when all he had was a flesh wound. I would assist in the operation and of course I knew how needless the amputation was, but I could only obey orders. The contract doctors at that time received $50 for every amputation and, of course, much less for merely bandaging a wound, so they usually decided on amputation, frequently explaining to me, as a justification, that gangrene might set in, so they would play safe and take off the wounded arm or leg. The soldiers called those contract doctors the 'Iowa Butchers.'

"For a while I nursed where wounded Confederate prisoners were treated, and many a young chap who had been marked to have his leg or arm amputated was spirited away through my help.

"While I was nursing at Keokuk, Iowa, a Mrs. Astone, an Englishwoman, whose husband was in the Confederate Army, appealed to me to help her join her husband. She had two small children. I secured a skiff, and, waiting for a moonless night, we launched the skiff and started down the river for St. Louis. She cared for her two babies while I rowed the skiff. We hid during the daytime and traveled at night. She found friends at St. Louis who assisted her in rejoining her husband. I made my way back up the river to Navon, and from there I made my way home, but my career as an army nurse was over, for I couldn't explain my apparent desertion from duty.

"My brother, Henry Chapman, was eight years older than I. He was born in 1833. He was a frail and sickly child, and he was never strong. I was a light sleeper, so from the time I was a little tot I slept on a pallet beside his bed so as to cover his feet at night or give him his medicine. The doctor said a complete change of climate might be beneficial to him, so, in 1853, when I was 12 years old, he and my brother Daniel started across the plains for Oregon. Daniel got a job driving a prairie schooner for Enoch Walker, while Henry, who was 20, drove a wagon for Enoch's brother, Fruit Walker. I cried because I could not go to Oregon with my brother Henry. I remember they laughed at me when I cried and said, 'Poor Henry! Who will cover his feet and give him his medicine if I do not go along?'

"On the way across the plains, one of Fruit Walker's drivers, a man named Griffiths, quarreled with another teamster and, picking up an ox yoke, tried to brain him. Fruit Walker grabbed the yoke in time to save the man from being killed. This made Griffiths crazy with anger, so, pulling an Allen pepperbox revolver from his pocket, he shot Fruit Walker through the groin, killing him. Fruit Walker's young widow had two small children and was expecting another shortly. My brother Henry took charge for her and brought her safe through to Oregon. Shortly after she reached the Willamette Valley she gave birth to a son who, of course, never saw his father and knew of him only by hearsay. Not long after arriving in Oregon she married Fruit Walker's brother John.

"My brother Daniel Chapman settled near Ashland. Some of his children and grandchildren still reside in Jackson County. My brother Henry went to Yreka, California, to work in the mines, but his health was so impaired that he could not do hard work, so he came back to Southern Oregon and took up a donation land claim on Emigrant Creek, seven miles from Ashland.

"During the second Rogue River War, in 1855–56, Henry, with two neighbors, was out in the hills looking for hostile Indians. He saw several grizzly bears on the hillside eating service berries. Henry was a good shot. He had a hard-shooting muzzle-loading gun. He took careful aim and shot at one of the largest of the bears. It fell in its tracks. He loaded his gun and shot another bear, which made off in the direction taken by the other bears.

"Henry, carelessly, did not reload his gun, but went up to examine the dead bear, which was a huge one. Just as he got to it the bear came to and made for Henry.

Henry started to run. The bear struck at him, tearing Henry's coat nearly off. Henry ran for a tree, which proved too large for him to climb. He ran toward a smaller tree, but the bear overtook him and with one blow knocked him down and tore his shoulder blade loose. The bear with one or two strokes of his claws tore Henry's clothes off. Henry had heard an Indian say that if a grizzly attacked you if you 'memaloosed' the bear would leave you alone, so Henry played dead. The bear had never heard that bears do not molest dead men, for he bit my brother in the loins and back so that Henry screamed from the pain. Then the bear clawed his head and turned him over to bite his neck. My brother rammed his fist into the bear's mouth. The bear crushed the bones in his hand and wrist. Then the bear bit him through the shoulder and stripped the flesh from one leg from the thigh to the knee.

"The two young men with my brother heard him scream when the bear bit him in the loins, and hurried back. They shot and killed the grizzly.

"My brother was still conscious, and as they rolled the bear off him he said, 'I'll never see Mother or Father or old Kentucky again.' Then he fainted. They thought he was dead, so they tied him across his horse to bring him in for Christian burial. The motion of the horse brought him to.

"They took him to the home of 'Daddy' Wells, a nearby settler. There was no doctor nearer than Jacksonville, so one of the boys rode at full speed to get the doctor, while Daddy Wells washed my brother's wounds and with a sack needle and twine sewed the flesh that was hanging loose back into place. When the doctor came he had to rip out all the stitches so as to wash the torn flesh better.

"Henry's neck was terribly lacerated. They thought he could not live, but he kept alive day after day and at last they decided to send him to San Francisco to secure the services of a surgeon to fix his shoulder, which was so badly shattered when the bear crunched it that the local doctor could not fix it. Even the San Francisco surgeon could not restore its strength and usefulness.

"My brother proved up on his donation claim, and in 1862 went back home by way of the Isthmus. They still call the mountain where the bear and my brother had their fight, Grizzly Butte. Come out on the porch and I will point out Grizzly Butte to you.

"In 1862, because I have always had a knack of nursing and because I loved my brother dearly and was sorry for him, I took him under my wing and did for him, earning money at whatever I could find to do to support both of us.

"Henry was restless and wanted to travel, so I bought a team and light rig and we traveled all over the Middle West. I acted as traveling correspondent and field editor of one of the St. Louis papers. Later I added several other papers to my list, and made good money. Henry could do light work, so he took subscriptions for the papers on a commission basis, which brought us several extra dollars daily and helped pay expenses.

"In our travels we visited Colorado. Henry thought the climate there would help him, so I landed a position as cashier at the Southern Hotel at Trinidad.

Times were flush in the early '70s in Colorado. They paid me $225 a month and board. I was young, good-looking, and vivacious. Scores of wealthy cattlemen or miners who had struck it rich would put up at the Southern. The rates were $10 a day and up. When they paid their bills they would toss back a $5 gold piece and say, 'Keep that for yourself, Bright Eyes,' or 'Here, Sunshine, is a gold piece to remember me by.' I took in as much from tips as I received in salary or more. Quite a few of these miners and cattlemen tried their best to persuade me to quit the state of single blessedness, but I felt that my first duty was to my sick brother. I knew he would feel, in a way, as though he were playing second fiddle if I devoted my attention to any other man, either a sweetheart or a husband, so I promised to be a sister to my various ardent suitors.

"Presently Henry became restless to be on the go, so we started by team again. Henry believed we could make big money by buying a bunch of blooded cattle. Henry got in touch with a stock man who was willing to put up most of the money, so we gathered up a bunch of cattle consisting of about 200 head and started for southern Oregon.

Near the base of the Spanish peaks in Colorado we ran into a lot of grief. The Utes left the reservation and began killing emigrants and settlers and burning ranch houses. A runner came and warned us. We hurried our stock into the mountains. Henry and his partner left me in charge of the stock while they went to secure help.

"I shall never forget the lonesome night I spent. The cougars and wolves were bad there, so with a six-shooter hanging in the holster from my belt and with a Winchester on my shoulder, I kept guard over the cattle all night. We decided that it would be too dangerous to try to drive the stock through the hostile country, so we drove them down into New Mexico and sold the herd at $100 a head straight through.

"The Ute outbreak enabled me to drop back into my old job as correspondent, so I sent accounts of the Indian troubles and also travel letters to the Eastern papers.

"In work of that kind one meets many charming people. I believe two of the most delightful persons I ever met were General George A. Custer and Elizabeth Custer, his wife. They were simple, unaffected, friendly, and most charming. Mrs. Custer always called me Pussy.

"I saw some rough times in the late '70s at Trinidad, Pueblo, and Colorado Springs. The towns were wide open and a 'man for breakfast' was a common occurrence.

"In September, 1880, 44 years ago, Henry and I came to southern Oregon. We went out to Henry's place in the foothills—the claim he had taken up near Ashland in 1855—and I divided my attention between caring for Henry and raising Percheron horses. Henry died 19 years ago at the age of 72.

"In 1890, when I was 49 years old, I married Michael Mickelson. I would not have married him, but he was sick and needed careful nursing, and I could care for him better as his wife than in any other way. Ever since I served as nurse during the Civil War people who are helpless or dependent or who need nursing have made a strong appeal to me. I guess it is the maternal instinct in me.

"Mr. Mickelson was an old-time Nevada miner. He was a silversmith and also a blacksmith. In the early days in the mines he used to get as high as $10 for shoeing a saddle horse. I married Mr. Mickelson on October 14, 1890. I traveled all over California with him for his health, but he died on October 5, 1894.

"After my husband's death I ran my brother's ranch and also my husband's. They were nine miles apart and I rode from one to the other on horseback through the mountains every day to superintend the work. I bought this place and built my home in Ashland 21 years ago. Some years ago I sold both of the ranches, as I found it hard to get reliable help to run them.

"I am 83 years—I will not say old, except in experience—and as I sit here alone of an evening, I find I have plenty to think of, though, of course, I would like to have young folks of my own flesh and blood about me."

YOUNG AND BRAVE

TOP HAND

Luke Short

Gus Irby was out on the boardwalk in front of the Elite, giving his swamper hell for staving in an empty beer barrel, when the kid passed on his way to the feed stable. His horse was a good one and it was tired, Gus saw, and the kid had a little hump in his back from the cold of a mountain October morning. In spite of the ample layer of flesh that Gus wore carefully like an uncomfortable shroud, he shivered in his shirt sleeves and turned into the saloon, thinking without much interest, *Another fiddle-footed dry-country kid that's been paid off after round-up*.

Later, while he was taking out the cash for the day and opening up some fresh cigars, Gus saw the kid go into the Pride Café for breakfast, and afterward come out, toothpick in mouth, and cruise both sides of Wagon Mound's main street in aimless curiosity.

After that, Gus wasn't surprised when he looked around at the sound of the door opening, and saw the kid coming toward the bar. He was in a clean and faded shirt and looked as if he'd been cold for a good many hours. Gus said good morning and took down his best whisky and a glass and put them in front of the kid.

"First customer in the morning gets a drink on the house," Gus announced.

"Now I know why I rode all night," the kid said, and he grinned at Gus. He was a pleasant-faced kid with pale eyes that weren't shy or sullen or bold, and maybe because of this he didn't fit readily into any of Gus' handy character pigeonholes. Gus had seen them young and fiddle-footed before, but they were the tough kids, and for a man with no truculence in him, like Gus, talking with them was like trying to pet a tiger.

Gus leaned against the back bar and watched the kid take his whisky and wipe his mouth on his sleeve, and Gus found himself getting curious. Half a lifetime of asking skillful questions that didn't seem like questions at all, prompted Gus to observe now, "If you're goin' on through you better pick up a coat. This high country's cold now."

"I figure this is far enough," the kid said.

"Oh, well, if somebody sent for you, that's different." Gus reached lazily for a cigar.

The kid pulled out a silver dollar from his pocket and put it on the bar top, and then poured himself another whisky, which Gus was sure he didn't want, but which courtesy dictated he should buy. "Nobody sent fur me, either," the kid observed. "I ain't got any money."

Gus picked up the dollar and got change from the cash drawer and put it in front of the kid, afterward lighting his cigar. This was when the announcement came.

"I'm a top hand," the kid said quietly, looking levelly at Gus. "Who's lookin' for one?"

Gus was glad he was still lighting his cigar, else he might have smiled. If there had been a third man here, Gus would have winked at him surreptitiously; but since there wasn't, Gus kept his face expressionless, drew on his cigar a moment, and then observed gently, "You look pretty young for a top hand."

"The best cow pony I ever saw was four years old," the kid answered pointedly.

Gus smiled faintly and shook his head. "You picked a bad time. Round-up's over."

The kid nodded, and drank down his second whisky quickly, waited for his breath to come normally. Then he said, "Much obliged. I'll see you again," and turned toward the door.

A mild cussedness stirred within Gus, and after a moment's hesitation he called out, "Wait a minute."

The kid hauled up and came back to the bar. He moved with an easy grace that suggested quickness and work-hardened muscle, and for a moment Gus, a careful man, was undecided. But the kid's face, so young and without caution, reassured him, and he folded his heavy arms on the bar top and pulled his nose thoughtfully. "You figure to hit all the outfits, one by one, don't you?"

The kid nodded, and Gus frowned and was silent a moment, and then he murmured, almost to himself, "I had a notion—oh, hell, I don't know."

"Go ahead," the kid said, and then his swift grin came again. "I'll try anything once."

"Look," Gus said, as if his mind were made up. "We got a newspaper here—the Wickford County Free Press. Comes out Thursday, that's today." He looked soberly at the kid. "Whyn't you put a piece in there and say 'top hand wants a job at forty dollars a month'? Tell 'em what you can do and tell 'em to come see you in here if they want a hand. They'll all get it in a couple days. That way you'll save yourself a hundred miles of ridin'. Won't cost much either."

The kid thought awhile and then asked, without smiling, "Where's this newspaper at?"

Gus told him and the kid went out. Gus put the bottle away and doused the glass in water, and he was smiling slyly at his thoughts. Wait till the boys read that in the Free Press. They were going to have some fun with that kid, Gus reflected.

Johnny McSorley stepped out into the chill thin sunshine. The last silver dollar in his pants pocket was a solid weight against his leg, and he was aware that he'd probably spend it in the next few minutes on the newspaper piece. He wondered about that, and figured shrewdly it had an off chance of working.

Four riders dismounted at a tie rail ahead and paused a moment, talking. Johnny looked them over and picked out their leader, a tall, heavy, scowling man in his middle thirties who was wearing a mackinaw unbuttoned.

Johnny stopped and said, "You know anybody lookin' for a top hand?" and grinned pleasantly at the big man.

For a second Johnny thought he was going to smile. He didn't think he'd have liked the smile, once he saw it, but the man's face settled into the scowl again. "I never saw a top hand that couldn't vote," he said.

Johnny looked at him carefully, not smiling, and said, "Look at one now, then," and went on, and by the time he'd taken two steps he thought, *Voted, huh? A man must grow pretty slow in this high country.*

He crossed the street and paused before a window marked WICKFORD COUNTY FREE PRESS. JOB PRINTING. D. MELAVEN, IED. AND PROP. He went inside, then. A girl was seated at a cluttered desk, staring at the street, tapping a pencil against her teeth. Johnny tramped over to her, noting the infernal racket made by one of two men at a small press under the lamp behind the railed-off office space.

Johnny said "Hello," and the girl turned tiredly and said, "Hello, bub." She had on a plain blue dress with a high bodice and a narrow lace collar, and she was a very pretty girl, but tired, Johnny noticed. Her long yellow hair was worn in braids that crossed almost atop her head, and she looked, Johnny thought, like a small kid who has pinned her hair up out of the way for her Saturday night bath. He thought all this and then remembered her greeting, and he reflected without rancor, Damn, that's twice, and he said, "I got a piece for the paper, sis."

"Don't call me sis," the girl said. "Anybody's

name I don't know, I call him bub. No offense. I got that from pa, I guess."

That's likely, Johnny thought, and he said amiably, "Any girl's name I don't know, I call her sis. I got that from ma."

The cheerful effrontery of the remark widened the girl's eyes. She held out her hand now and said with dignity, "Give it to me. I'll see it gets in next week."

"That's too late," Johnny said. "I got to get it in this week."

"Why?"

"I ain't got money enough to hang around another week."

The girl stared carefully at him. "What is it?"

"I want to put a piece in about myself. I'm a top hand, and I'm lookin' for work. The fella over there at the saloon says why don't I put a piece in the paper about wantin' work, instead of ridin' out lookin' for it."

The girl was silent a full five seconds and then said, "You don't look that simple. Gus was having fun with you."

"I figured that," Johnny agreed. "Still, it might work. If you're caught short-handed, you take anything."

The girl shook her head. "It's too late. The paper's made up." Her voice was meant to hold a note of finality, but Johnny regarded her curiously, with a maddening placidity.

"You D. Melaven?" he asked.

"No. That's pa."

"Where's he?"

"Back there. Busy."

Johnny saw the gate in the rail that separated the office from the shop and headed toward it. He heard the girl's chair scrape on the floor and her urgent command, "Don't go back there. It's not allowed."

Johnny looked over his shoulder and grinned and said, "I'll try anything once," and went on through the gate, hearing the girl's swift steps behind him. He halted along a square-built and solid man with a thatch of stiff hair more gray than black, and said, "You D. Melaven?"

"Dan Melaven, bub. What can I do for you?"

That's three times, Johnny thought, and regarded Melaven's square face without anger. He liked the face; it was homely and stubborn and intelligent, and the eyes were both sharp and kindly. Hearing the girl stop beside him, Johnny said, "I got a piece for the paper today."

The girl put in quickly, "I told him it was too late, pa. Now you tell him and maybe he'll get out."

"Cassie," Melaven said in surprised protest.

"I don't care. We can't unlock the forms for every out-at-the-pants puncher that asks us. Besides, I think he's one of Alec Barr's bunch." She spoke vehemently, angrily, and Johnny listened to her with growing amazement.

"Alec who?" he asked.

"I saw you talking to him, and then you came straight over here from him," Cassie said hotly.

"I hit him for work."

"I don't believe it."

"Cassie," Melaven said grimly, "come back here a minute." He took her by the arm and led her toward the back of the shop, where they halted and engaged in a quiet, earnest conversation.

Johnny shook his head in bewilderment, and then looked around him. The biggest press, he observed, was idle. And on a stone-topped table where Melaven had been working was a metal form almost filled with lines of type and gray metal pieces of assorted sizes and shapes. Now, Johnny McSorley did not know any more than the average person about the workings of a newspaper, but his common sense told him that Cassie had lied to him when she said it was too late to accept his advertisement. Why, there was space and to spare in that form for the few lines of type his message would need. Turning this over in his mind, he wondered what was behind her refusal.

Presently, the argument settled, Melaven and Cassie came back to him, and Johnny observed that Cassie, while chastened, was still mad.

"All right, what do you want printed, bub?" Melaven asked.

Johnny told him and Melaven nodded when he

was finished, said, "Pay her," and went over to the type case.

Cassie went back to the desk and Johnny followed her, and when she was seated he said, "What do I owe you?"

Cassie looked speculatively at him, her face still flushed with anger. "How much money have you got?"

"A dollar some."

"It'll be two dollars," Cassie said.

Johnny pulled out his lone silver dollar and put it on the desk. "You print it just the same; I'll be back with the rest later."

Cassie said with open malice, "You'd have it now, bub, if you hadn't been drinking before ten o'clock."

Johnny didn't do anything for a moment, and then he put both hands on the desk and leaned close to her. "How old are you?" he asked quietly.

"Seventeen."

"I'm older'n you," Johnny murmured. "So the next time you call me 'bub' I'm goin' to take down your pigtails and pull 'em. I'll try anything once."

Once he was in the sunlight, crossing toward the Elite, he felt better. He smiled—partly at himself but mostly at Cassie. She was a real spitfire, kind of pretty and kind of nice, and he wished he knew what her father said to her that made her so mad, and why she'd been mad in the first place.

Gus was breaking out a new case of whisky and stacking bottles against the back mirror as Johnny came in and went up to the bar. Neither of them spoke while Gus finished, and Johnny gazed absently at the poker game at one of the tables and now yawned sleepily.

Gus said finally, "You get it in all right?"

Johnny nodded thoughtfully and said, "She mad like that at everybody?"

"Who? Cassie?"

"First she didn't want to take the piece, but her old man made her. Then she charges me more for it than I got in my pocket. Then she combs me over like I got my head stuck in the cookie crock for drinkin' in the morning. She calls me bub, to boot."

"She calls everybody bub."

"Not me no more," Johnny said firmly, and yawned again.

Gus grinned and sauntered over to the cash box. When he came back he put ten silver dollars on the bar top and said, "Pay me back when you get your job. And I got rooms upstairs if you want to sleep."

Johnny grinned. "Sleep, hunh? I'll try anything once." He took the money, said "Much obliged" and started away from the bar and then paused. "Say, who's this Alec Barr?"

Johnny saw Gus' eyes shift swiftly to the poker game and then shuttle back to him. Gus didn't say anything.

"See you later," Johnny said.

He climbed the stairs whose entrance was at the end of the bar, wondering why Gus was so careful about Alec Barr.

A gunshot somewhere out in the street woke him. The sun was gone from the room, so it must be afternoon, he thought. He pulled on his boots, slopped some water into the washbowl and washed up, pulled his hand across his cheek and decided he should shave, and went downstairs. There wasn't anybody in the saloon, not even behind the bar. On the tables and on the bar top, however, were several newspapers, all fresh. He was reminded at once that he was in debt to the Wickford County Free Press for the sum of one dollar. He pulled one of the newspapers toward him and turned to the page where all the advertisements were.

When, after some minutes, he finished, he saw that his advertisement was not there. A slow wrath grew in him as he thought of the girl and her father taking his money, and when it had come to full flower, he went out of the Elite and cut across toward the newspaper office. He saw, without really noticing it, the group of men clustered in front of the store across from the newspaper office. He swung under the tie rail and reached the opposite boardwalk

Overleaf: Nick Eggenhofer, *Gunfight at the O.K. Corral.* Date unknown. Oil, 20 x 30"

just this side of the newspaper office and a man who was lounging against the building. He was a puncher and when he saw Johnny heading up the walk he said, "Don't go across there."

Johnny said grimly, "You stop me," and went on, and he heard the puncher say, "All right, getcher head blown off."

His boots crunched broken glass in front of the office and he came to a gingerly halt, looking down at his feet. His glance raised to the window, and he saw where there was a big jag of glass out of the window, neatly wiping out the Wickford except for the W on the sign and ribboning cracks to all four corners of the frame. This surprised him motionless for a moment, and then he heard a voice calling from across the street, "Clear out of there, son."

That makes four times, Johnny thought resignedly, and he glanced across the street and saw Alec Barr, several men clotted around him, looking his way.

Johnny went on and turned into the newspaper office and it was like walking into a dark cave. The lamp was extinguished.

And then he saw the dim forms of Cassie Melaven and her father back of the railing beside the job press, and the reason for his errand came back to him with a rush. Walking through the gate, he began firmly, "I got a dollar—" and ceased talking and halted abruptly. There was a six-shooter in Dan Melaven's hand hanging at his side. Johnny looked at it, and then raised his glance to Melaven's face and found the man watching him with a bitter amusement in his eyes. His glance shuttled to Cassie, and she was looking at him as if she didn't see him, and her face seemed very pale in that gloom. He half gestured toward the gun and said, "What's that for?"

"A little trouble, bub," Melaven said mildly. "Come back for your money?"

"Yeah," Johnny said slowly.

Suddenly it came to him, and he wheeled and looked out through the broken window and saw Alec Barr across the street in conversation with two men, his own hands, Johnny supposed. That explained the shot that wakened him. A little trouble.

He looked back at Melaven now in time to hear him say to Cassie, "Give him his money."

Cassie came past him to the desk and pulled open a drawer and opened the cash box. While she was doing it, Johnny strolled soberly over to the desk. She gave him the dollar and he took it, and their glances met. *She's been crying*, he thought, with a strange distress.

"That's what I tried to tell you," Cassie said. "We didn't want to take your money, but you wouldn't have it. That's why I was so mean."

"What's it all about?" Johnny asked soberly.

"Didn't you read the paper?"

Johnny shook his head in negation, and Cassie said dully, "It's right there on page one. There's a big chunk of Government land out on Artillery Creek coming up for sale. Alec Barr wanted it, but he didn't want anybody bidding against him. He knew pa would have to publish a notice of sale. He tried to get pa to hold off publication of the date of sale until it would be too late for other bidders to make it. Pa was to get a piece of the land in return for the favor, or money. I guess we needed it all right, but pa told him no."

Johnny looked over at Melaven, who had come up to the rail now and was listening. Melaven said, "I knew Barr'd be in today with his bunch, and they'd want a look at a pull sheet before the press got busy, just to make sure the notice wasn't there. Well, Cassie and Dad Hopper worked with me all last night to turn out the real paper, with the notice of sale and a front-page editorial about Barr's proposition to me, to boot."

"We got it printed and hid it out in the shed early this morning," Cassie explained.

Melaven grinned faintly at Cassie, and there was a kind of open admiration for the job in the way he smiled. He said to Johnny now, "So what you saw in the forms this mornin' was a fake, bub. That's why Cassie didn't want your money. The paper was already printed." He smiled again, that rather proud smile. "After you'd gone, Barr came in. He wanted a pull sheet and we gave it to him, and he had a man out front watching us most of the morning. But he pulled him off later. We got the real paper out of the shed onto the Willow Valley stage, and we got it delivered all over town before Barr saw it."

Johnny was silent a moment, thinking this over. Then he nodded toward the window. "Barr do that?"

"I did," Melaven said quietly. "I reckon I can keep him out until someone in this town gets the guts to run him off."

Johnny looked down at the dollar in his hand and stared at it a moment and put it in his pocket. When he looked up at Cassie, he surprised her watching him, and she smiled a little, as if to ask forgiveness.

Johnny said, "Want any help?" to Melaven, and the man looked at him thoughtfully and then nodded. "Yes. You can take Cassie home."

"Oh, no," Cassie said. She backed away from the desk and put her back against the wall, looking from one to the other. "I don't go. As long as I'm here, he'll stay there."

"Sooner or later, he'll come in," Melaven said grimly. "I don't want you hurt."

"Let him come," Cassie said stubbornly. "I can swing a wrench better than some of his crew can shoot."

"Please go with him."

Cassie shook her head. "No, pa. There's some men left in this town. They'll turn up."

Melaven said "Hell," quietly, angrily, and went back into the shop. Johnny and the girl looked at each other for a long moment, and Johnny saw the fear in her eyes. She was fighting it, but she didn't have it licked, and he couldn't blame her. He said, "If I'd had a gun on me, I don't reckon they'd of let me in here, would they?"

"Don't try it again," Cassie said. "Don't try the back either. They're out there."

Johnny said, "Sure you won't come with me?"

"I'm sure."

"Good," Johnny said quietly. He stepped outside and turned up the street, glancing over at Barr and the three men with him, who were watching him wordlessly. The man leaning against the building straightened up and asked, "She comin' out?"

"She's thinkin' it over," Johnny said.

The man called across the street to Barr, "She's

thinkin' it over," and Johnny headed obliquely across the wide street toward the Elite. *What kind of a town is this, where they'd let this happen?* he thought angrily, and then he caught sight of Gus Irby standing under the wooden awning in front of the Elite, watching the show. Everybody else was doing the same thing. A man behind Johnny yelled, "Send her out, Melaven," and Johnny vaulted up onto the boardwalk and halted in front of Gus.

"What do you aim to do?" he asked Gus.

"Mind my own business, same as you," Gus growled, but he couldn't hold Johnny's gaze.

There was shame in his face, and when Johnny saw it his mind was made up. He shouldered past him and went into the Elite and saw it was empty. He stepped behind the bar now and, bent over so he could look under it, slowly traveled down it. Right beside the beer taps he found what he was looking for. It was a sawed-off shotgun and he lifted it up and broke it and saw that both barrels were loaded. Standing motionless, he thought about this now, and presently he moved on toward the back and went out the rear door. It opened onto an alley, and he turned left and went by it, thinking, *It was brick, and the one next to it was painted brown, at least in front.* And then he saw it up ahead, a low brick store with a big loading platform running across its rear.

He went up to it, and looked down the narrow passageway he'd remembered was between this building and the brown one beside it. There was a small areaway here, this end cluttered with weeds and bottles and tin cans. Looking through it he could see a man's elbow and segment of leg at the boardwalk, and he stepped as noiselessly as he could over the trash and worked forward to the boardwalk.

At the end of the areaway, he hauled up and looked out and saw Alec Barr some ten feet to his right and teetering on the edge of the high boardwalk, gun in hand. He was engaged in low conversation with three other men on either side of him. There was a supreme insolence in the way he exposed himself, as if he knew Melaven would not shoot at him and could not hit him if he did.

Johnny raised the shotgun hip high and stepped out and said quietly, "Barr, you goin' to throw away that gun and get on your horse or am I goin' to burn you down?"

The four men turned slowly, not moving anything except their heads. It was Barr whom Johnny watched, and he saw the man's bold baleful eyes gauge his chances and decline the risk, and Johnny smiled. The three other men were watching Barr for a clue to their moves.

Johnny said "Now," and on the heel of it he heard the faint clatter of a kicked tin can in the areaway behind him. He lunged out of the areaway just as a pistol shot erupted with a savage roar between the two buildings.

Barr half turned now with the swiftness with which he lifted his gun across his front and Johnny, watching him, didn't even raise the shotgun in his haste; he let go from the hip. He saw Barr rammed off the high boardwalk into the tie rail, and heard it crack and splinter and break with the big man's weight, and then Barr fell in the street out of sight.

The three other men scattered into the street, running blindly for the opposite sidewalk. And at the same time, the men who had been standing in front of the buildings watching this now ran toward Barr, and Gus Irby was in the van. Johnny poked the shotgun into the areaway and without even taking sight he pulled the trigger and listened to the bellow of the explosion and the rattling raking of the buckshot as it caromed between the two buildings. Afterward, he turned down the street and let Gus and the others run past him, and he went into the Elite.

It was empty, and he put the shotgun on the bar and got himself a glass of water and stood there drinking it, thinking, *I feel some different, but not much.*

He was still drinking water when Gus came in later. Gus looked at him long and hard, as he poured himself a stout glass of whisky and downed it. Finally, Gus said, "There ain't a right thing about it, but they won't pay you a bounty for him. They should."

Johnny didn't say anything, only rinsed out his glass.

"Melaven wants to see you," Gus said then.

"All right." Johnny walked past him and Gus let him get past him ten feet, and then said, "Kid, look."

Johnny halted and turned around and Gus, looking sheepish, said, "About that there newspaper piece. That was meant to be a rawhide, but damned if it didn't backfire on me."

Johnny just waited, and Gus went on. "You remember the man that was standing this side of Barr? He works for me, runs some cows for me. Did, I mean, because he stood there all afternoon sickin' Barr on Melaven. You want his job? Forty a month, top hand."

"Sure," Johnny said promptly.

Gus smiled expansively and said, "Let's have a drink on it."

"Tomorrow," Johnny said. "I don't aim to get a reputation for drinkin' all day long."

Gus looked puzzled, and then laughed. "Reputation? Who with? Who knows—" His talk faded off, and then he said quietly, "Oh."

Johnny waited long enough to see if Gus would smile, and when Gus didn't, he went out. Gus didn't smile after he'd gone either.

LUKE SHORT *(1908–1975), wrote popular Western fiction during the 1950s and into the '70s, until he died in 1975. His stories appeared in* The Saturday Evening Post*, and "Top Hand" is considered to be one of the finest.*

FROM MISSOURI

ZANE GREY

With jingling spurs a tall cowboy stalked out of the post office to confront three punchers who were just then crossing the wide street from the saloon opposite. "Look heah," he said, shoving a letter under their noses. "Which one of you longhorns wrote her again?"

From a gay, careless trio his listeners suddenly looked blank, then intensely curious. They stared at the handwriting on the letter.

"Tex, I'm a son-of-a-gun if it ain't from Missouri!" exclaimed Andy Smith, his lean red face bursting into a smile.

"It shore is," declared Nevada.

"From Missouri!" echoed Panhandle Hanes.

"Well?" asked Tex, almost with a snort.

The three cowboys drew back to look from Tex to one another, and then back at Tex.

"It's from her," went on Tex, his voice hushing on the pronoun. "You all know that handwritin'. Now how about this deal? We swore none of us would write to this schoolmarm. But some one of you has doublecrossed the outfit."

Loud and simultaneous protestations of innocence arose from them. But it was evident that Tex did not trust them, and that they did not trust him or each other.

"Say, boys," said Panhandle suddenly. "I see Beady Jones in here lookin' darn sharp at us. Let's get off in the woods somewhere."

"Back to the bar," said Nevada. "I reckon we'll all need bracers."

"Beady!" exclaimed Tex as they turned across the street. "He could be to blame as much as any of us. An' he was still at Stringer's when we wrote the first letter."

"Shore. It'd be more like Beady," said Nevada. "But Tex, your mind ain't workin'. Our lady friend from Missouri wrote before without gettin' any letter from us."

"How do we know thet?" asked Tex suspiciously. "Shore the boss' typewriter is a puzzle, but it could hide tracks. Savvy, pards?"

"Doggone it, Tex, you need a drink," said Panhandle peevishly.

They entered the saloon and strode up to the bar, where from all appearances Tex was not the only one to seek artificial strength. Then they repaired to a corner, where they took seats and stared at the letter Tex threw down before them.

"From Missouri, all right," said Panhandle, studying the postmark. "Kansas City, Missouri."

"It's her writin'," said Nevada, in awe. "Shore I'd know that out of a million letters."

"Ain't you goin' to read it to us?" asked Andy Smith.

"Mr. Frank Owens," said Tex, reading from the address on the letter. "Springer's Ranch, Beacon, Arizona...Boys, this Frank Owens is all of us."

"Huh! Mebbe he's a darn sight more," added Andy.

"Looks like a lowdown trick we're to blame for," resumed Tex, seriously shaking his hawklike head. "Heah we reads in a Kansas City paper about a schoolteacher wantin' a job out in dry Arizona. An' we writes her an' gets her a-rarin' to come. Then when she writes and tells us she's not over forty—then we quits like yellow coyotes. An' we four anyhow shook hands on never writin' her agin. Well, somebody did, an' I reckon you all think me as big a liar as I think you are. But that ain't the point. Heah's another letter to Mr. Owens an' I'll bet my saddle it means trouble."

Tex impressively spread out the letter and read laboriously:

> Kansas City, Mo.
> June 15
>
> Dear Mr. Owens:
> Your last letter has explained away much that was vague and perplexing in your other letters.
>
> It has inspired me with hope and anticipation. I shall not take time now to express my thanks, but hasten to get ready to go west. I shall leave tomorrow and arrive at Beacon on June 19, at 4:30 P.M. You see I have studied the timetable.
>
> Yours very truly,
> Jane Stacey

Profound silence followed Tex's reading of the letter. The cowboys were struck completely dumb. Then suddenly Nevada exploded:

"My Gawd, fellers, today's the nineteenth!"

"Well, Springer needs a schoolmarm at the ranch," finally spoke up the more practical Andy. "There's half a dozen kids growin' up without schoolin', not to talk about other ranches. I heard the boss say so himself."

Tex spoke up. "I've an idea. It's too late now to turn this poor schoolmarm back. An' somebody'll have to meet her. You all come with me. I'll get a

buckboard. I'll meet the lady and do the talkin'. I'll let her down easy. And if I cain't head her back to Missouri we'll fetch her out to the ranch an' then leave it up to Springer. Only we won't tell her or him or anybody who's the real Frank Owens."

"Tex, that ain't so plumb bad," said Andy admiringly.

"What I want to know is who's goin' to do the talkin' to the boss?" asked Panhandle. "It mightn't be so hard to explain now. But after drivin' up to the ranch with a woman! You all know Springer's shy. Young an' rich, like he is, an' a bachelor—he's been fussed over so he's plumb afraid of girls. An' here you're fetchin' a middle-aged schoolmarm who's romantic an' mushy!—My Gawd;...I say send her home on the next train."

"Pan, you're wise as far as horses an' cattle goes, but you don't know human nature, an' you're dead wrong about the boss," said Tex. "We're in a bad fix, I'll admit. But I lean more to fetchin' the lady up than sendin' her back. Somebody down Beacon way would get wise. Mebbe the schoolmarm might talk. She'd shore have cause. An' suppose Springer hears about it—that some of us or all of us has played a lowdown trick on a woman. He'd be madder at that than if we fetched her up.

"Likely he'll try to make amends. The boss may be shy on girls but he's the squarest man in Arizona. My idea is that we'll deny any of us is Frank Owens, and we'll meet Miss—Miss—what was her name?—Miss Jane Stacey and fetch her up to the ranch, an' let her do the talkin' to Springer."

During the next several hours while Tex searched the town for a buckboard and team he could borrow, the other cowboys wandered from the saloon to the post office and back again, and then to the store, the restaurant and back again, and finally settled in the saloon.

When they emerged some time later they were arm in arm, and far from steady on their feet. They paraded up the one main street of Beacon not in the least conspicious on a Saturday afternoon. As they were neither hilarious nor dangerous, nobody paid any particular attention to them. Springer, their boss, met them, gazed at them casually, and passed by without sign of recognition. If he had studied the boys closely he might have received an impression that they were clinging to a secret, as well as to each other.

In due time the trio presented themselves at the railroad station. Tex was there, nervously striding up and down the platform, now and then looking at his watch. The afternoon train was nearly due. At the hitching rail below the platform stood a new buckboard and a rather spirited team of horses.

The boys, coming across the wide square, encountered this evidence of Tex's extremity, and struck a posture before it.

"Livery shtable outfit, my gosh," said Andy.

"Shon of a gun if it ain't," added Panhandle with a huge grin.

"This here Tex spendin' his money royal," agreed Nevada.

Then Tex saw them. He stared. Suddenly he jumped straight up. Striding to the edge of the platform, with face red as a beet, he began to curse them.

"Whash masher, ole pard?" asked Andy, who appeared a little less stable than his two comrades.

Tex's reply was another volley of expressive profanity. And he ended with: "—you all yellow quitters to get drunk and leave me in the lurch. But you gotta get away from here. I shore won't have you about when the train comes in."

"But pard, we jist want to shee you meet our Jane from Missouri," said Andy.

"If you all ain't a lot of fourflushers I'll eat my chaps!" burst out Tex hotly.

Just then a shrill whistle announced the arrival of the train.

"You can sneak off now," he went on, "an' leave me to face the music. Always knew I was the only gentleman in Springer's outfit."

The three cowboys did not act upon Tex's sarcastic suggestion, but they hung back, looking at once excited and sheepish and hugely delighted.

The long gray dusty train pulled into the station and stopped with a complaining of brakes. There was

only one passenger for Springer—a woman—and she alighted from the coach near where the cowboys stood waiting. She wore a long linen coat and a brown veil that completely hid her face. She was not tall and she was much too slight for the heavy valise the porter handed down to her.

Tex strode swaggeringly toward her.

"Miss—Miss Stacey, ma'am?" he asked, removing his sombrero.

"Yes," she replied. "Are you Mr. Owens?"

Evidently the voice was not what Tex had expected and it disconcerted him.

"No, ma'am,—I'm not Mister Owens," he said. "Please let me take your bag . . . I'm Tex Dillon, one of Springer's cowboys. An' I've come to meet you—and fetch you out to the ranch."

"Thank you, but—I expected to be met by Mr. Owens," she replied.

"Ma'am, there's been a mistake—I've got to tell you—there ain't any Mister Owens," blurted out Tex manfully.

"Oh!" she said, with a little start.

"You see, it was this way," went on the confused cowboy. "One of Springer's cowboys—not me—wrote them letters to you, signin' his name Owens. There ain't no such named cowboy in this whole country. Your last letter—an' here it is—fell into my hands—all by accident, ma'am, it shore was. I took my three friends heah—I took them into my confidence. An' we all came down to meet you."

She moved her head and evidently looked at the strange trio of cowboys Tex pointed out as his friends. They shuffled forward, not too eagerly, and they still held on to each other. Their condition, not to consider their state of excitement, could not have been lost even upon a tenderfoot from Missouri.

"Please return my—my letter," she said, turning again to Tex, and she put out a small gloved hand to take it from him. "Then—there is no Mr. Frank Owens?"

Overleaf: James E. Reynolds, *The Good Life*, 1971. Oil, 24 x 36"

"No ma'am, there shore ain't," said Tex miserably.

"Is there—no—no truth in his—is there no schoolteacher wanted here?" she faltered.

"I think so, ma'am," he replied. "Springer said he needed one. That's what started us answerin' the advertisement an' the letters to you. You can see the boss an'—an' explain. I'm shore it will be all right. He's one swell feller. He won't stand for no joke on a poor old schoolmarm."

In his bewilderment Tex had spoken his thoughts, and his last slip made him look more miserable than ever, and made the boys appear ready to burst.

"Poor old schoolmarm" echoed Miss Stacey. "Perhaps the deceit has not been wholly on one side."

Whereupon she swept aside the enveloping veil to reveal a pale yet extremely pretty face. She was young. She had clear gray eyes and a sweet sensitive mouth. Little curls of chestnut hair straggled down from under her veil, and she had tiny freckles.

Tex stared at this lovely apparition.

"But you—you—the letter says she wasn't over forty," he exclaimed.

"She's not," rejoined Miss Stacey curtly.

Then there were visible and remarkable indications of a transformation in the attitude of the cowboy. But the approach of a stranger suddenly seemed to paralyze him. The newcomer was very tall. He strolled up to them. He was hooted and spurred. He halted before the group and looked expectantly from the boys to the strange young woman and back again. But for the moment the four cowboys appeared dumb.

"Are—are you Mr. Springer?" asked Miss Stacey.

"Yes," he replied, and he took off his sombrero. He had a deeply tanned frank face and keen blue eyes.

"I am Jane Stacey," she explained hurriedly. "I'm a schoolteacher. I answered an advertisement. And I've come from Missouri because of letters I received from a Mr. Frank Owens, of Springer's Ranch. This young man met me. He has not been very explicit. I gather there is no Mr. Owens—that I'm the victim of a cowboy joke...But he said that Mr. Springer wouldn't stand for a joke on a poor old schoolmarm."

"I sure am glad to meet you, Miss Stacey," said the rancher, with an easy Western courtesy that must have been comforting to her. "Please let me see the letters."

She opened a handbag, and searching in it, presently held out several letters. Springer never even glanced at his stricken cowboys. He took the letters.

"No, not that one," said Miss Stacey, blushing scarlet. "That's one I wrote to Mr. Owens, but didn't mail. It's—hardly necessary to read that."

While Springer read the others she looked at him. Presently he asked her for the letter she had taken back. Miss Stacey hesitated, then refused. He looked cool, serious, businesslike. Then his keen eyes swept over the four ill-at-ease cowboys.

"Tex, are you Mr. Frank Owens?" he asked sharply.

"I—shore—ain't," gasped Tex.

Springer asked each of the other boys the same question and received decidedly maudlin but negative answers. Then he turned to the girl.

"Miss Stacey, I regret to say that you are indeed the victim of a lowdown cowboy trick," he said. "I'd apologize for such heathen if I knew how. All I can say is I'm sorry."

"Then—then there isn't any school to teach—any place for me—out here?" she asked, and there were tears in her eyes.

"That's another matter," he said, with a pleasant smile. "Of course there's a place for you. I've wanted a schoolteacher for a long time. Some of the men out at the ranch have kids and they sure need a teacher badly."

"Oh, I'm—so glad," she murmured, in evident relief. "I was afraid I'd have to go all the way back. You see I'm not so strong as I used to be—and my doctor advised a change of climate—dry Western air."

"You don't look sick," he said, with his keen eyes on her. "You look very well to me."

"Oh, indeed, but I'm not very strong," she said quickly. "But I must confess I wasn't altogether truthful about my age."

I was wondering about that," he said, gravely. There seemed just a glint of a twinkle in his eye. "Not over forty."

Again she blushed and this time with confusion.

"It wasn't altogether a lie. I was afraid to mention that I was only—young. And I wanted to get the position so much.... I'm a good—a competent teacher, unless the scholars are too grown up."

"The scholars you'll have at my ranch are children," he replied. "Well, we'd better be starting if we are to get there before dark. It's a long ride."

A FEW WEEKS ALTERED many things at Springer's Ranch. There was a marvelous change in the dress and deportment of the cowboys when off duty. There were some clean and happy and interested children. There was a rather taciturn and lonely young rancher who was given to thoughtful dreams and whose keen blue eyes kept watch on the little adobe schoolhouse under the cottonwoods. And in Jane Stacey's face a rich bloom and tan had begun to drive out the city pallor.

It was not often that Jane left the schoolhouse without meeting one of Springer's cowboys. She met Tex most frequently, and according to Andy, that fact was because Tex was foreman and could send the boys off to the end of the range when he had the notion.

One afternoon Jane encountered the foreman. He was clean-shaven, bright and eager, a superb figure of a man. Tex had been lucky enough to have a gun with him one day when a rattlesnake had frightened the schoolteacher and he had shot the reptile. Miss Stacey had leaned against him in her fright. She had been grateful; she had admired his wonderful skill with a gun, and had murmured that a woman always would be safe with such a man. Thereafter Tex packed his gun, unmindful of the ridicule of his rivals.

"Miss Stacey, come for a little ride, won't you?" he asked eagerly.

The cowboys had already taught her how to handle a horse and to ride; and if all they said of her appearance and accomplishment were true she was indeed worth watching.

"I'm sorry," said Jane. "I promised Nevada I'd ride with him today."

"I reckon Nevada is miles and miles up the valley by now," replied Tex. "He won't be back till long after dark."

"But he made an engagement with me," protested the schoolmistress.

"An' shore he has to work. He's ridin' for Springer, an' I'm foreman of this ranch," said Tex.

"You sent him off on some long chase," said Jane severely. "Now didn't you?"

"I shore did. He comes crowin' down to the bunkhouse—about how he's goin' to ride with you an' how we all are not in the runnin'."

"Oh! he did— And what did you say?"

"I says, 'Nevada, I reckon there's a steer mired in the sand up in Cedar Wash. You ride up there and pull him out.'"

"And then what did he say?" inquired Jane curiously.

"Why, Miss Stacey, shore I hate to tell you. I didn't think he was so—so bad. He just used the most awful language as was ever heard on this here ranch. Then he rode off."

"But was there a steer mired up in the wash?"

"I reckon so," replied Tex, rather shamefacedly. "Most always is one."

Jane let scornful eyes rest upon the foreman. "That was a mean trick," she said.

"There's been worse done to me by him, an' all of them. An' all's fair in love an' war...Will you ride with me?"

"No."

"Why not?"

"Because I think I'll ride off alone up Cedar Wash and help Nevada find that mired steer."

"Miss Stacey, you're shore not goin' to ride off alone. Savvy that."

"Who'll keep me from it?" demanded Jane with spirit.

"I will. Or any of the boys, for that matter. Springer's orders."

Jane started with surprise and then blushed rosy red. Tex, also, appeared confused at his disclosure.

"Miss Stacey, I oughtn't have said that. It slipped

out the boss said we needn't tell you, but you were to be watched an' taken care of. It's a wild range. You could get lost or thrown from a hoss."

"Mr. Springer is very kind and thoughtful," murmured Jane.

"The fact is, this ranch is a different place since you came," went on Tex as if suddenly emboldened. "An' this beatin' around the bush doesn't suit me. All the boys have lost their heads over you."

"Indeed? How flattering!" said Jane, with just a hint of mockery. She was fond of all her admirers, but there were four of them she had not yet forgiven.

The tall foreman was not without spirit. "It's true all right, as you'll find out pretty quick," he replied. "If you had any eyes you'd see that cattle raisin' on this ranch is about to halt till somethin' is decided. Why, even Springer himself is sweet on you!"

"How dare you!" flashed Jane, blushing furiously.

"I ain't afraid to tell the truth," said Tex stoutly. "He is. The boys all say so. He's grouchier than ever. He's jealous. Lord! he's jealous! He watches you—"

"Suppose I told him you had dared to say such things?" interrupted Jane, trembling on the verge of a strange emotion.

"Why, he'd be tickled to death. He hasn't got nerve enough to tell you himself."

Jane shook her head, but her face was still flushed. This cowboy, like all his comrades, was hopeless. She was about to change the topic of conversation when Tex suddenly took her into his arms. She struggled—and fought with all her might. But he succeeded in kissing her cheek and then the tip of her ear. Finally she broke away from him.

"Now—" she panted. "You've done it—you've insulted me! Now I'll never ride with you again—never even speak to you."

"Shore I didn't insult you," replied Tex. "Jane—won't you marry me?"

"No."

"Won't you be my sweetheart—till you care enough to—to—"

"No."

"But, Jane, you'll forgive me, an' be good friends with me again?"

"Never!"

Jane did not mean all she said. She had come to understand these men of the range—their loneliness—their hunger for love. But in spite of her sympathy and affection she needed sometimes to appear cold and severe with them.

"Jane, you owe me a great deal—more than you got any idea of," said Tex seriously.

"How so?"

"Didn't you ever guess about me?"

"My wildest flight at guessing would never make anything of you, Texas Jack."

"You'd never have been here but for me," he said solemnly.

Jane could only stare at him.

"I meant to tell you long ago. But I shore didn't have the nerve. Jane I—I was that there letter-writin' feller. I wrote them letters you got. I am Frank Owens."

"No!" exclaimed Jane.

She was startled. That matter of Frank Owens had never been cleared up to her satisfaction. It had ceased to rankle within her breast, but it had never been completely forgotten. She looked up earnestly into the big fellow's face. It was like a mask. But she saw through it. He was lying. He was brazen. Almost, she thought, she saw a laugh deep in his eyes.

"I shore am that lucky man who found you a job when you was sick an' needed a change…An' that you've grown so pretty an' so well you owe all to me."

"Tex, if you really were Frank Owens, that would make a great difference; indeed I do owe him everything, I would—but I don't believe you are he."

"It's shore honest Gospel fact," declared Tex. "I hope to die if it ain't!"

Jane shook her head sadly at his monstrous prevarication. "I don't believe you," she said, and left him standing there.

It might have been coincidence that the next few days both Nevada and Panhandle waylaid the pretty schoolteacher and conveyed to her intelligence the astounding fact that each was none other than Mr. Frank Owens. More likely, however, was it attributable to the unerring instinct of lovers who had sensed the importance and significance of this mysterious correspondent's part in bringing health and happiness into Jane Stacey's life. She listened to them with both anger and amusement at their deceit, and she had the same answer for both. "I don't believe you."

Because of these clumsy machinations of the cowboys, Jane had begun to entertain some vague, sweet, and disturbing suspicions of her own as to the identity of that mysterious cowboy, Frank Owens.

IT CAME ABOUT THAT a dance was to be held at Beacon during the late summer. The cowboys let Jane know that it was something she could not very well afford to miss. She had not attended either of the cowboy dances which had been given since her arrival. This next one, however, appeared to be an annual affair, at which all the ranching fraternity for miles around would be attending.

Jane, as a matter of fact, was wild to go. However, she felt that she could not accept the escort of any one of her cowboy admirers without alienating the others. And she began to have visions of this wonderful dance fading away without a chance of her attending, when Springer accosted her one day.

"Who's the lucky cowboy to take you to our dance?" he asked.

"He seems to be as mysterious and doubtful as Mr. Frank Owens," replied Jane.

"Oh, you still remember him," said the rancher, his keen dark eyes quizzically on her.

"Indeed I do," sighed Jane.

"Too bad! He was a villain . . . But you don't mean you haven't been asked to go?"

"They've all asked me. That's the trouble."

"I see. But you mustn't miss it. It'd be pleasant for you to meet some of the ranchers and their wives. Suppose you go with me?"

"Oh, Mr. Springer, I—I'd be delighted," replied Jane.

Jane's first sight of that dance hall astonished her. It was a big barnlike room, crudely raftered and sided, decorated with colored bunting which took away some of the bareness. The oil lamps were not bright, but there were plenty of them hung in brackets around the room. The volume of sound amazed her. Music and the trample of boots, gay laughter, the deep voices of men and the high-pitched voices of the children—all seemed to merge into a loud, confused uproar. A swaying, wheeling horde of dancers circled past her.

"Sure it's something pretty fine for old Bill Springer to have the prettiest girl here," her escort said.

"Thank you—but, Mr. Springer—I can easily see that you were a cowboy before you became a rancher," she replied archly.

"Sure I was. And that you will be dead sure to find out," he laughed. "Of course I could never compete with—say—Frank Owens. But let's dance. I shall have little enough of you in this outfit."

So he swung her into the circle of dancers. Jane found him easy to dance with, though he was far from expert. It was a jostling mob, and she soon acquired a conviction that if her gown did outlast the entire dance her feet never would. Springer took his dancing seriously and had little to say. She felt strange and uncertain with him. Presently she became aware of the cessation of hum and movement. The music had stopped.

"That sure was the best dance I ever had," said Springer, with a glow of excitement on his dark face. "An' now I must lose you to this outfit just coming."

Manifestly he meant his cowboys, Tex, Nevada, Panhandle, and Andy, who were presenting themselves four abreast shiny of hair and face.

"Good luck," he whispered. "If you get into a jam, let me know."

What he meant quickly dawned upon Jane. Right then it began. She saw there was absolutely no use in trying to avoid or refuse these young men. The wisest and safest course was to surrender, which she did.

"Boys, don't all talk at once. I can dance with only

one of you at a time. So I'll take you in alphabetical
order. I'm a poor old schoolmarm from Missouri, you
know. It'll be Andy, Nevada, Panhandle, and Tex."

Despite their protests she held rigidly to this rule.
Each one of the cowboys took shameless advantage of
his opportunity. Outrageously as they all hugged her,
Tex was the worst offender. She tried to stop dancing,
but he carried her along as if she had been a child. He
was rapt, and yet there seemed a devil in him.

"Tex—how dare—you!" she panted, when at last
the dance ended.

"Well, I reckon I'd about dare anythin' for you,
Jane," he replied, towering over her.

"You ought to be—ashamed," she went on. "I'll
not dance with you again."

"Aw, now," he pleaded.

"I won't, Tex, so there. You're no gentleman."

"Ahuh!" he retorted, drawing himself up stiffly.
"All right, I'll go out an' get drunk, an' when I come
back I'll clean out this hall so quick that you'll get
dizzy watchin'."

"Tex! Don't go," she called hurriedly, as he started
to stride away. "I'll take that back. I will give you
another dance—if you promise to—to behave."

With this hasty promise she got rid of him, and
was carried off by Mrs. Hartwell to be introduced to
the various ranchers and their wives, and to all the
girls and their escorts. She found herself a center of
admiring eyes. She promised more dances than she
could ever hope to remember or keep.

Her next partner was a tall handsome cowboy
named Jones. She did not know quite what to make
of him. But he was an unusually good dancer, and he
did not hold her in such a manner that she had difficulty in breathing. He talked all the time. He was
witty and engaging and he had a most subtly flattering tongue. Jane could not fail to grasp that he might
even be more outrageous than Tex, but at least he
did not make love to her with physical violence.

She enjoyed that dance and admitted to herself

Frank Tenney Johnson, *Rough Riding Rancheros*, 1935.
Oil, 36 x 46"

that the singular forceful charm about this Mr. Jones was appealing. If he was a little too bold of glance and somehow too primitively self-assured and debonair she passed it by in the excitement and joy of the hour, and in the conviction that she was now a long way from Missouri. Jones demanded, rather than begged for, another dance, and though she laughingly explained her predicament in regard to partners he said he would come after her anyhow.

Then followed several dances with new partners, and Jane became more than ever the center of attraction. It all went to the schoolteacher's head like wine. She was having a perfectly wonderful time. Jones claimed her again, in fact whirled her away from the man to whom she was talking and out on the floor. Twice again before the supper hour at midnight she found herself dancing with Jones. How he managed it she did not know. He just took her, carrying her off by storm.

She did not awaken to this unpardonable conduct of hers until she suddenly recalled that a little before she had promised Tex his second dance, and then she had given it to Jones, or at least had danced it with him. But, after all, what could she do when he had walked right off with her? It was a glimpse of Tex's face, as she whirled past in Jones' arms, that filled Jane with sudden remorse.

Then came the supper hour. It was a gala occasion, for which evidently the children had heroically kept awake. Jane enjoyed the children immensely. She sat with the numerous Hartwells, all of whom were most pleasantly attentive to her. Jane wondered why Mr. Springer did not put in an appearance, but considered his absence due to numerous duties on the dance committee!

When the supper hour ended and the people were stirring about the hall again, and the musicians were turning up, Jane caught sight of Andy. He looked rather pale and almost sick. Jane tried to catch his eye, but failing that she went to him.

"Andy, please find Tex for me. I owe him a dance, and I'll give him the very first, unless Mr. Springer comes for it."

Andy regarded her with an aloofness totally new to her.

"Well, I'll tell him. But I reckon Tex ain't presentable just now. An' all of us boys are through dancin' for tonight."

"What's happened?" asked Jane, swift to divine trouble.

"There's been a little fight."

"Oh, no!" cried Jane. "Who? Why?—Andy, please tell me."

"Well, when you cut Tex's dance for Beady Jones, you shore put our outfit in bad," replied Andy coldly. "At that there wouldn't have been anything come of it here if Beady Jones hadn't got to shootin' off his chin. Tex slapped his face an' that shore started a fight. Beady licked Tex, too, I'm sorry to say. He's a pretty bad hombre, Beady is, an' he's bigger'n Tex. Well, he had a hell of a time keepin' Nevada out of it. That would have been a worse fight. I'd like to have seen it. But we kept them apart till Springer come out. An' what the boss said to that outfit was sure aplenty.

"Beady Jones kept talkin' back, nastylike—you know he was once foreman for us—till Springer got good an' mad. An' he said: 'Jones, I fired you once because you were a little too slick for our outfit, an' I'll tell you this, if it come to a pinch I'll give you the damnedest thrashin' any smart-aleck cowboy ever got.' . . . Judas, the boss was riled. It sort of surprised me, an' tickled me pink. You can bet that shut Beady Jones' loud mouth and mighty quick!"

After his rather lengthy speech, Andy left her unceremoniously standing there alone. She was not alone long, but it was long enough for her to feel a rush of bitter dissatisfaction with herself.

Jane looked for Springer, hoping yet fearing he would come to her. But he did not. She had another uninterrupted dizzy round of dancing until her strength completely failed. By four o'clock she was scarcely able to walk. Her pretty dress was torn and mussed; her white stockings were no longer white; her slippers were worn ragged. And her feet were dead. She dragged herself to a chair where she sat looking on, and trying to keep awake. The wonderful dance that had begun so promisingly had ended sadly for her.

At length the exodus began, though Jane did not see many of the dancers leaving. She went out to be received by Springer, who had evidently made arrangements for their leaving. He seemed decidedly cool to the remorseful Jane.

All during the long ride to the ranch he never addressed her or looked toward her. Daylight came, appearing cold and gray to Jane. She felt as if she wanted to cry.

Springer's sister and the matronly housekeeper were waiting for them, with a cherry welcome, and an invitation to a hot breakfast.

Presently Jane found herself momentarily alone with the taciturn rancher.

"Miss Stacey," he said, in a voice she had never heard, "your crude flirting with Beady Jones made trouble for the Springer outfit last night."

"*Mr. Springer!*" she exclaimed, her head going up.

"Excuse me," he returned, in a cutting, dry tone that recalled Tex. After all, this Westerner was still a cowboy, just exactly like those who rode for him, only a little older, and therefore more reserved and careful of his speech. "If it wasn't that—then you sure appeared to be pretty much taken with Mr. Beady Jones."

"If that was anybody's business, it might have appeared so," she cried, tingling all over with some feeling which she could not control.

"Sure. But are you denying it?" he asked soberly, eyeing her with a grave frown and obvious disapproval. It was this more than his question that roused hot anger and contrariness in Jane.

"I admired Mr. Jones very much," she replied haughtily. "He was a splendid dancer. He did not maul me like a bear. I really had a chance to breathe during my dances with him. Then too he could talk. He was a gentleman."

Springer bowed with dignity. His dark face paled. It dawned upon Jane that the situation had become serious for everyone concerned. She began to repent her hasty pride.

"Thanks," he said. "Please excuse my impertinence. I see you have found your Mr. Frank Owens in this cowboy Jones, and it sure is not my place to say any more."

"But—but—Mr. Springer—" faltered Jane, quite unstrung by the rancher's amazing speech.

However, he merely bowed again and left her. Jane felt too miserable and weary for anything but rest and a good cry. She went to her room, and flinging off her hateful finery, she crawled into bed, and buried her head in her pillow.

About mid-afternoon Jane awakened greatly refreshed and relieved and strangely repentant. She invaded the kitchen, where the goodnatured housekeeper, who had become fond of her, gave her some wild-turkey sandwiches and cookies and sweet rich milk. While Jane appeased her hunger the woman gossiped about the cowboys and Springer, and the information she imparted renewed Jane's concern over the last night's affair.

From the kitchen Jane went out into the court-yard, and naturally, as always, gravitated toward the corrals and barns. Springer appeared in company of a rancher Jane did not know. She expected Springer to stop her for a few pleasant words as was his wont. This time, however, he merely touched his sombrero and passed on. Jane felt the incident almost as a slight. And it hurt.

As she went on down the lane she became very thoughtful. A cloud suddenly had appeared above the horizon of her happy life there at the Springer ranch. It did not seem to her that what she had done deserved the change in everyone's attitude. The lane opened out onto a wide square, around which were the gates to the corrals, the entrances to several barns, the forge, granaries, and the commodious bunkhouse of the cowboys.

Jane's sharp eyes caught sight of the boys before they saw her. But when she looked up again every broad back was turned. They allowed her to pass with-

Overleaf: Edward Borein, *Untitled*, 1945.
Oil, 11½ x 20"

out any apparent knowledge of her existence. This obvious snub was unprecedented. It offended her bitterly. She knew that she was being unreasonable, but could not or would not help it. She strolled on down to the pasture gate and watched the colts and calves.

Upon her return she passed even closer to the cowboys. But again they apparently did not see her. Jane added resentment to her wounded vanity and pride. Yet even then a still small voice tormented and accused her. She went back to her room, meaning to read or sew, or prepare schoolwork. But instead she sat down in a chair and burst into tears.

Next day was Sunday. Heretofore every Sunday had been a full day for Jane. This one, however, bade fair to be an empty one. Company came as usual, neighbors from nearby ranches. The cowboys were off duty and other cowboys came over to visit them.

Jane's attention was attracted by the sight of a superb horseman riding up the lane to the ranch house. He seemed familiar, somehow, but she could not place him. What a picture he made as he dismounted slick and shiny, booted and spurred, to doff his huge sombrero! Jane heard him ask for Miss Stacey. Then she recognized him. Beady Jones! She was at once horrified and yet attracted to this cowboy. She remembered how he had asked if he might call Sunday and she had certainly not refused to see him. But for him to come here after the fight with Tex and the bitter scene with Springer!

It seemed almost an unparalleled affront. What manner of man was this cowboy Jones? He certainly did not lack courage. But more to the point what idea had he of her? Jane rose to the occasion. She had let herself in for this, and she would see it through, come what might. Looming disaster stimulated her. She would show these indifferent, deceitful, firespirited, incomprehensible cowboys! She would let Springer see that she had indeed taken Beady Jones for Mr. Frank Owens.

With this thought in mind, Jane made her way down to the porch to greet her cowboy visitor. She made herself charming and gracious, and carried off the embarrassing situation—for Springer was pre-sent—just as if it were the most natural thing in the world. And she led Jones to one of the rustic benches farther down the porch.

Obvious, indeed, was it in all his actions that young Jones felt he had made a conquest. He was the most forceful and bold person Jane had ever met, quite incapable of appreciating her as a lady. It was not long before he was waxing ardent. Jane had become accustomed to the sentimental talk of cowboys, but this fellow was neither amusing nor interesting. He was dangerous. When she pulled her hand, by main force, free from his, and said she was not accustomed to allow men such privileges, he grinned at her like the handsome devil he was. Her conquest was only a matter of time.

"Sure, sweetheart, you have missed a heap of fun," Beady Jones said. "An' I reckon I'll have to break you in."

Jane could not really feel insulted at this brazen, conceited fool, but she certainly could feel enraged with herself. Her instant impulse was to excuse herself and abruptly leave him. But Springer was close by. She had caught his dark, speculative, covert glances. And the cowboys were at the other end of the long porch. Jane feared another fight. She had brought this situation upon herself, and she must stick it out. The ensuing hour was an increasing torment.

At last it seemed to her that she could not bear the false situation any longer. And when Jones again importuned her to meet him out on horseback some time, she stooped to deception to end the interview. She really did not concentrate her attention on his plan or really take stock of what she was agreeing to do, but she got rid of him with ease and dignity in the presence of Springer and the others. After that she did not have the courage to stay out there and face them, and stole off to the darkness and loneliness of her room.

The schoolteaching went on just the same, and the cowboys thawed out perceptibly, and Springer returned somewhat to his friendly manner, but Jane missed something from her work and in them, and her heart was sad the way everything was changed. Would it ever be the same again? What had happened? She had only been an emotional little tenderfoot, unused to Western ways. After all, she had not failed, at least in gratitude and affection, though now it seemed they would never know.

There came a day, when Jane rode off toward the hills. She forgot the risk and all of the admonitions of the cowboys. She wanted to be alone to think.

She rode fast until her horse was hot and she was out of breath. Then she slowed down. The foothills seemed so close now. But they were not really close. Still she could smell the fragrant dry cedar aroma on the air.

Then for the first time she looked back toward the ranch. It was a long way off—ten miles—a mere green spot in the gray. Suddenly she caught sight of a horseman coming. As usual, some one of the cowboys had observed her, let her think she had slipped away, and was now following her. Today it angered Jane. She wanted to be alone. She could take care of herself. And as was unusual with her, she used her quirt on the horse. He broke into a gallop.

She did not look back again for a long time. When she did it was to discover that the horseman had not only gained, but was now quite close to her. Jane looked intently, but she could not recognize the rider. Once she imagined it was Tex and again Andy. It did not make any difference which one of the cowboys it was. She was angry, and if he caught up with her he would be sorry.

Jane rode the longest and fastest race she had ever ridden. She reached the low foothills, and without heeding the fact that she might speedily become lost, she entered the cedars and began to climb.

What was her amazement when she heard a thud of hoofs and crackling of branches in the opposite direction from which she was expecting her pursuer, and saw a rider emerge from the cedars and trot his horse toward her. Jane needed only a second glance to recognize Beady Jones. Surely she had met him by chance. Suddenly she knew he was not the pursuer she had been so angrily aware of. Jones's horse was white. That checked her mounting anger.

Jones rode straight at her, and as he came close she saw his bold tanned face and gleaming eyes. Instantly she realized that she had been mad to ride so far into the wild country, to expose herself to something from which the cowboys on the ranch had always tried to save her.

"Howdy, sweetheart," sang out Jones, in his cool devil-may-care way. "Reckon it took you a long time to make up your mind t' meet me as you promised."

"I didn't ride out to meet you, Mr. Jones," said Jane spiritedly. "I know I agreed to something or other, but even then I didn't mean it."

"Yes, I had a hunch you were just playin' with me," he said darkly, riding his white mount right up against her horse.

He reached out a long gloved hand and grasped her arm.

"What do you mean, sir?" demanded Jane, trying to wrench her arm free.

"Shore I mean a lot," he said grimly. "You stood for the lovemakin' of that Springer outfit. Now you're goin' to get a taste of somethin' not quite so easy."

"Let go of me—you—you utter fool!" cried Jane, struggling fiercely. She was both furious and terrified. But she seemed to be a child in the grasp of a giant.

"Hell! Your fightin' will only make it more interestin'. Come here, you sassy little cat."

And he lifted her out of her saddle over onto his horse in front of him. Jane's mount, that had been frightened and plunging, ran away into the cedars. Then Jones proceeded to embrace Jane. She managed to keep her mouth from contact with his, but he kissed her face and neck, kisses that seemed to fill her with shame and disgust.

"Jane, I'm ridin' out of this country for good," he said. "An' I've just been waitin' for this chance. You bet you'll remember Beady Jones."

Jane realized that Jones would stop at nothing. Frantically she fought to get away from him, and to pitch herself to the ground. She screamed. She beat and tore at him. She scratched his face till the blood flowed. And as her struggles increased with her

fright, she gradually slipped down between him and the pommel of his saddle, with her head hanging down on one side and her feet on the other. This position was awkward and painful, hut infinitely preferable to being crushed in his arms. He was riding off with her as if she had been a half-empty sack.

Suddenly Jane's hands, while trying to hold on to something to lessen the severe jolting her position was giving her, came in contact with Jones's gun. Dare she draw it and try to shoot him? Then all at once her ears filled with the approaching gallop of another horse. Inverted as she was, she was able to see and recognize Springer riding directly at Jones and yelling hoarsely.

Next she felt Jones's hard jerk at his gun. But Jane had hold of it, and suddenly her little hands had the strength of steel. The fierce energy with which Jones was wrestling to draw his gun threw Jane from the saddle. And when she dropped clear of the horse the gun came with her.

"Hands up, Beady!" she heard Springer call out, as she lay momentarily face down in the dust. Then she struggled to her knees, and crawled to get away from the danger of the horse's hoofs. She still clung to the heavy gun. And when breathless and almost collapsing she fell back on the ground, she saw Jones with his hands above his head and Springer on foot with leveled gun.

"Sit tight, cowboy," ordered the rancher, in a hard tone. "It'll take damn little more to make me bore you."

Then while still covering Jones, evidently ready for any sudden move, Springer spoke again.

"Jane, did you come out here to meet this cowboy?" he asked.

"Oh, no! How can you ask that?" cried Jane, almost sobbing.

"She's a liar, boss," spoke up Jones coolly. "She let me make love to her. An' she agreed to ride out an' meet me. Well it shore took her a spell, an' when she did come she was shy on the lovemakin'. I was packin' her off to scare some sense into her when you rode in."

"Beady, I know your way with women. You can save your breath, for I've a hunch you're going to need it."

"Mr. Springer," faltered Jane, getting to her knees. "I—I was foolishly attracted to this cowboy—at first. Then—that Sunday after the dance when he called on me at the ranch—I saw through him then. I heartily despised him. To get rid of him I did say I'd meet him. But I never meant to. Then I forgot all about it. Today I rode alone for the first time. I saw someone following me and thought it must be Tex or one of the boys. Finally I waited, and presently Jones rode up to me . . . And, Mr. Springer, he—he grabbed me off my horse—and handled me shamefully. I fought him with all my might, but what could I do?"

Springer's face changed markedly during Jane's long explanation. Then he threw his gun on the ground in front of Jane.

"Jones, I'm going to beat you within an inch of your life," he said grimly; and leaping at the cowboy, he jerked him out of the saddle and sent him sprawling on the ground. Next Springer threw aside his sombrero, his vest, his spurs. But he kept on his gloves. The cowboy rose to one knee, and he measured the distance between him and Springer, and then the gun that lay on the ground. Suddenly he swung toward it. Springer intercepted him with a powerful kick that tripped Jones and laid him flat.

"Jones, you're sure about as lowdown as they come," he said, in a tone of disgust. "I've got to be satisfied with beating you when I ought to kill you!"

"Ahuh! Well, boss, it ain't any safe bet that you can do either," cried Beady Jones sullenly, as he got up.

As they rushed together Jane had wit enough to pick up the gun, and then with it and Jones', to get back a safe distance. She wanted to run away out of sight. But she could not keep her fascinated gaze from the combatants. Even in her distraught condition she could see that the cowboy, young and active and strong as he was, could not hold his own with Springer. They fought all over the open space, and

crashed into the cedars and out again. The time came when Jones was on the ground about as much as he was erect. Bloody, dishevelled, beaten, he kept on trying to stem the onslaught of blows.

Suddenly he broke off a dead branch of cedar, and brandishing it rushed at the rancher. Jane uttered a cry, closed her eyes, and sank to the ground.

She heard fierce muttered imprecations and savage blows. When at length she opened her eyes again, fearing something dreadful, she saw Springer erect, wiping his face with the back of one hand and Jones lying on the ground.

Then Jane saw him go to his horse, untie a canteen from the saddle, remove his bloody gloves, and wash his face with a wet scarf. Next he poured some water on Jones' face.

"Come on, Jane," he called. "I reckon it's all over."

He tied the bridle of Jones's horse to a cedar, and leading his own animal turned to meet Jane.

I want to compliment you on getting that cowboy's gun, he said warmly. "But for that there'd sure have been something bad. I'd have had to kill him, Jane…Here, give me the guns…You poor little tenderfoot from Missouri. No, not tenderfoot any longer. You became a Westerner today."

His face was bruised and cut, his clothes dirty and bloody, but he did not appear the worse for such a desperate fight. Jane found her legs scarcely able to support her, and she had apparently lost her voice.

"Let me put you on my saddle till we find your horse," he said, and lifted her lightly as a feather to a seat crosswise in the saddle. Then he walked with a hand on the bridle.

Jane saw him examining the ground, evidently searching for horse tracks. "Here we are." And he led off in another direction through the cedars. Soon Jane saw her horse, calmly nibbling at the bleached grass.

Springer stood beside her with a hand on her horse. He looked frankly into her face. The keen eyes were softer than usual. He looked so fine and strong and splendid that she found herself breathing with difficulty. She was afraid of her betraying eyes and looked away.

"When the boys found out that you were gone, they all saddled up to find you," he said. "But I asked them if they didn't think the boss ought to have one chance. So they let me come."

Right about then something completely unforeseen happened to Jane's heart. She was overwhelmed by a strange happiness that she knew she ought to hide, but could not. She could not speak. The silence grew. She felt Springer there, but she could not look at him.

"Do you like it out here in the West?" he asked presently.

"Oh, I love it! I'll never want to leave it," she replied impulsively.

"I reckon I'm glad to hear you say that."

Then there fell another silence. He pressed closer to her and seemed now to be leaning against the horse. She wondered if he heard the thunderous knocking of her heart against her side.

"Will you be my wife an' stay here always?" he asked simply. "I'm in love with you. I've been lonely since my mother died…You'll sure have to marry some of us. Because, as Tex says, if you don't, ranchin' can't go on much longer. These boys don't seem to get anywhere with you. Have I any chance—Jane?"

He possessed himself of her gloved hand and gave her a gentle tug. Jane knew it was gentle because she scarcely felt it. Yet it had irresistible power. She was swayed by that gentle pull. She moved into his arms.

A little later he smiled at her and said, "Jane, they call me Bill for short. Same as they call me boss. But my two front names are Frank Owens."

"Oh!" cried Jane. "Then you—"

"Yes, I'm the guilty one," he said happily. "It happened this way. My bedroom, you know is next to my office. I often heard the boys pounding the typewriter. I had a hunch they were up to some trick. So I spied upon them—heard about Frank Owens and the letters to the little schoolmarm.

At Beacon I got the postmistress to give me your address. And, of course, I intercepted some of your letters. It sure has turned out great."

"I—I don't know about you or those terrible cowboys," said Jane dubiously. "How did they happen on the name Frank Owens?"

"That's sure a stumper. I reckon they put a job up on me."

"Frank—tell me—did you write the—the love letters?" she asked appealingly. "There were two kinds of letters. That's what I never could understand."

"Jane, I reckon I did," he confessed. "Something about your little notes made me fall in love with you clear back there in Missouri. Does that make it all right?"

"Yes, Frank, I reckon it does—now," she said.

"Let's ride back home and tell the boys," said Springer gayly. "The joke's sure on them. I've corralled the little 'under-forty schoolmarm from Missouri.' "

ZANE GREY *(1875–1939), born in Zanesville, Ohio, was a dentist before he took up writing at age thirty-two. After his bestseller,* Riders of the Purple Sage *(1912), he became a million-copy author. His stories often contrast a decadent East with a decent, rugged, morally superior West.*

THE GIFT OF COCHISE

LOUIS L'AMOUR

Tense, and white to the lips, Angie Lowe stood in the door of her cabin with a double-barreled shotgun in her hands. Beside the door was a Winchester '73, and on the table inside the house were two Walker Colts.

Facing the cabin were twelve Apaches on ragged calico ponies, and one of the Indians had lifted his hand palm outward. The Apache sitting the white-splashed bay pony was Cochise.

Beside Angie were her seven-year-old son Jimmy and her five-year-old daughter Jane.

Cochise sat his pony in silence; his black, unreadable eyes studied the woman, the children, the cabin, and the small garden. He looked at the two ponies in the corral and the three cows. His eyes strayed to the small stack of hay cut from the meadow, and to the few steers farther up the canyon.

Three times the warriors of Cochise had attacked this solitary cabin and three times they had been turned back. In all, they had lost seven men, and three had been wounded. Four ponies had been killed. His braves reported that there was no man in the house, only a woman and two children, so Cochise had come to see for himself this woman who was so certain a shot with a rifle and who killed his fighting men.

These were some of the same fighting men who had outfought, outguessed and outrun the finest American army on record, an army outnumbering the Apaches by a hundred to one. Yet a lone woman with two small children had fought them off, and the

woman was scarcely more than a girl. And she was prepared to fight now. There was a glint of admiration in the old eyes that appraised her. The Apache was a fighting man, and he respected fighting blood.

"Where is your man?"

"He has gone to El Paso." Angie's voice was steady, but she was frightened as she had never been before. She recognized Cochise from descriptions, and she knew that if he decided to kill or capture her it would be done. Until now, the sporadic attacks she had fought off had been those of casual bands of warriors who raided her in passing.

"He has been gone a long time. How long?"

Angie hesitated, but it was not in her to lie. "He has been gone four months."

Cochise considered that. No one but a fool would leave such a woman or such fine children. Only one thing could have prevented his return. "Your man is dead," he said.

Angie waited, her heart pounding with heavy, measured beats. She had guessed long ago that Ed had been killed but the way Cochise spoke did not imply that Apaches had killed him, only that he must be dead or he would have returned.

"You fight well," Cochise said. "You have killed my young men."

"Your young men attacked me." She hesitated then added, "They stole my horses."

"Your man is gone. Why do you not leave?"

Angie looked at him with surprise. "Leave? Why,

this is my home. This land is mine. This spring is mine. I shall not leave."

"This was an Apache spring," Cochise reminded her reasonably.

"The Apache lives in the mountains," Angie replied. "He does not need this spring. I have two children, and I do need it."

"But when the Apache comes this way, where shall he drink? His throat is dry and you keep him from water."

The very fact that Cochise was willing to talk raised her hopes. There had been a time when the Apache made no war on the white man. "Cochise speaks with a forked tongue," she said. "There is water yonder." She gestured toward the hills, where Ed had told her there were springs. "But if the people of Cochise come in peace they may drink at this spring."

The Apache leader smiled faintly. Such a woman would rear a nation of warriors. He nodded at Jimmy. "The small one—does he also shoot?"

"He does," Angie said proudly, "and well, too." She pointed at an upthrust leaf of prickly pear. "Show them, Jimmy."

The prickly pear was an easy two hundred yards away, and the Winchester was long and heavy, but he lifted it eagerly and steadied it against the door-jamb as his father had taught him, held his sight an instant, then fired. The bud on top of the prickly pear disintegrated.

There were grunts of appreciation from the dark-faced warriors. Cochise chuckled.

"The little warrior shoots well. It is well you have no man. One might raise an army of little warriors to fight my people."

"I have no wish to fight your people," Angie said quietly. Your people have your ways, and I have mine. I live in peace when I am left in peace. I did not think," she added with dignity, "that the great Cochise made war on women!"

Tom Lovell, *Target Practice*, 1986.
Oil, 34 x 24"

The Apache looked at her, then turned his pony away. "My people will trouble you no longer," he said. "You are the mother of a strong son."

"What about my two ponies?" she called after him. "Your young men took them from me."

Cochise did not turn or look back, and the little cavalcade of riders followed him away. Angie stepped back into the cabin and closed the door. Then she sat down abruptly, her face white, the muscles in her legs trembling.

When morning came, she went cautiously to the spring for water. Her ponies were back in the corral. They had been returned during the night.

Slowly, the days drew on. Angie broke a small piece of the meadow and planted it. Alone, she cut hay in the meadow and built another stack. She saw Indians several times, but they did not bother her. One morning, when she opened her door, a quarter of antelope lay on the step, but no Indian was in sight. Several times, during the weeks that followed, she saw moccasin tracks near the spring.

Once, going out at daybreak, she saw an Indian girl dipping water from the spring. Angie called to her, and the girl turned quickly, facing her. Angie walked toward her, offering a bright red silk ribbon. Pleased at the gift, the Apache girl left.

And the following morning there was another quarter of antelope on her step—but she saw no Indian.

Ed Lowe had built the cabin in West Dog Canyon in the spring of 1871, but it was Angie who chose the spot, not Ed. In Santa Fe they would have told you that Ed Lowe was good-looking, shiftless and agreeable. He was, also, unfortunately handy with a pistol.

Angie's father had come from County Mayo to New York and from New York to the Mississippi, where he became a tough, brawling river boatman. In New Orleans, he met a beautiful Cajun girl and married her. Together, they started west for Santa Fe, and Angie was born en route. Both parents died of cholera when Angie was fourteen. She lived with an Irish family for the following three years, then married Ed Lowe when she was seventeen.

Santa Fe was not good for Ed, and Angie kept after

him until they started south. It was Apache country, but they kept on until they reached the old Spanish ruin in West Dog. Here there were grass, water, and shelter from the wind.

There was fuel, and there were pinons and game. And Angie, with an Irish eye for the land, saw that it would grow crops.

The house itself was built on the ruins of the old Spanish building, using the thick walls and the floor. The location had been admirably chosen for defense. The house was built in a corner of the cliff, under the sheltering overhang, and that approach was possible from only two directions, both covered by an easy field of fire from the door and windows.

For seven months, Ed worked hard and steadily. He put in the first crop, he built the house, and proved himself a handy man with tools. He repaired the old plow they had bought, cleaned out the spring, and paved and walled it with slabs of stone. If he was lonely for the carefree companions of Santa Fe, he gave no indication of it. Provisions were low, and when he finally started off to the south, Angie watched him go with an ache in her heart.

She did not know whether she loved Ed. The first rush of enthusiasm had passed, and Ed Lowe had proved something less than she had believed. But he had tried, she admitted. And it had not been easy for him. He was an amiable soul, given to whittling and idle talk, all of which he missed in the loneliness of the Apache country. And when he rode away, she had no idea whether she would ever see him again. She never did.

Santa Fe was far and away to the north, but the growing village of El Paso was less than a hundred miles to the west, and it was there Ed Lowe rode for supplies and seed.

He had several drinks—his first in months—in one of the saloons. As the liquor warmed his stomach, Ed Lowe looked around agreeably. For a moment, his eyes clouded with worry as he thought of his wife and children back in Apache country, but it was not in Ed Lowe to worry for long. He had another drink and leaned on the bar, talking to the bartender. All

Ed had ever asked of life was enough to eat, a horse to ride, an occasional drink, and companions to talk with. Not that he had anything important to say. He just liked to talk.

Suddenly a chair grated on the floor, and Ed turned. A lean, powerful man with a shock of uncut black hair and a torn, weather-faded shirt stood at bay. Facing him across the table were three hard-faced men, obviously brothers.

Ches Lane did not notice Ed Lowe watching from the bar. He had eyes only for the men facing him. "You done that deliberate!" The statement was a challenge.

The broad-chested man on the left grinned through broken teeth. "That's right, Ches. I done it deliberate. You killed Dan Tolliver on the Brazos."

"He made the quarrel." Comprehension came to Ches. He was boxed, and by three of the fighting, blood-hungry Tollivers.

"Don't make no difference," the broad-chested Tolliver said. " 'Who sheds a Tolliver's blood, by a Tolliver's hand must die!' "

Ed Lowe moved suddenly from the bar. "Three to one is long odds," he said, his voice low and friendly. "If the gent in the corner is willin', I'll side him."

Two Tollivers turned toward him. Ed Lowe was smiling easily, his hand hovering near his gun. "You stay out of this!" one of the brothers said harshly.

"I'm in," Ed replied. "Why don't you boys light a shuck?"

"No, by—!" The man's hand dropped for his gun, and the room thundered with sound.

Ed was smiling easily, unworried as always. His gun flashed up. He felt it leap in his hand, saw the nearest Tolliver smashed back, and he shot him again as he dropped. He had only time to see Ches Lane with two guns out and another Tolliver down when something struck him through the stomach and he stepped back against the bar, suddenly sick.

The sound stopped, and the room was quiet, and there was the acrid smell of powder smoke. Three Tollivers were down and dead, and Ed Lowe was dying. Ches Lane crossed to him.

"We got 'em," Ed said, "we sure did. But they got me."

Suddenly his face changed. "Oh Lord in heaven, what'll Angie do?" And then he crumpled over on the floor and lay still, the blood staining his shirt and mingling with the sawdust.

Stiff-faced, Ches looked up. "Who was Angie?" he asked.

"His wife," the bartender told him. "She's up northeast somewhere, in Apache country. He was tellin' me about her. Two kids, too."

Ches Lane stared down at the crumpled, used-up body of Ed Lowe. The man had saved his life.

One he could have beaten, two he might have beaten; three would have killed him. Ed Lowe, stepping in when he did, had saved the life of Ches Lane.

"He didn't say where?"

"No."

Ches Lane shoved his hat back on his head. "What's northeast of here?"

The bartender rested his hands on the bar. "Cochise," he said...

For more than three months, whenever he could rustle the grub, Ches Lane quartered the country over and back. The trouble was, he had no lead to the location of Ed Lowe's homestead. An examination of Ed's horse revealed nothing. Lowe had bought seed and ammunition, and the seed indicated a good water supply, and the ammunition implied trouble. But in the country there was always trouble.

A man had died to save his life, and Ches Lane had a deep sense of obligation. Somewhere that wife waited, if she was still alive, and it was up to him to find her and look out for her. He rode northeast, cutting for sign, but found none. Sandstorms had wiped out any hope of back-trailing Lowe. Actually, West Dog Canyon was more east than north, but this he had no way of knowing.

North he went, skirting the rugged San Andreas Mountains. Heat baked him hot, dry winds parched his skin. His hair grew dry and stiff and alkali-whitened. He rode north, and soon the Apaches knew of him. He fought them at a lonely water hole, and he fought them on the run. They killed his horse, and he switched his saddle to the spare and rode on. They cornered him in the rocks, and he killed two of them and escaped by night.

They trailed him through the White Sands, and he left two more for dead. He fought fiercely and bitterly, and would not be turned from his quest. He turned east through the lava beds and still more east to the Pecos. He saw only two white men, and neither knew of a white woman.

The bearded man laughed harshly. "A woman alone? She wouldn't last a month! By now the Apaches got her, or she's dead. Don't be a fool! Leave this country before you die here."

Lean, wind-whipped and savage, Ches Lane pushed on. The Mescaleros concerned him in Rawhide Draw and he fought them to a standstill. Grimly, the Apaches clung to his trail.

The sheer determination of the man fascinated them. Bred and born in a rugged and lonely land, the Apaches knew the difficulties of survival. They knew how a man could live, how he must live. Even as they tried to kill this man, they loved him, for he was one of their own.

Lane's jeans grew ragged. Two bullet holes were added to the old black hat. The slicker was torn; the saddle, so carefully kept until now, was scratched by gravel and brush. At night he cleaned his guns and by day he scouted the trails. Three times he found lonely ranch houses burned to the ground, the buzzard- and coyote-stripped bones of their owners lying nearby.

Once he found a covered wagon, its canvas flopping in the wind, a man lying sprawled on the seat with a pistol near his hand. He was dead and his wife was dead, and their canteens rattled like empty skulls.

Leaner every day, Ches Lane pushed on. He camped one night in a canyon near some white oaks. He heard a hoof click on stone and he backed away from his tiny fire, gun in hand.

The riders were white men, and there were two of them. Joe Tompkins and Wiley Lynn were headed west, and Ches Lane could have guessed why. They were men he had known before, and he told them what he was doing.

Lynn chuckled. He was a thin-faced man with lank yellow hair and dirty fingers. "Seems a mighty strange way to get a woman. There's some as comes easier."

"This ain't for fun," Ches replied shortly. "I got to find her."

Tompkins stared at him. "Ches, you're crazy! That gent declared himself in of his own wish and desire. Far's that goes, the gal's dead. No woman could last this long in Apache country."

At daylight, the two men headed west, and Ches Lane turned south.

Antelope and deer are curious creatures, often led to their death by curiosity. The longhorn, soon going wild on the plains, acquires the same characteristic. He is essentially curious. Any new thing or strange action will bring his head up and his ears alert. Often a longhorn, like a deer, can be lured within a stone's throw by some queer antic, by a handkerchief waving, by a man under a hide, by a man on foot.

This character of the wild things holds true of the Indian. The lonely rider who fought so desperately and knew the desert so well soon became a subject of gossip among the Apaches. Over the fires of many a rancheria they discussed this strange rider who seemed to be going nowhere, but always riding, like a lean wolf dog on a trail. He rode across the mesas and down the canyons, he studied sign at every water hole; he looked long from every ridge. It was obvious to the Indians that he searched for something—but what?

Cochise had come again to the cabin in West Dog Canyon. "Little warrior too small," he said, "too small for hunt. You join my people. Take Apache for man."

"No." Angie shook her head. "Apache ways are good for the Apache, and the white man's ways are good for white men—and women."

They rode away and said no more, but that night, as she had on many other nights after the children were asleep, Angie cried. She wept silently, her head pillowed on her arms. She was as pretty as ever, but her face was thin, showing the worry and struggle of the months gone by, the weeks and months without hope.

The crops were small but good. Little Jimmy worked beside her. At night, Angie sat alone on the steps and watched the shadows gather down the long canyon, listening to the coyotes yapping from the rim of the Guadalupes, hearing the horses blowing in the corral. She watched, still hopeful, but now she knew that Cochise was right: Ed would not return.

But even if she had been ready to give up this, the first home she had known, there could be no escape. Here she was protected by Cochise. Other Apaches from other tribes would not so willingly grant her peace.

At daylight she was up. The morning air was bright and balmy, but soon it would be hot again. Jimmy went to the spring for water, and when breakfast was over, the children played while Angie sat in the shade of a huge old cottonwood and sewed. It was a Sunday, warm and lovely. From time to time, she lifted her eyes to look down the canyon, half smiling at her own foolishness.

The hard-packed earth of the yard was swept clean of dust; the pans hanging on the kitchen wall were neat and shining. The children's hair had been clipped, and there was a small bouquet on the kitchen table.

After a while, Angie put aside her sewing and changed her dress. She did her hair carefully, and then, looking in her mirror, she reflected with sudden pain that she *was* pretty, and that she was only a girl.

Resolutely, she turned from the mirror and, taking up her Bible, went back to the seat under the cottonwood. The children left their playing and came to her, for this was a Sunday ritual, their only one. Opening the Bible, she read slowly,

"*. . . though I walk through the valley of the shadow of death, I will fear no evil for thou art with me; thy rod and thy staff, they comfort me. Thou preparest a table before me in the presence of mine enemies: thou . . .*"

"Mommy." Jimmy tugged at her sleeve. "Look!"

CHES LANE HAD REACHED a narrow canyon by midafternoon and decided to make camp. There was small possibility he would find another such spot, and he was dead tired, his muscles sodden with fatigue. The canyon was one of those unexpected gashes in the cap rock that gave no indication of its presence until you came right on it. After some searching, Ches found a route to the bottom and made camp under a wind-hollowed overhang. There was water, and there was a small patch of grass.

After his horse had a drink and a roll on the ground, it began cropping eagerly at the rich, green grass, and Ches built a smokeless fire of some ancient driftwood in the canyon bottom. It was his first hot meal in days, and when he had finished he put out his fire, rolled a smoke, and leaned back contentedly.

Before darkness settled, he climbed to the rim and looked over the country. The sun had gone down, and the shadows were growing long. After a half hour of study, he decided there was no living thing within miles, except for the usual desert life. Returning to the bottom, he moved his horse to fresh grass, then rolled in his blanket. For the first time in a month, he slept without fear.

He woke up suddenly in the broad daylight. The horse was listening to something, his head up. Swiftly, Ches went to the horse and led it back under the overhang. Then he drew on his boots, rolled his blankets, and saddled the horse. Still he heard no sound.

Climbing the rim again, he studied the desert and found nothing. Returning to his horse, he mounted up and rode down the canyon toward the flatland beyond. Coming out of the canyon mouth, he rode right into the middle of a war party of more than twenty Apaches—invisible until suddenly they stood up behind rocks, their rifles leveled. And he didn't have a chance.

Swiftly, they bound his wrists to the saddle horn and tied his feet. Only then did he see the man who led the party. It was Cochise.

He was a lean, wiry Indian of past fifty, his black hair streaked with gray, his features strong and clean-cut. He stared at Lane, and there was nothing in his face to reveal what he might be thinking.

Several of the younger warriors pushed forward, talking excitedly and waving their arms. Ches Lane understood some of it, but he sat straight in the saddle, his head up, waiting. Then Cochise spoke and the party turned, and, leading his horse, they rode away.

The miles grew long and the sun was hot. He was offered no water and he asked for none. The Indians ignored him. Once a young brave rode near and struck him viciously. Lane made no sound, gave no indication of pain. When they finally stopped, it was beside a huge anthill swarming with big red desert ants.

Roughly, they quickly untied him and jerked him from his horse. He dug in his heels and shouted at them in Spanish: "The Apaches are women! They tie me to the ants because they are afraid to fight me!"

An Indian struck him, and Ches glared at the man. If he must die, he would show them how it should be done. Yet he knew the unpredictable nature of the Indian, of his great respect for courage.

"Give me a knife, and I'll kill any of your warriors!"

They stared at him, and one powerfully built Apache angrily ordered them to get on with it. Cochise spoke, and the big warrior replied angrily.

Ches Lane nodded at the anthill. "Is this the death for a fighting man? I have fought your strong men and beaten them. I have left no trail for them to follow, and for months I have lived among you, and now only by accident have you captured me. Give me a knife," he added grimly, "and I will fight him!" He indicated the big, black-faced Apache.

The warrior's cruel mouth hardened, and he struck Ches across the face.

The white man tasted blood and fury. "Woman!" Ches said. "Coyote! You are afraid!" Ches turned on Cochise, as the Indians stood irresolute. "Free my hands and let me fight!" he demanded. "If I win, let me go free."

Cochise said something to the big Indian. Instantly, there was stillness. Then an Apache sprang forward and, with a slash of his knife, freed Lane's hands. Shaking loose the thongs, Ches Lane chafed

Overleaf: John Clymer, *Land of Plenty*, 1970.
Oil, 20 x 40"

his wrists to bring back the circulation. An Indian threw a knife at his feet. It was his own bowie knife.

Ches took off his riding boots. In sock feet, his knife gripped low in his hand, its cutting edge up, he looked at the big warrior.

"I promise you nothing," Cochise said in Spanish, "but an honorable death."

The big warrior came at him on cat feet. Warily, Ches turned. He had not only to defeat this Apache but to escape. He permitted himself a side glance toward his horse. It stood alone. No Indian held him.

The Apache closed swiftly, thrusting wickedly with the knife. Ches, who had learned knife-fighting in the bayou country of Louisiana, turned his hip sharply, and the blade slid past him. He struck swiftly, but the Apache's forward movement deflected the blade, and it failed to penetrate. However, as it swept up between the Indian's body and arm, it cut a deep gash in the warrior's left armpit.

The Indian sprang again, like a clawing cat, streaming blood. Ches moved aside, but a backhand sweep nicked him, and he felt the sharp bite of the blade. Turning, he paused on the balls of his feet.

He had had no water in hours. His lips were cracked. But he sweated now, and the salt of it stung his eyes. He stared into the malevolent black eyes of the Apache, then moved to meet him. The Indian lunged, and Ches sidestepped like a boxer and spun on the ball of his foot.

The sudden sidestep threw the Indian past him, but Ches failed to drive the knife into the Apache's kidney when his foot rolled on a stone. The point left a thin red line across the Indian's back. The Indian was quick. Before Ches could recover his balance, he grasped the white man's knife wrist. Desperately, Ches grabbed for the Indian's knife hand and got the wrist, and they stood there straining, chest to chest.

Seeing his chance, Ches suddenly let his knees buckle, then brought up his knee and fell back, throwing the Apache over his head to the sand. Instantly, he whirled and was on his feet, standing over the Apache. The warrior had lost his knife, and he lay there, staring up, his eyes black with hatred.

Coolly, Ches stepped back, picked up the Indian's knife, and tossed it to him contemptuously. There was a grunt from the watching Indians and then his antagonist rushed. But loss of blood had weakened the warrior, and Ches stepped in swiftly, struck the blade aside, then thrust the point of his blade hard against the Indian's belly.

Black eyes glared into his without yielding. A thrust, and the man would be disemboweled, but Ches stepped back. "He is a strong man," Ches said in Spanish. "It is enough that I have won."

Deliberately, he walked to his horse and swung into the saddle. He looked around, and every rifle covered him.

So he had gained nothing. He had hoped that mercy might lead to mercy, that the Apache's respect for a fighting man would win his freedom. He had failed. Again they bound him to his horse, but they did not take his knife from him.

When they camped at last, he was given food and drink. He was bound again, and a blanket was thrown over him. At daylight they were again in the saddle. In Spanish he asked where they were taking him, but they gave no indication of hearing. When they stopped again, it was beside a pole corral, near a stone cabin.

WHEN JIMMY SPOKE, ANGIE got quickly to her feet. She recognized Cochise with a start of relief, but she saw instantly that this was a war party. And then she saw the prisoner.

Their eyes met and she felt a distinct shock. He was a white man, a big, unshaven man who badly needed both a bath and a haircut, his clothes ragged and bloody. Cochise gestured at the prisoner.

"No take Apache man, you take white man. This man good for hunt, good for fight. He strong warrior. You take 'em."

Flushed and startled, Angie stared at the prisoner and caught a faint glint of humor in his dark eyes.

"Is this here the fate worse than death I hear tell of?" he inquired gently.

"Who are you?" she asked, and was immediately

conscious that it was an extremely silly question.

The Apaches had drawn back and were watching curiously. She could do nothing for the present but accept the situation. Obviously they intended to do her a kindness, and it would not do to offend them. If they had not brought this man to her, he might have been killed.

"Name's Ches Lane, ma'am," he said. "Will you untie me? I'd feel a lot safer."

"Of course." Still flustered, she went to him and untied his hands. One Indian said something, and the others chuckled, then, with a whoop, they swung their horses and galloped off down the canyon.

Their departure left her suddenly helpless, the shadowy globe of her loneliness shattered by this utterly strange man standing before her, this big, bearded man brought to her out of the desert.

She smoothed her apron, suddenly pale as she realized what his delivery to her implied. What must he think of her? She turned away quickly.

"There's hot water," she said hastily, to prevent his speaking. "Dinner is almost ready."

She walked quickly into the house and stopped before the stove, her mind a blank. She looked around her as if she had suddenly waked up in a strange place. She heard water being poured into the basin by the door, and heard him take Ed's razor. She had never moved the box. To have moved it would—

"Sight of work done here, ma'am."

She hesitated, then turned with determination and stepped into the doorway. "Yes, Ed—"

"You're Angie Lowe."

Surprised, she turned toward him, and recognized his own startled awareness of her. As he shaved, he told her about Ed, and what had happened that day in the saloon.

"He—Ed was like that. He never considered consequences until it too late."

"Lucky for me he didn't."

He was younger looking with his beard gone. There was a certain quiet dignity in his face. She went back inside and began putting plates on the table. She was conscious that he had moved to the door and was watching her.

"You don't have to stay," she said. "You owe me nothing. Whatever Ed did, he did because he was that kind of person. You aren't responsible."

He did not answer, and when she turned again to the stove, she glanced swiftly at him. He was looking across the valley.

There was a studied deference about him when he moved to a place at the table. The children stared, wide-eyed and silent; it had been so long since a man sat at this table.

Angie could not remember when she had felt like this. She was awkwardly conscious of her hands, which never seemed to be in the right place or doing the right things. She scarcely tasted her food, nor did the children.

Ches Lane had no such inhibitions. For the first time, he realized how hungry he was. After the half-cooked meat of lonely, trailside fires, this was tender and flavored. Hot biscuits, desert honey . . . Suddenly he looked up, embarrassed at his appetite.

"You were really hungry," she said.

"Man can't fix much, out on the trail."

Later, after he'd got his bedroll from his saddle and unrolled it on the hay in the barn, he walked back to the house and sat on the lowest step. The sun was gone, and they watched the cliffs stretch their red shadows across the valley. A quail called plaintively, a mellow sound of twilight.

"You needn't worry about Cochise," she said. "He'll soon be crossing into Mexico."

"I wasn't thinking about Cochise."

That left her with nothing to say, and she listened again to the quail and watched a lone bright star in the sky.

"A man could get to like it here," he said quietly.

LOUIS L'AMOUR *(1908–1988), a self-educated man, is probably the most popular Western writer in modern times. He is known for his commitment to historical accuracy and his enormous ability as a storyteller.*

GOLD DIGGIN'

ALL GOLD CANYON

Jack London

It was the green heart of the canyon, where the walls swerved back from the rigid plains and relieved their harshness of line by making a little sheltered nook and filling it to the brim with sweetness and roundness and softness. Here all things rested. Even the narrow stream ceased its turbulent down-rush long enough to form a quiet pool. Knee-deep in the water, with drooping head and half-shut eyes, drowsed a red-coated, many-antlered buck.

On one side, beginning at the very lip of the pool, was a tiny meadow, a cool, resilient surface of green that extended to the base of the frowning wall. Beyond the pool a gentle slope of earth ran up and up to meet the opposing wall. Fine grass covered the slope—grass that was spangled with flowers, with here-and-there patches of color, orange and purple and golden. Below, the canyon was shut in. There was no view. The walls leaned together abruptly, and the canyon ended in a chaos of rocks, moss-covered and hidden by a green screen of vines and creepers and boughs of trees. Up the canyon rose far hills and peaks, the big foothills, pine-covered and remote. And far beyond, like clouds upon the border of the sky, towered minarets of white, where the Sierra's eternal snows flashed austerely the blazes of the sun.

There was no dust in the canyon. The leaves and flowers were clean and virginal. The grass was young velvet. Over the pool three cottonwoods sent their snowy fluffs fluttering down the quiet air. On the slope the blossoms of the wine-wooded manzanita filled the air with springtime odors, while the leaves, wise with experience, were already beginning their vertical twist against the coming aridity of summer. In the open spaces on the slope, beyond the farthest shadow-reach of the manzanita, poised the mariposa lilies, like so many flights of jewelled moths suddenly arrested and on the verge of trembling into flight again. Here and there that woods harlequin, the madrone, permitting itself to be caught in the act of changing its pea green trunk to madder red, breathed its fragrance into the air from great clusters of waxen bells. Creamy white were these bells, shaped like lilies of the valley, with the sweetness of perfume that is of the springtime.

There was not a sigh of wind. The air was drowsy with its weight of perfume. It was a sweetness that would have been cloying had the air been heavy and humid. But the air was sharp and thin. It was as starlight transmuted into atmosphere, shot through and warmed by sunshine, and flower-drenched with sweetness.

An occasional butterfly drifted in and out through the patches of light and shade. And from all about rose the low and sleepy hum of mountain bees—feasting Sybarites that jostled one another good-naturedly at the board, nor found time for rough discourtesy. So quietly did the little stream drip and

Previous pages: A.D.O. Browere, *Mines of Placerville*, 1855. Oil, 26 x 36"

ripple its way through the canyon that it spoke only in faint and occasional gurgles. The voice of the stream was as a drowsy whisper, ever interrupted by dozings and silences, ever lifted again in the awakenings.

The motion of all things was a drifting in the heart of the canyon. Sunshine and butterflies drifted in and out among the trees. The hum of the bees and the whisper of the stream were a drifting of sound. And the drifting sound and drifting color seemed to weave together in the making of a delicate and intangible fabric which was the spirit of the place. It was a spirit of peace that was not of death, but of smooth-pulsing life, of quietude that was not silence, of movement that was not action, of repose that was quick with existence without being violent with struggle and travail. The spirit of the place was the spirit of the peace of the living, somnolent with the easement and content of prosperity, and undisturbed by rumors of far wars.

The red-coated, many-antlered buck acknowledged the lordship of the spirit of the place and dozed knee-deep in the cool, shaded pool. There seemed no flies to vex him and he was languid with rest. Sometimes his ears moved when the stream awoke and whispered; but they moved lazily, with foreknowledge that it was merely the stream grown garrulous at discovery that it had slept.

But there came a time when the buck's ears lifted and tensed with swift eagerness for sound. His head was turned down the canyon. His sensitive, quivering nostrils scented the air. His eyes could not pierce the green screen through which the stream rippled away, but to his ears came the voice of a man. It was a steady, monotonous, singsong voice. Once the buck heard the harsh clash of metal upon rock. At the sound he snorted with a sudden start that jerked him through the air from water to meadow, and his feet sank into the young velvet while he pricked his ears and again scented the air. Then he stole across the tiny meadow, pausing once and again to listen, and faded away out of the canyon like a wraith, soft-footed and without sound.

The clash of steel-shod soles against the rocks began to be heard, and the man's voice grew louder. It was raised in a sort of chant and became distinct with nearness, so that the words could be heard.

> *"Tu'n around an' tu'n yo' face*
> *Unto them sweet hills of grace*
> *(D' pow'rs of sin yo' am scornin'!).*
> *Look about an' look aroun'*
> *Fling yo' sin-pack on d' groun'*
> *(Yo' will meet wid d' Lord in d' mornin'!)."*

A sound of scrambling accompanied the song, and the spirit of the place fled away on the heels of the red-coated buck. The green screen was burst asunder, and a man peered out at the meadow and the pool and the sloping side-hill. He was a deliberate sort of man. He took in the scene with one embracing glance, then ran his eyes over the details to verify the general impression. Then, and not until then, did he open his mouth in vivid and solemn approval.

"Smoke of life an' snakes of purgatory! Will you just look at that! Wood an' water an' grass an' a side-hill! A pocket-hunter's delight an' a cayuse's paradise! Cool green for tired eyes! Pink pills for pale people ain't in it. A secret pasture for prospectors and a resting-place for tired burros. It's just boofull!"

He was a sandy-complexioned man in whose face geniality and humor seemed the salient characteristics. It was a mobile face, quick-changing to inward mood and thought. Thinking was in him a visible process. Ideas chased across his face like wind flaws across the surface of a lake. His hair, sparse and unkempt of growth, was as indeterminate and colorless as his complexion. It would seem that all the color of his frame had gone into his eyes, for they were startlingly blue. Also, they were laughing and merry eyes, within them much of the naivete and wonder of the child; and yet, in an unassertive way, they contained much of calm self-reliance and strength of purpose founded upon self-experience and experience of the world.

From out the screen of vines and creepers, he flung ahead of him a miner's pick and shovel and gold-pan. Then he crawled out himself into the open. He was clad in faded overalls and black cotton shirt, with hobnailed brogans on his feet, and on his head a hat whose shapelessness and stains advertised the rough usage of wind and rain and sun and camp smoke. He stood erect, seeing wide-eyed the secrecy of the scene and sensuously inhaling the warm, sweet breath of the canyon garden through nostrils that dilated and quivered with delight. His eyes narrowed to laughing slits of blue, his face wreathed itself in joy, and his mouth curled in a smile as he cried aloud, "lumping dandelions and happy hollyhocks, but that smells good to me! Talk about your attar o' roses an' cologne factories! They ain't in it!"

He had the habit of soliloquy. His quick-changing facial expressions might tell every thought and mood, but the tongue, perforce, ran hard after, repeating, like a second Boswell.

The man lay down on the lip of the pool and drank long and deep of its water. "Tastes good to me," he murmured, lifting his head and gazing across the pool at the side-hill, while he wiped his mouth with the back of his hand. The side-hill attracted his attention. Still lying on his stomach, he studied the hill formation long and carefully. It was a practiced eye that traveled up the slope to the crumbling canyon wall and back and down again to the edge of the pool. He scrambled to his feet and favored the side-hill with a second survey.

"Looks good to me," he concluded, picking up his pick and shovel and gold-pan.

He crossed the stream below the pool, stepping agilely from stone to stone. Where the side-hill touched the water he dug up a shovelful of dirt and put it into the gold-pan. He squatted down, holding the pan in his two hands, and partly immersing it in the stream. Then he imparted to the pan a deft circular motion that sent the water sluicing in and out through the dirt and gravel. The larger and the lighter particles worked to the surface, and these, by a skillful dipping movement of the pan, he spilled out and over the edge. Occasionally, to expedite matters, he rested the pan and with his fingers raked out the large pebbles and pieces of rock.

The contents of the pan diminished rapidly until only fine dirt and the smallest bits of gravel remained. At this stage he began to work very deliberately and carefully. It was fine washing, and he washed fine and finer, with a keen scrutiny and delicate and fastidious touch. At last the pan seemed empty of everything but water; but with a quick semicircular flirt that sent the water flying over the shallow rim into the stream, he disclosed a layer of black sand on the bottom of the pan. So thin was this layer that it was like a streak of paint. He examined it closely. In the midst of it was a tiny golden speck. He dribbled a little water in over the depressed edge of the pan. With a quick flirt he sent the water sluicing across the bottom, turning the grains of black sand over and over. A second tiny golden speck rewarded his effort.

The washing had now become very fine—fine beyond all need of ordinary placer mining. He worked the black sand, a small portion at a time, up the shallow rim of the pan. Each small portion he examined sharply, so that his eyes saw every grain of it before he allowed it to slide over the edge and away. Jealously, bit by bit, he let the black sand slip away. A golden speck, no larger than a pinpoint, appeared on the rim, and by his manipulation of the water it returned to the bottom of the pan. And in such fashion another speck was disclosed, and another. Great was his care of them. Like a shepherd he herded his flock of golden specks so that not one should be lost. At last, of the pan of dirt nothing remained but his golden herd. He counted it, and then, after all his labor, sent it flying out of the pan with one final swirl of water.

But his blue eyes were shining with desire as he rose to his feet. "Seven," he muttered aloud, asserting the sum of the specks for which he had toiled so hard and which he had so wantonly thrown away. "Seven," he repeated, with the emphasis of one trying to impress a number on his memory.

He stood still a long while, surveying the hillside. In his eyes was a curiosity, new-aroused and burning. There was an exultance about his bearing and a keenness like that of a hunting animal catching the fresh scent of game.

He moved down the stream a few steps and took a second panful of dirt.

Again came the careful washing, the jealous herding of the golden specks, and the wantonness with which he sent them flying into the stream. His golden herd diminished. "Four, five," he muttered, and repeated, "five."

He could not forbear another survey of the hill before filling the pan farther down the stream. His golden herds diminished. "Four, three, two, two, one," were his memory tabulations as he moved down the stream. When but one speck of gold rewarded his washing, he stopped and built a fire of dry twigs. Into this he thrust the gold-pan and burned it till it was blue black. He held up the pan and examined it critically. Then he nodded approbation. Against such a color-background he could defy the tiniest yellow speck to elude him.

Still moving down the stream, he panned again. A single speck was his reward. A third pan contained no gold at all. Not satisfied with this, he panned three times again, taking his shovels of dirt within a foot of one another. Each pan proved empty of gold, and the fact, instead of discouraging him, seemed to give him satisfaction. His elation increased with each barren washing, until he arose, exclaiming jubilantly:

"If it ain't the real thing, may God knock off my head with sour apples!"

Returning to where he had started operations, he began to pan up the stream. At first his golden herds increased—increased prodigiously. "Fourteen, eighteen, twenty-one, twenty-six," ran his memory tabulations. Just above the pool he struck his richest pan—thirty-five colors.

"Almost enough to save," he remarked regretfully as he allowed the water to sweep them away.

The sun climbed to the top of the sky. The man worked on. Pan by pan, he went up the stream, the tally of results steadily decreasing.

"It's just booful, the way it peters out," he exulted when a shovelful of dirt contained no more than a single speck of gold. And when no specks at all were found in several pans, he straightened up and favored the hillside with a confident glance. "Ah, ha! Mr. Pocket!" he cried out, as though to an auditor hidden somewhere above him beneath the surface of the slope.

"Ah, ha! Mr. Pocket! I'm a-comin', I'm a-comin', an' I'm shorely gwine to get yer! You heah me, Mr. Pocket? I'm gwine to get yer as shore as punkins ain't cauliflowers!"

He turned and flung a measuring glance at the sun poised above him in the azure of the cloudless sky. Then he went down the canyon, following the line of shovel holes he had made in filling the pans. He crossed the stream below the pool and disappeared through the green screen. There was little opportunity for the spirit of the place to return with its quietude and repose, for the man's voice, raised in ragtime song, still dominated the canyon with possession.

After a time, with a greater clashing of steel-shod feet on rock, he returned. The green screen was tremendously agitated. It surged back and forth in the throes of a struggle. There was a loud grating and clanging of metal. The man's voice leaped to a higher pitch and was sharp with imperativeness. A large body plunged and panted. There was a snapping and ripping and rending, and amid a shower of falling leaves a horse burst through the screen. On its back was a pack, and from this trailed broken vines and torn creepers. The animal gazed with astonished eyes at the scene into which it had been precipitated, then dropped its head to the grass and began contentedly to graze. A second horse scrambled into view, slipping once on the mossy rocks and regaining equilibrium when its hoofs sank into the yielding surface of the meadow. It was riderless, though on its back was a high-horned Mexican saddle, scarred and discolored by long usage.

The man brought up the rear. He threw off pack and saddle, with an eye to camp location, and gave the animals their freedom to graze. He unpacked his food and got out frying pan and coffeepot. He gathered an armful of dry wood, and with a few stones made a place for his fire.

"My!" he said, "but I've got an appetite. I could scoff ironfilings an' horseshoe nails an' thank you kindly, ma'am, for a second helpin'."

He straightened up, and while he reached for matches in the pocket of his overalls, his eyes traveled across the pool to the side-hill. His fingers had clutched the matchbox, but they relaxed their hold and the hand came out empty. The man wavered perceptibly. He looked at his preparations for cooking and he looked at the hill.

"Guess I'll take another whack at her," he concluded, starting to cross the stream.

"They ain't no sense in it, I know," he mumbled apologetically. "But keepin' grub back an hour ain't goin' to hurt none, I reckon."

A few feet back from his first of test pans he started a second line. The sun dropped down the western sky, the shadows lengthened, but the man worked on. He began a third line of test pans. He was crosscutting the hillside, line by line, as he ascended. The center of each line produced the richest pans, while the ends came where no colors showed in the pan. And as he ascended the hillside the lines grew perceptibly shorter. The regularity with which their length diminished served to indicate that somewhere up the slope the last line would be so short as to have scarcely length at all, and that beyond could come only a point. The design was growing into an inverted V. The converging sides of this V marked the boundaries of the gold-bearing dirt.

The apex of the V was evidently the man's goal. Often he ran his eye along the converging sides and on up the hill, trying to divine the apex, the point where the gold-bearing dirt must cease. Here resided Mr. Pocket—for so the man familiarly addressed the imaginary point above him on the slope, crying out, "Come down out o' that, Mr. Pocket! Be right smart an' agreeable, an' come down!

"All right," he would add later, in a voice resigned to determination. "All right, Mr. Pocket. It's plain to me I got to come right up an' snatch you out bald headed. An' I'll do it! I'll do it!" he would threaten still later.

Each pan he carried down to the water to wash, and as he went higher up the hill the pans grew richer, until he began to save the gold in an empty baking-powder can which he carried carelessly in his hip-pocket. So engrossed was he in his toil that he did not notice the long twilight of oncoming night. It was not until he tried vainly to see the gold colors in the bottom of the pan that he realized the passage of time. He straightened up abruptly. An expression of whimsical wonderment and awe overspread his face as he drawled, "Gosh darn my buttons! If I didn't plumb forget dinner!"

He stumbled across the stream in the darkness and lighted his long-delayed fire. Flapjacks and bacon and warmed-over beans constituted his supper. Then he smoked a pipe by the smoldering coals, listening to the night noises and watching the moonlight stream through the canyon. After that he unrolled his bed, took off his heavy shoes and pulled the blankets up to his chin. His face showed white in the moonlight, like the face of a corpse. But it was a corpse that knew its resurrection, for the man rose suddenly on one elbow and gazed across at his hillside.

"Good night, Mr. Pocket," he called sleepily. "Good night."

He slept through the early gray of morning until the direct rays of the sun smote his closed eyelids, when he awoke with a start and looked about him until he had established the continuity of his existence and identified his present self with the days previously lived.

To dress, he had merely to buckle on his shoes. He glanced at his fireplace and at his hillside, wavered, but fought down the temptation and started the fire.

"Keep yer shirt on, Bill; keep yer shirt on," he admonished himself. "What's the good of rushin'? No use in gettin' all het up an' sweaty. Mr. Pocket'll wait for you. He ain't a-runnin' away before you can get your breakfast. Now, what you want, Bill, is something fresh in yer bill o' fare. So it's up to you to go an' get it."

He cut a short pole at the water's edge and drew from one of his pockets a bit of line and a draggled fly that had once been a royal coachman.

Charles M. Russell, *When Mules Wear Diamonds*, 1921. Oil, 30 x 33"

"Mebbe they'll bite in the early morning," he muttered, as he made his first cast into the pool. And a moment later he was gleefully crying, "What'd I tell you, eh? What'd I tell you?"

He had no reel nor any inclination to waste time, and by main strength, and swiftly, he drew out of the water a flashing ten-inch trout. Three more, caught in rapid succession, furnished his breakfast. When he came to the stepping-stones on his way to his hillside, he was struck by a sudden thought, and paused.

"I'd just better take a hike downstream a ways," he said. "There's no tellin' who may be snoopin' around."

But he crossed over on the stones, and with a "I really oughter take that hike," the need of the precaution passed out of his mind, and he fell to work.

At nightfall he straightened up. The small of his back was stiff from stooping toil, and as he put his hand behind him to soothe the protesting muscles, he said; "Now what d'ye think of that? I clean forgot my dinner again! If I don't watch out, I'll sure be degeneratin' into a two-meal-a-day crank."

"Pockets is the hangedest things I ever see for makin' a man absent-minded," he communed that night, as he crawled into his blankets. Nor did he forget to call up the hillside, "Good night, Mr. Pocket! Good night!"

Rising with the sun, and snatching a hasty breakfast, he was early at work. A fever seemed to be growing in him, nor did the increasing richness of the test pans allay this fever. There was a flush in his cheek other than that made by the heat of the sun, and he was oblivious to fatigue and the passage of time. When he filled a pan with dirt, he ran down the hill to wash it; nor could he forbear running up the hill again, panting and stumbling profanely, to refill the pan.

He was now a hundred yards from the water, and the inverted V was assuming definite proportions. The width of the paydirt steadily decreased, and the man extended in his mind's eye the sides of the V to their meeting place far up the hill. This was his goal, the apex of the V, and he panned many times to locate it.

"Just about two yards above that manzanita bush an' a yard to the right," he finally concluded.

Then the temptation seized him. "As plain as the nose on your face," he said, as he abandoned his laborious crosscutting and climbed to the indicated apex. He filled a pan and carried it down the hill to wash. It contained no trace of gold. He dug deep, and he dug shallow, filling and washing a dozen pans, and was unrewarded even by the tiniest golden speck. He was enraged at having yielded to the temptation, and berated himself blasphemously and pridelessly. Then he went down the hill and took up the crosscutting.

"Slow an' certain, Bill; slow an' certain," he crooned. "Shortcuts to fortune ain't in your line, an' it's about time you know it. Get wise, Bill; get wise. Slow an' certain's the only hand you can play; so get to it, an' keep to it, too."

As the crosscuts decreased, showing that the sides of the V were converging, the depth of the V increased. The gold trace was dipping into the hill. It was only at thirty inches beneath the surface that he could get colors in his pan. The dirt he found at twenty-five inches from the surface, and at thirty-five inches, yielded barren pans. At the base of the V, by the water's edge, he had found the gold colors at the grass roots. The higher he went up the hill, the deeper the gold dipped. To dig a hole three feet deep in order to get one test pan was a task of no mean magnitude; while between the man and the apex intervened an untold number of such holes to be dug. "An' there's no tellin' how much deeper it'll pitch," he sighed in a moment's pause while his fingers soothed his aching back.

Feverish with desire, with aching back and stiffening muscles, with pick and shovel gouging and mauling the soft brown earth, the man toiled up the hill. Before him was the smooth slope, spangled with flowers and made sweet with their breath. Behind him was devastation. It looked like some terrible eruption breaking out on the smooth skin of the hill. His slow progress was like that of a slug, befouling beauty with a monstrous trail.

Though the dipping gold trace increased the man's work, he found consolation in the increasing richness of the pans. Twenty cents, thirty cents, fifty cents, sixty cents, were the values of the gold found in the pans, and at nightfall he washed his banner pan, which gave him a dollar's worth of gold dust from a shovelful of dirt.

"I'll just bet it's my luck to have some inquisitive one come buttin' in here on my pasture," he mumbled sleepily that night as he pulled the blankets up to his chin.

Suddenly he sat upright. "Bill!" he called sharply. "Now, listen to me, Bill; d'ye hear! It's up to you, tomorrow mornin', to mosey round an' see what you can see. Understand? Tomorrow morning, an' don't you forget it!"

He yawned and glanced across at his side-hill. "Good night, Mr. Pocket," he called.

In the morning he stole a march on the sun, for he had finished breakfast when its first rays caught him, and he was climbing the wall of the canyon where it crumbled away and gave footing. From the outlook at the top he found himself in the midst of loneliness. As far as he could see, chain after chain of mountains heaved themselves into his vision. To the east his eyes, leaping the miles between range and range and between many ranges, brought up at last against the white-peaked Sierras—the main crest, where the backbone of the Western world reared itself against the sky! To the north and south he could see more distinctly the cross systems that broke through the main trend of the sea of mountains. To the west the ranges fell away, one behind the other, diminishing and fading into the gentle foothills that, in turn, descended into the great valley which he could not see.

And in all that mighty sweep of earth he saw no sign of man nor of the handiwork of man—save only the torn bosom of the hillside at his feet. The man looked long and carefully. Once, far down his own canyon, he thought he saw in the air a faint hint of smoke. He looked again and decided that it was the purple haze of the hills made dark by a convolution of the canyon wall at its back.

"Hey, you, Mr. Pocket!" he called down into the canyon. "Stand out from under! I'm a-comin', Mr. Pocket! I'm a-comin'!"

The heavy brogans on the man's feet made him appear clumsyfooted, but he swung down from the giddy height as lightly and airily as a mountain goat. A rock, turning under his foot on the edge of the precipice, did not disconcert him. He seemed to know the precise time required for the turn to culminate in disaster, and in the meantime he utilized the false footing itself for the momentary earth contact necessary to carry him on into safety. Where the earth sloped so steeply that it was impossible to stand for a second upright, the man did not hesitate. His foot pressed the impossible surface for but a fraction of the fatal second and gave him the bound that carried him onward. Again, where even the fraction of a second's footing was out of the question, he would swing his body past by a moment's handgrip on a jutting knob of rock, a crevice or a precariously rooted shrub. At last, with a wild leap and yell, he exchanged the face of the wall for an earthslide and finished the descent in the midst of several tons of sliding earth and gravel.

His first pan of the morning washed out over two dollars in coarse gold. It was from the center of the V. To either side the diminution in the values of the pans was swift. His lines of crosscutting holes were growing very short. The converging sides of the inverted V were only a few yards apart. Their meeting point was only a few yards above him. But the pay streak was dipping deeper and deeper into the earth. By early afternoon he was sinking the test holes five feet before the pans could show the gold trace.

For that matter, the gold trace had become something more than a trace; it was a placer mine in itself, and the man resolved to come back after he had found the pocket and work over the ground. But the increasing richness of the pans began to worry him. By late afternoon the worth of the pans had grown to three and four dollars. The man scratched his head perplexedly and looked a few feet up the hill at the manzanita bush that marked approximately the apex of the V. He nodded his head and said oracularly:

"It's one o' two things, Bill; one o' two things. Either Mr. Pocket's spilled himself all out an' down the hill, or else Mr. Pocket's so rich you maybe won't

Frederic Remington, *Miners Prospecting for Gold*, 1888.

be able to carry him all away with you. And that'd be an awful shame, wouldn't it, now?" He chuckled at contemplation of so pleasant a dilemma.

Nightfall found him by the edge of the stream, his eyes wrestling with the gathering darkness over the washing of a five-dollar pan.

"Wisht I had an electric light to go on working," he said.

He found sleep difficult that night: Many times he composed himself and closed his eyes for slumber to overtake him; but his blood pounded with too strong desire, and as many times his eyes opened and he murmured wearily, "Wisht it was sunup."

Sleep came to him in the end, but his eyes were open with the first paling of the stars, and the gray of dawn caught him with breakfast finished and climbing the hillside in the direction of the secret abiding place of Mr. Pocket.

The first crosscut the man made, there was space for only three holes, so narrow had become the pay streak and so close was he to the fountainhead of the golden stream he had been following for four days.

"Be ca'm, Bill; be ca'm," he admonished himself, as he broke ground for the final hole where the sides of the V had at last come together in a point.

"I've got the almighty cinch on you, Mr. Pocket, an' you can't lose me," he said many times as he sank the hole deeper and deeper.

Four feet, five feet, six feet, he dug his way down into the earth. The digging grew harder. His pick grated on broken rock. He examined the rock. "Rotten quartz" was his conclusion as, with the shovel, he cleared the bottom of the hole of loose dirt. He attacked the crumbling quartz with the pick, bursting the disintegrating rock asunder with every stroke.

He thrust his shovel into the loose mass. His eye caught a gleam of yellow. He dropped the shovel and squatted suddenly on his heels. As a farmer rubs the clinging earth from fresh-dug potatoes, so the man, a piece of rotten quartz held in both hands, rubbed the dirt away.

"Sufferin' Sardanopolis!" he cried. "Lumps an'

chunks of it! lumps an' chunks of it!"

It was only half rock he held in his hand. The other half was virgin gold. He dropped it into his pan and examined another piece. Little yellow was to be seen, but with his strong fingers he crumbled the rotten quartz away till both hands were filled with glowing yellow. He rubbed the dirt away from fragment after fragment, tossing them into the gold-pan. It was a treasure hole. So much had the quartz rotted away that there was less of it than there was of gold. Now and again he found a piece to which no rock clung—a piece that was all gold. A chunk where the pick had laid open the heart of the gold glittered like a handful of yellow jewels, and he cocked his head at it and slowly turned it around and over to observe the rich play of the light upon it.

"Talk about yer too-much-gold diggin's!" the man snorted contemptuously. "Why, this diggin'd make it look like thirty cents. This diggin' is all gold. An' right here an' now I name this here canyon All Gold Canyon, b' gosh!"

Still squatting on his heels, he continued examining the fragments and tossing them into the pan. Suddenly there came to him a premonition of danger. It seemed a shadow had fallen upon him. But there was no shadow. His heart had given a great jump up into his throat and was choking him. Then his blood slowly chilled, and he felt the sweat of his shirt cold against his flesh.

He did not spring up nor look around. He did not move. He was considering the nature of the premonition he had received, trying to locate the source of the mysterious force that had warned him, striving to sense the imperative presence of the unseen thing that threatened him. There is an aura of things hostile, made manifest by messengers too refined for the senses to know; and this aura he felt, but knew not how he felt it. His was the feeling as when a cloud passes over the sun. It seemed that between him and life had passed something dark and smothering and menacing; a gloom, as it were, that swallowed up life and made for death—his death.

Every force of his being impelled him to spring up and confront the unseen danger, but his soul dominated the panic, and he remained squatting on his heels, in his hands a chunk of gold. He did not dare to look around, but he knew by now that there was something behind him and above him. He made believe to be interested in the gold in his hand. He examined it critically, turned it over and over, and rubbed the dirt from it. And all the time he knew that something behind him was looking at the gold over his shoulder.

Still feigning interest in the chunk of gold in his hand, he listened intently and he heard the breathing of the thing behind him. His eyes searched the ground in front of him for a weapon, but they saw only the uprooted gold, worthless to him now in his extremity. There was his pick, a handy weapon on occasion; but this was not such an occasion. The man realized his predicament. He was in a narrow hole that was seven feet deep. His head did not come to the surface of the ground. He was in a trap.

He remained squatting on his heels. He was quite cool and collected; but his mind, considering every factor, showed him only his helplessness. He continued rubbing the dirt from the quartz fragments and throwing the gold into the pan. There was nothing else for him to do. Yet he knew that he would have to rise up, sooner or later, and face the danger that breathed at his back. The minutes passed, and with the passage of each minute he knew that by so much he was nearer the time when he must stand up, or else—and his wet shirt went cold against his flesh again at the thought—or else he might receive death as he stooped there over his treasure.

Still he squatted on his heels, rubbing dirt from gold and debating in just what manner he should rise up. He might rise up with a rush and claw his way out of the hole to meet whatever threatened on the even footing above ground. Or he might rise up slowly and carelessly, and feign casually to discover the thing that breathed at his back. His instinct and every fighting fiber of his body favored the mad, clawing rush to the surface.

His intellect, and the craft thereof, favored the slow

and cautious meeting with the thing that menaced and which he could not see. And while he debated, a loud, crashing noise burst on his ear. At the same instant he received a stunning blow on the left side of his back, and from the point of impact felt a rush of flame through his flesh. He sprang up in the air but, halfway to his feet, collapsed. His body crumpled in like a leaf withered in sudden heat, and he came down, his chest across his pan of gold, his face in the dirt and rock, his legs tangled and twisted because of the restricted space at the bottom of the hole. His legs twitched convulsively several times. His body was shaken with a mighty ague. There was a slow expansion of the lungs, accompanied by a deep sigh. Then the air was slowly, very slowly, exhaled, and his body as slowly flattened itself down into inertness.

Above, revolver in hand, a man was peering down over the edge of the hole. He peered for a long time at the prone and motionless body beneath him. After a while the stranger sat down on the edge of the hole so that he could see into it, and rested the revolver on his knee. Reaching his hand into a pocket, he drew out a wisp of brown paper. Into this he dropped a few crumbs of tobacco. The combination became a cigarette, brown and squat, with the ends turned in. Not once did he take his eyes from the body at the bottom of the hole. He lighted the cigarette and drew its smoke into his lungs with a caressing intake of the breath. He smoked slowly. Once the cigarette went out and he relighted it. And all the while he studied the body beneath him.

In the end he tossed the cigarette stub away and rose to his feet. He moved to the edge of the hole. Spanning it, a hand resting on each edge, and with the revolver still in the right hand, he muscled his body down into the hole. While his feet were yet a yard from the bottom, he released his hands and dropped down.

At the instant his feet struck bottom he saw the pocket-miner's arm leap out, and his own legs knew a swift, jerking grip that overthrew him. In the nature of the jump his revolver-hand was above his head. Swiftly as the grip had flashed about his legs, just as

swiftly he brought the revolver down. He was still in the air, his fall in process of completion, when he pulled the trigger. The explosion was deafening in the confined space. The smoke filled the hole so that he could see nothing. He struck the bottom on his back, and, like a cat's the pocket-miner's body was on top of him. Even as the miner's body passed on top, the stranger crooked in his right arm to fire; and even in that instant the miner, with a quick thrust of elbow, struck his wrist. The muzzle was thrown up and the bullet thudded into the dirt of the side of the hole.

The next instant the stranger felt the miner's hand grip his wrist. The struggle was now for the revolver. Each man strove to turn it against the other's body. The smoke in the hole was clearing. The stranger, lying on his back, was beginning to see dimly. But suddenly he was blinded by a handful of dirt deliberately flung into his eyes by his antagonist. In that moment of shock his grip on the revolver was broken. In the next moment he felt a smashing darkness descend upon his brain, and in the midst of the darkness even the darkness ceased.

But the pocket miner fired again and again, until the revolver was empty. Then he tossed it from him and, breathing heavily, sat down on the dead man's legs.

The miner was sobbing and struggling for breath. "Measly skunk!" he panted, "a-campin' on my trail an' lettin' me do the work, an' then shootin' me in the back!"

He was half crying from anger and exhaustion. He peered at the face of the dead man. It was sprinkled with loose dirt and gravel, and it was difficult to distinguish the features.

"Never laid eyes on him before," the miner concluded his scrutiny. "Just a common an' ordinary thief, hang him! An' he shot me in the back! He shot me in the back!"

He opened his shirt and felt himself, front and back, on his left side.

"Went clean through, and no harm done!" he cried jubilantly. "I'll bet he aimed all right; but he drew the gun over when he pulled the trigger—the cur! But I fixed 'm! Oh, I fixed 'm!"

His fingers were investigating the bullet hole in his side, and a shade of regret passed over his face. "It's goin' to be stiffer'n hell," he said. "An' it's up to me to get mended an' get out o' here."

He crawled out of the hole and went down the hill to his camp. Half an hour later he returned, leading his packhorse. His open shirt disclosed the rude bandages with which he had dressed his wound. He was slow and awkward with his left-hand movements, but that did not prevent his using the arm.

The bight of the pack rope under the dead man's shoulders enabled him to heave the body out of the hole. Then he set to work gathering up his gold. He worked steadily for several hours, pausing often to rest his stiffening shoulder and to exclaim, "He shot me in the back, the measly skunk! He shot me in the back!"

When his treasure was quite cleaned up and wrapped securely into a number of blanket-covered parcels, he made an estimate of its value.

"Four hundred pounds, or I'm a Hottentot," he concluded. "Say two hundred in quartz an' dirt—that leaves two hundred pounds of gold. Bill! Wake up! Two hundred pounds of gold! Forty thousand dollars! An' it's yourn—all yourn!"

He scratched his head delightedly and his fingers blundered into an unfamiliar groove. They quested along it for several inches. It was a crease through his scalp where the second bullet had ploughed.

He walked angrily over to the dead man.

"You would, would you?" he bullied. "You would, eh? Well, I fixed you good an' plenty, an' I'll give you a decent burial, too. That's more'n you'd have done for me."

He dragged the body to the edge of the hole and toppled it in. It struck the bottom with a dull crash, on its side, the face twisted up to the light. The miner peered down at it.

"An' you shot me in the back!" he said accusingly.

With pick and shovel he filled the hole. Then he loaded the gold on his horse. It was too great a load for the animal, and when he had gained his camp he transferred part of it to his saddle horse. Even so, he was compelled to abandon a portion of his outfit—pick and shovel and gold-pan, extra food and cooking utensils, and divers odds and ends.

The sun was at the zenith when the man forced the horses at the screen of vines and creepers. To climb the huge boulders the animals were compelled to uprear and struggle blindly through the tangled mass of vegetation. Once the saddle horse fell heavily and the man removed the pack to get the animal on its feet. After it started on its way again the man thrust his head out from among the leaves and peered up at the hillside.

"The measly skunk!" he said, and disappeared.

There was a ripping and tearing of vines and boughs. The trees surged back and forth, marking the passage of the animals through the midst of them. There was a clashing of steel-shod hoofs on stone, and now and again a sharp cry of command. Then the voice of the man was raised in song.

"Tu'n around an' tu'n yo' face
Unto them sweet hills of grace
(D' pow'rs of sin yo' am scornin'!).
Look about an' look aroun'
Fling yo' sin-pack on d' groun'
(Yo' will meet wid d' Lord in d' mornin'!)."

The song grew faint and fainter, and through the silence crept back the spirit of the place. The stream once more drowsed and whispered; the hum of the mountain bees rose sleepily. Down through the perfume-weighted air fluttered the snowy fluffs of the cottonwoods. The butterflies drifted in and out among the trees, and over all blazed the quiet sunshine. Only remained the hoof marks in the meadow and the torn hillside to mark the boisterous trail of the life that had broken the peace of the place and passed on.

JACK LONDON *(1876–1916), born in San Francisco possibly as an illegitimate son of an itinerant astrologist, grew up tough and lawless and was an oyster pirate by age fifteen. He tells harsh tales of life at sea and of the gold rush and is best known for his novel* Call of the Wild *(1903).*

TREACHERY

THE FOOL'S HEART

EUGENE MANLOVE RHODES

Charley Ellis did not know where he was; he did not know where he was going; he was not even cheered by any hope of damnation. His worldly goods were the clothes he wore, the six-shooter on his thigh, the horse between his legs, and his saddle, bridle and spurs. He had no money; no friend closer than five hundred miles. Therefore, he whistled and sang; he sat jauntily; his wide hat took on the cant joyous; he cocked a bright eye appreciatively at a pleasant world—a lonesome world just now, but great fun.

By years, few-and-twenty; by size, of the great upper-middle class; blond, tanned, down-cheeked. Add a shock of tow-colored hair, a pug nose of engaging impudence—and you have the inventory.

All day he had ridden slowly across a dreary land of rolling hills, northward and ever northward; a steepest, interminable gray ridge of limestone on his right, knife-sharp, bleak and bare; the vast black bulk of San Mateo on the west; and all the long day the rider had seen no house, or road, or any man.

One thing troubled him a little: his big roan horse was roadweary and had lost his aforetime pleasing plumpness. He had also lost a shoe to-day and was intending to be very tender-footed at once.

Charley was pleased, then, topping a hill, to observe that somebody had chopped a deep notch into the stubborn limestone ridge; and to see, framed in that tremendous notch, a low square of ranch buildings on a high tableland beyond. A dark and crooked chasm lay between—Ellis could see only the upper walls of it, but the steep angle of the sides gave the depth.

A deep and broad basin fell away before his feet. Westward it broke into misty branches between ridges blue-black with pine. Plainly the waters of these many valleys drained away through the deep-notched chasm.

It was late. The valley was dark with shadow. Beyond, the lonely ranch loomed high and mysterious in a blaze of the dying sunlight. Ellis felt his blood stir and thrill to watch it higher and higher above him as he followed down a plunging ridge. Higher and higher it rose; another downward step and it was gone.

Ellis led his horse now, to favor the unshod foot on the stony way. He came to a road in the valley; the road took him to a swift and noisy stream, brawling, foaming white and narrow.

They drank; they splashed across.

A juniper stood beside the road. To it was nailed a signboard, with the rudely painted direction:

BOX O RANCH, FIVE MILES

Previous pages: Charles M. Russell, *The Call of the Law*, 1911. Oil, 24 x 36"

Below was a penciled injunction:

DON'T TRY THE BOX CANON.
IT'S FENCED. TOO ROUGH ANYWAY.
KEEP TO THE ROAD.

"Vinegaroan, you old skeesicks," said Charley, "I'm goin' to leave you here and hoof it in. Good grass here and you're right tired. Besides, that foot of yours'll be ruined with a little more of these rocks. I'll rustle a shoe and tack it on in the morning." He hung the saddle high in the juniper—for range cattle prefer a good sixty-dollar saddle to other feed. Tents and bedding are nutritious but dry. A line of washing has its points for delicate appetites; boots make dainty titbits; harness is excellent—harness is the good old stand-by—harness is worthy of high praise, though buckle-y; but for all around merit, wholesome, substantial, piquant, the saddle has no equal. Bridle and blankets are the customary relishes for the saddle, but the best cattle often omit them.

Charley hobbled old Vinegaroan and set out smartly, hobbling himself in his high-heeled boots. As the dim road wound into the falling dusk he regaled himself with the immortal saga of Sam Bass:

"Sam Bass he came from Indiana—it was his native state;
He came out here to Texas, and there he met his fate.
Sam always drank good liquor and spent his money free,
And a kinder-hearted fellow you'd seldom ever see!"

The Box O Ranch stands on a bone-dry mesa, two miles from living water. It is a hollow square of adobe; within is a mighty cistern, large enough to store the filtered rain water from all the roofs. The site was chosen for shelter in Indian times; there is neither hill nor ridge within gunshot. One lonely cedar fronts the house, and no other tree is in sight; for that one tree the ranch was built there and not in another place. A mile away you come to the brink of Nogales Canyon, narrow and deep and dark; a thousand feet below the sunless waters carve their way to the far-off river. The ranch buildings and corrals now mark one corner of a fenced pasture, three miles square, the farther cliffs of Nogales Canyon make the southern fence.

The great mesas pyramid against the west, step on step; on that heaven-high pedestal San Mateo Peak basks in the sun, a sleeping lion. But the wonder and beauty of San Mateo are unprized. San Mateo is in America.

Two men came to the Box O in the glare of afternoon—a tall man, great of bone and coarse of face, hawk-nosed; a shorter man and younger, dark, thin-lipped, with little restless eyes, gray and shifting. He had broad eyebrows and a sharp, thin nose.

A heavy revolver swung at the tall man's thigh—the short man had an automatic; each had a rifle under his knee. They were weary and thirst-parched; the horses stumbled as they walked—they were streaked and splashed with the white salt of sweat, caked with a mire of dust and lather, dried now by the last slow miles, so that no man might know their color.

The unlocked house lay silent and empty; the stove was cold; the dust of days lay on the table. "Good enough!" croaked the shorter man. "Luck's with us."

He led the way to the cistern. They drank eagerly, prudently; they sluiced the stinging dust from face and neck and hair.

"Ain't it good?" said the short man.

"Huh! That wasn't such a much. Wait till you're good and dry once—till your lips crack to the quick and your tongue swells black."

"Never for mine! I'm for getting out of this. I'm hunting the rainiest country I can find; and I stay there."

"If we get away! What if we don't find fresh horses in the pasture? There's none in sight."

"Reed's always got horses in the pasture. They're down in the canyon, where the sun hasn't dried up the grass. Oh, we'll get away, all right!'

"They've got to track us, Laxon—and we've left a

mighty crooked trail. They can't follow our trail at night and the Angel Gabriel couldn't guess where we are headed for."

"You don't allow much for chance? Or for—anything else? We sure don't deserve to get away," said Laxon.

He led his horse in, took off the bridle and pumped up a bucket of water. The poor beast drank greedily and his eyes begged for more.

"Not now, Bill. Another in ten minutes," he said in answer to a feeble nickering. He unsaddled; he sighed at the scalded back. "I'll douse a few bucketfuls on you quick as your pard gets his."

He turned his head. The younger man leaned sullenly against the wall. He had not moved. Laxon's face hardened. It was an ugly and brutal face at best— the uglier that he was slightly cross-eyed. Now it was the face of a devil.

"You worthless cur, get your horse! I thought you was yellow when you killed poor Mims last night— and now I know it! No need of it—not a bit. We could 'a got his gun and his box of money without. Sink me to hell if I've not half a mind to give you up! If I was sure they'd hang you first I'd do it!"

"Don't let's quarrel, Jess. I'll get the horse, of course," said Moss wearily. "I'm just about all in— that's all. I could sleep a week!"

"Guess your horse ain't tired, you swine! I ought to kick you through the gate! Quarrel? You! Wish you'd try it. Wish you'd just raise your voice at me! Sleep, says he! Sleep, when somebody may drop in on us any time! All the sleep you get is the next hour. We ride to-night and sleep all day to-morrow in some hollow of the deep hills, over beyond the Divide. No more daylight for us till we strike the Gila."

Moss made no answer. Laxon hobbled stiffly into the house and brought back canned tomatoes, corned beef and a butcher knife. They wolfed their food in silence.

"Sleep now, baby!" said Laxon. "I'll stand watch."

James Boren, *When Saddles Creak*, 1970.
Watercolor, 30 x 40"

He spread the heavy saddle blankets in the sun; he gave the horses water, a little at a time, until they had their fill; with a gunny sack and pail he washed them carefully. Their sides were raw with spurring; there were ridges and welts where a doubled rope had lashed.

A cruel day to the northward two other horses lay stark and cold by Bluewater Corral; a cruel night beyond Bluewater the paymaster of the Harqua Hala Mine lay by the broken box of his trust, with a bullet in his heart.

Laxon found a can of baking powder and sprinkled it on the scalded backs.

"Pretty hard lines, Bill," he said, with a pat for the drooping neck. "All that heft of coin heaped up behind the cantle—that made it bad. Never mind! You'll come out all right—both of you!"

His thoughts went back to those other horses at Bluewater. They had shot them at sunrise. He could not turn them loose to drink the icy water and die in agony; he could not stay; he could not shut them in the corral to endure the agony of thirst until the pursuit came up—a pursuit that so easily might lose the trail in the rock country and never come to Bluewater. It had been a bitter choice.

He built a fire and investigated the chuck room; he put on the coffeepot, took a careful look across the mesa and came back to Moss. The hour was up.

Moss slept heavily; his arms sprawled wide, his fingers jerking; he moaned and muttered in his sleep; his eyes were sunken and on his check the skin was stretched skintight. The watcher was in less evil ease; his reserves of stored-up vitality were scarcely touched as yet. Conscious of this, his anger for the outworn man gave way to rough compassion; the hour had stretched to nearly two before he shook the sleeper's shoulder.

"Come, Moss! You're rested a little and so's your horse. I've got some good hot coffee ready for you. Get a cup of that into your belly and you'll be as good as new. Then you go drive all the horses up out of the pasture—just about time before dark. While you're gone I'll cook a hot supper, bake up a few pones of

bread for us to take along and pack up enough other truck to do us. I'd go, but you're fifty pounds lighter'n me. Besides, you know the pasture."

"Oh, I'll go," said Moss as he drank his coffee. "There's a little corral down in the bottom. Guess I can ease a bunch in there and get me a new mount. The rest'll be easy."

"We'll pick out the likeliest, turn the others out and throw a scare into 'em," said Laxon. "We don't want to leave any fresh horses for them fellows, if they come. And, of course, they'll come."

"Yes, and they'll have a time finding out which is our tracks. I'll just leave this money here, and the rifle," said Moss, in the corral. "That'll be so much weight off, anyway." He untied a slicker from behind the saddle. Unrolling it he took out an ore sack and tossed it over beside Laxon's saddle; it fell with a heavy clink of coins. "Say, Jess! Look over my doin' the baby act a while ago, will you? I should have taken care of my horse, of course—poor devil; but I was all in—so tired I hardly knew what I was about." He hesitated. "And—honest, Jess—I thought Mim was going after his gun."

"Guess I didn't sense how tired you was," said Jess, and there was relief in his voice. "Let it all slide. We're in bad and we got to stick together—us two."

At sundown Moss drove back twelve head of saddle stock. He had caught a big rangy sorrel at the horse pen in the canyon.

"This one'll do for me," he announced as he swung down.

"I'll take the big black," said Laxon. "Trot along now and eat your supper. I'll be ready by the time you're done. I've got our stuff all packed—and two canteens. Say, Moss, I've got two bed blankets. I'm goin' to carry my share of grub behind my saddle. My sack of money I'll wad up in my blanket and sling it across in front of me, see? We don't want any more sore-backed horses. You'd better do the same."

"All right!" said Moss. "You fix it up while I eat."

Laxon roped and saddled the black, and tied one of the grub sacks behind the cantle; he made a neat roll of his own sack of money and the blanket and tied it across behind the horn. Then he fixed his partner's money sack and grub sack the same way and thrust the rifle into the scabbard. He opened the outer gate of the corral and let the loose horses out on the eastern mesa.

"Hike, you! We'll fall in behind you in a pair of minutes and make you burn the breeze!…Now for Bill, the very tired horse, and we'll be all ready to hit the trail."

Bill was lying down in a corner. Laxon stirred him up and led him by the foretop out through the pasture gate. The saddlehouse door opened noiselessly; Moss steadied his automatic against the doorframe and waited.

"You go hunt up your pardner, old Bill. You and him orter be good pals from now on. So long! Good luck!" said Laxon. He closed the gate.

Moss shot him between the shoulder blades. Laxon whirled and fell on his face; the swift automatic cracked. Laxon rose to his elbow, riddled and torn; bullet after bullet crashed through his body. He shot the sorrel horse between the eyes; the black reared up and broke his rope. As he fell backward a ball from Laxon's forty-five pierced his breast; falling, another shot broke his neck. Then Laxon laughed— and died.

WHITE, FRANTIC, CURSING, THE trapped murderer staggered out from his ambush. Shaking horribly he made sure that Laxon was dead.

"The squint-eyed devil!" he screamed.

He ran to the outer gate. The band of freed horses was close by and unalarmed, but twilight was deepening fast. What was to be done must be done quickly.

He set the outer gate open. He bridled old Bill and leaped on, bareback; with infinite caution he made a wide circle beyond the little bunch of horses and worked them slowly toward the gate.

They came readily enough and, at first, it seemed that there would be no trouble; but at the gate they stopped, sniffed, saw those dim, mysterious forms stretched out at the farther side, huddled, recoiled and broke away in a little, slow trot.

Moss could not stop them. Poor old Bill could only shuffle. The trot became a walk; they nibbled at the young grass.

Once he turned them back, but before they reached the gate they edged away uneasily. Twilight was done. Twice he turned them back. All the stars were out and blazing clear; a cool night breeze sprang up. Nearing the gate the horses sniffed the air; they snorted, wheeled and broke away; the trot became a gallop, the gallop a run.

Moss slipped the bridle off and walked back to the corral. His whole body was shaking in a passion of rage and fear.

He drank deeply at the cistern; he reloaded the automatic; he went to the dead horses. Whatever came, he would not abandon that money. After all, there was a chance. He would keep the notes with him; he would hide the gold somewhere in the rocky cliffs of the canyon; he would climb out over the cliffs, where he would leave no track to follow; he would keep in the impassable hills, hiding by day; he would carry food and water; he would take the rifle and the first time he saw a horseman alone he would have a horse.

Eagerly he untied the two treasure sacks and emptied one into the other. He started for the house. Then his heart stopped beating. It was a voice, faint and far away:

"Rabbit Rabbit! Tail mighty white!
Yes, good Lord—he'll take it out o' sight!
Take it out o'sight!"

In a frenzy of fear the murderer dropped his treasure and matched up the rifle. He ran to the gate and crouched in the shadow. His hair stood up; his heart pounded at his ribs; his knees knocked together.

"Rabbit! Rabbit! Ears mighty long!
Yes, good Lord—you set 'em on wrong!
Set 'em on wrong!"

It was a gay young voice, coming from the westward, nearer and nearer. Slinking in the shadows, Moss came to the corner. In the starlight he saw a man very near now, coming down the road afoot, singing as he came:

> *"Sam Bass he came from Indiana—*
> *it was his native state."*

From the west? His pursuers would be coming from the north along his track—they would not be singing, and there would be more than one. Why was this man afoot? With a desperate effort of the will Moss pulled himself together. He slipped back into the kitchen and lit the lamp. He threw dry sticks on the glowing coals—they broke into a crackling flame; the pleasant tingling incense of cedar filled the room. He dabbed at his burning face with a wet towel; he smoothed his hair hastily. Drawn, pale and haggard, the face in the glass gave him his cue—he was an invalid.

Would the man never come? He felt the mounting impulse to struggle no longer—to shriek out all the ghastly truth; to give up anything, so he might sleep and die and rest. But he had no choice; he must fight on. Someway he must use this newcomer for his need. But why afoot? Why could not the man have a horse? Then his way would have been so easy. His throat and mouth were dust-dry—he drank deep of the cool water and felt new life steal along his veins.

Then—because he must busy himself to bridge the dreadful interval—he forced his hands to steadiness; he filled and lit a pipe.

"Hello, the house!"

Moss threw open the door; the dancing light leaped out against the dark. Along that golden pathway a man came, smiling.

"Hello yourself, and see how you like it! You're late. Turn your horse in the corral while I warm up supper for you."

"I LEFT MY HORSE BACK up the road. I just love to walk," said Charley. At the door he held up a warning hand. "Before I come in, let's have a clear under-standing. No canned corn goes with me. I don't want anybody even to mention canned corn."

"Never heard of it," said Moss. "Sit ye down. How'd fried spuds, with onions and bacon, suit you?"

"Fine and dandy! Anything but ensilage." Ellis limped to a box by the fire and painfully removed a boot. "Cracky! Some blisters!"

Moss bent over the fire.

"You're not from round these parts, are you?" he asked. He raked out coals for the coffeepot and put the potatoes to warm.

"Nope. From Arizona—lookin' for work. What's the show to hook up with this outfit?"

"None. Everybody gone to the round-up. Oh, I don't live here myself. I'm just a-stayin' round for my health." . . . If I could only get to this man's horse—if I could leave this man in the trap! The pursuit must be here by to-morrow. Steady! I must feel my way . . . "Horse played out?"

"No; but he's right tired and he lost the shoe off his nigh forefoot to-day. Stake me to a new shoe, of course?"

"Sure!" . . . But this man will tell his story. I can never get away on a tired horse—they will overtake me; they will be here tomorrow. Shall I make it seem that Laxon and this man have killed each other? No; there will still be his tracks where he came—mine where I leave. How then? . . . "Sorry I can't let you have a horse to get yours. Just set myself afoot about sunset. Had all the saddle horses in the corral—saw a coyote—ran out to shoot at him—did you hear me, mister? I didn't get your name. Mine's Moss."

Ellis—Charley Ellis. No; I was 'way over behind that hill at sundown. You're sure looking peaked and pale, Mr. Moss."

"It's nothing—weak heart," said Moss. The heavy brows made a black bar across his white face . . . How then? I will stay here. I will be the dupe, the scapegoat—this man shall take my place, shall escape, shall be killed resisting arrest . . . "Just a little twinge. I'm used to it. Where was I?" Oh, yes—the horses. Well, I didn't shut the gate good. It blew open and away went my horses to the wild bunch. Idiotic, wasn't it? And I was planning to make a start to-night, ten mile or so, on a little hunting trip. That reminds me—I got a lot of bread baked up and it's out in my pack. You wash up and I'll go get it. There's the pan."...This man Ellis was the murderer! I left my horse. Ellis stole away while I was asleep. He tried to escape on my horse. He can't get far; the horse is about played out. When I woke and missed Ellis I found the dead man in the corral!

The black thought shaped and grew. He hugged it to his heart as he took bread from the pack sacks; he bettered it as he hid the sack of money. He struck a match and picked out a sheaf of five-dollar bills; he tore them part-way across, near one corner, perhaps an inch. Then he took one bill from the torn package, crumpled it up and wadded it in his pocket, putting the others back in the sack.

Next, he found the empty ore sack, the one that had carried Laxon's half of the plunder. With a corner of it he pressed lightly over the dead man's back, so that a tiny smear of drying blood showed on the sack.

Then he took the bread and hurried to the house dropping the ore sack outside the door. It was swiftly done. Ellis was just combing his hair when his host returned.

"There! Coffee's hot and potatoes will be in a jiffy. Sit up. Where'd you say you left your horse?"

"Where the wagon road crosses the creek west of the Box Canyon—where there's a sign nailed to a tree."

"Which sign? There's several different places."

" 'Five miles to the Box O Ranch,' it says."

"Hobbled your horse, I reckon?"

"Yep. Wasn't really no need of hobbling, either— he won't go far. Some gaunted up, he is. He'll be glad when I get a job. And I'll say this for old Vinegaroan— he's a son-of-a-gun to pitch; but he don't put on. When he shows tired he's tired for fair. Only for his wild fool ways, he'd be the best horse I ever owned. But, then, if it hadn't been for them wild fool ways the V R wouldn't never a' let me got my clutches on him. They never raised a better horse, but he was spoiled in breaking. He thinks you want him to buck. Don't mean no harm by it."

"I see! Roan horse, branded 'V R' and some devilish; you might say he named himself."

"That's it."

"What is he—red roan?"

"Naw—blue roan. Mighty fine looker when he's fat—the old scoundrel!"

"Old horse? Or is that just a love name?"

Charley laughed.

"Just a love name. He's seven years old."

Moss poured the coffee and dished up the potatoes.

"There! She's ready—pitch in! I'll take a cup of coffee with you. Big horse?"

"Fifteen hands. Say, this slumgullion tastes mighty ample after—you know—fodder. Last night I stayed in a little log shack south of the peak."

Moss interrupted.

"How many rooms? So I can know whose house it was."

"Two rooms—'H G' burned on the door. 'Chas. J. Graham, Cañada Mamosa,' stenciled on the boxes. No one at home but canned corn and flour and coffee. Night before at the Anchor X Ranch. No one at home. Note sayin' they'd gone to ship steers at Magdalena. Didn't say nothing about goin' after chuck— but I know. There wasn't one cussed thing to eat except canned corn—not even coffee. Blest if I've seen a man for three days. Before that I laid up a couple of days with an old Mexican, right on the tiptop of the Black Range—hunting, and resting up my horse."

"I knowed a V R brand once, up North," said Moss reflectively. "On the hip for mares, it was; thigh for geldings; side for cattle."

"That one's on the Gila—Old Man Hearn— shoulder for horses; hip for cattle."

"Let me fill your cup," said Moss. "Now I'll tell you what—I wish you could lay up with me. I'd be glad to have you. But if you want work bad, and your horse can make eighteen or twenty miles by noon to-morrow, I think you can catch onto a job. They're meetin' at Rosedale to-morrow to start for the north round-up. This country here has done been worked. They'll light out after dinner and make camp about twenty-five miles north. You follow back the road you came here for about a mile. When the road bends to come here, at the head of the draw, you bear off to the left across the mesa, northwest-like. In six or eight miles you'll hit a plain road from the river, running west, up into the mountains. That'll take you straight to Rosedale."

"Well! I'll have to be up and doin', then, and catch 'em before they move. Much obliged to you! Think I'm pretty sure of a job?"

"It's a cinch. Them V cross T cattle are a snaky lot, and they never have enough men."

"Look here! Stake me to a number-one shoe and some nails, will you? Loan me a rasp and a hammer? I'll stick the tools up in the tree where the sign is. Clap a shoe on at daylight and shack along while it's cool. I'll make it by ten o'clock or later."

"But you'll shy all night?"

"No—we might oversleep. I'll chin with you a while and then hike along back and sleep on my saddle blankets. Then I'll be stirrin' soon in the mawnin'."

"Well, I'm sorry to see you go; but you know your own business. No more? Smoke up, then?" He tossed papers and tobacco across. "Say, I want you to send a Mex. boy down here with a horse, so I can drive my runaways in off the flat. Don't forget!"

"I'll not. May I have a bucket and wash up these blistered feet of mine before I hike?"

"Sure you can! Sit still; I'll get the water. I'll rustle round and see if some of the boys ain't left some clean socks too; and I'll wrap you up a parcel of breakfast."

"Well, this is luck!" declared Charley a little later, soaking his feet luxuriously and blowing smoke rings while his host busied himself packing a lunch. "A job, horseshoe, socks, supper and breakfast—and no canned corn! I'll do somebody else a good turn sometime—see if I don't! I wasn't looking for much like this a spell back, either. About an hour by sun, I was countin' on maybe makin' supper on a cigarette and a few verses of The Boston Burglar—unless I could shoot me a cottontail at sundown—most

always you can find a rabbit at sundown. Then I sighted this dizzy old ranch peekin' through the gap at me. Bing! Just look at me now! Nobody's got nothin' on me! Right quaint, ain't it? What a difference a few hours'll make—the things that's waiting for a fellow and him not knowin' about it!"

Moss laughed.

"Well, I got to be steppin'," said Charley.

"Hold on! I'm not done with you yet. That's a good pair of boots you've got there—but they'll be just hell on those blistered feet. How'd you like to swap for my old ones? Sevens, mine are."

"So's mine. Why, I'll swap with you. Yours'll be a sight easier on me. I'm no great shakes on walkin' me."

"Why, man, did you think I meant to swap even? Your boots are worth ten dollars—almost new—and mine just hang together. I wouldn't take a mean advantage of you like that. Come! I'll make you an offer: Give me your boots and your forty-five, with the belt and scabbard, for my automatic, with its rigging and five dollars, and I'll throw in my boots."

"Shucks! You're cheating yourself! Trade boots and guns even—that'll be fair enough." Charley unbuckled his spurs.

"Don't be silly! Take the money. It's a long time till pay day. I've been all along that long road, my boy. If you're broke—I'm just guessing that, because I've been broke myself—why, you don't want to ask for an advance the first thing."

"I'll tell you what, then—swap spurs too. That'll make about an even break."

"Nonsense! Keep your spurs. You don't want these old petmakers of mine. They'd be a hoodoo to a cowboy. Take the money, son. I wish it was more. I've got plenty enough, but not here. If you feel that way about it, call it a loan and pay it back when you're flush. Better still, pass it on to somebody else that needs it."

Charley surrendered.

"I'll take it, then—that way. You're all right, Mr. Moss! Try on your new boots and see how they fit."

"Fine as silk! Couldn't be better if they was made

to order," said Moss. "Good boots. That's always the way with you young fellows. Every cent goes for a fancy outfit. Bet you've got a fire-new saddle—and you without a copper cent in your pocket."

"Well, purty nigh it," admitted Charley, grinning. "Set me back fifty-four pesos less'n a year ago. But she's a daisy."

"Swell fork?"

Charley snorted.

"Swell fork nothin'! No, sir; I don't need no roll. I ride 'em slick;—take off my spurs and grease my heels! I been throwed, of course—everybody has—but I never clawed leather yet and I don't need no swell fork!"

Moss smiled indulgently.

"Well, I must rig you out for horseshoein'. You stay here and rest up. Number one shoe, I think you said?"

He came back with the horseshoe and tools, bringing also the discarded ore sack, now bulging with a liberal feed of corn.

"For Vinegaroan, with my love!" he said, laughing, and clapping Ellis on the shoulder.

A lump came into Charley's throat.

"I reckon you're a real-for-certain white man, Mr. Moss. If old Vinegaroan could talk he'd sure thank you. I'm going now and let you go to bed. You don't look so clean beat out as you did, but you look right tired. *Adios!* And I hope to meet up with you again."

"Oh, you'll see me again! Good-by!"

They shook hands. Charley shouldered his pack and limped sturdily along the starlit road, turning once for a shouted "Good-by!" Moss waved a hand from the lighted doorway; a gay song floated back to him…

"Ada! Ada! Open that do',
Ada!

Add! Ada! Open that do'
This mawnin'.
Ada! Ada! Open that do'
Or I'll open it with a forty-fo'
This mawnin'!"

"Oh, yes! you'll see me again!" said Moss, smiling evilly. Then he closed the door. "Tired?" he said. "Tired? I've got to sleep if I swing for it!"

BOX O RANCH, AUGUST fifth.
Statement of Elmer Moss.

My name is Elmer Moss. I left Florence, Arizona, three weeks ago, looking for work. I did not find a place and drifted on to this ranch. I stayed here a week or two, six years ago, when George Sligh worked here.

Last night my horse was pretty well give out and had lost a shoe; so I left him at the crossing of Nogales Creek, west of the pasture fence, and walked in.

I got in soon after dark and found a man who said his name was Charley Ellis, and that he was working here. He was a young fellow, with rather a pleasant face. He was about my size, with light hair and blue eyes and a pug nose. He made me welcome. Said he couldn't say about the work, but for me to stay here till the boss came back. We talked quite late.

I woke up early in the morning. Ellis was not in his bed. I supposed he had gone to wrangle horses out of the pasture and I went back to sleep, for I was very tired from riding a slow horse. I woke again after a while and got up. Ellis was not back yet. I went out, into the corral. And there I found a dead man. He was shot all to pieces—I don't know how many times. There were two dead horses, both shot and both saddled.

I found the boot tracks where Ellis had gone back the way I came. He is trying to get away on my horse and leave me with a murdered man on my hands to explain.

I was so scared I didn't know what to do. I went out in the pasture to the rim, where I could see all over the canyon. If I could have got a horse I would have run away. There wasn't a horse in sight except one. That one was close up under the rim-rock. He had been ridden almost to death. He wouldn't have

Overleaf: Frederic Remington, *In From the Night Herd*, 1907. Oil, 27 x 40"

carried me five miles. After I came back I found another one, in worse shape than the first, outside the corral gates. I let him in and gave him water and hay. There were horse-tracks of all sizes round the corral.

I don't know what to do. I don't know what has happened here. It may be a week before anybody comes. If anyone comes to-day, or while the tracks are fresh that I made coming and that Ellis made going away, I'm all right. The story is all there, plain as print. My boots are new and his was all worn out. There's no chance for mistake. And my horse has lost a shoe from his left forefoot; so he will be easy tracked. And he's badly jaded—he can't go fast. If anybody comes to-day they can trail him up and catch him easy. If no one comes to-day I'm a goner.

I JUST NOW WENT and spread a tarp over the dead man. He was laughing when he died. He's laughing yet—and his eyes are wide open. It's horrible! Left everything else just as it was. Am writing this now, and taking my time at it, to get everything straight while there's no one to get me rattled and all mixed up. And in case I go out of my head. Or get hold of a horse somehow and try to get away. No, I won't try to run away. If I did it would be just the same as confessing that I was the murderer. If they caught me I'd hang sure.

Nothing can save me except the straight truth. And that won't help me none unless somebody comes along today. This man Ellis was about my size—but I told you that before. He wore blue overalls, pretty badly faded, and a gray flannel shirt. I didn't notice his hat; he didn't have it on much. I saw a revolver belt under his pillow and it's gone now; but I didn't see the gun.

THAT MADE ME THINK. I went back and looked round everywhere to see where Ellis had reloaded his gun. I found fresh shells—nine of them, thirty-twos, automatic shells, smokeless, rimless—scattered over the floor of the saddle room just as an automatic

would throw them. He killed his man from ambush. I went back and looked at the dead man. He was shot in the back—twice anyway. Hit six times in all, as near as I could see. I couldn't bear to touch him. He looked too terrible, laughing that way—and I'm about to break down. There was a hole in his neck about the size a thirty-two would make.

There was a six-shooter in the sand near his hand with three empty shells in it. Them shells was what killed the horses—after the dead man was first shot, I reckon. I covered him up again. I see now that I shouldn't have gone near him. I see now—too late—that I never should have made one single foot-track in that corral. If I had only known—if I had only thought in time—the tracks in there would have cleared me. All I had to do was to stay out. But how could I think of that?

LATER: THERE IS A tree in front of the house and I have started a grave there. If no one comes by sundown I'll bury the poor fellow. I will rig up some sort of a sled and put the body on it and make the give-out pony drag it out to the grave.

The work of digging has done me good and steadied my nerves. I am half done and now I am able to set a little. I will go back and finish it now.

LATER—TEN O'CLOCK: Thank God! When the grave was done and I climbed out I saw a big dust off in the north coming this way. I am saved! They are closer now and coming very fast—ten or twelve men on horseback. I have looked over this statement carefully and don't think I have forgotten anything. This is the truth and nothing but the truth, so help me God.

I want to make one thing straight: Moss is not my right name. I have used that name for nine years. I was of good family and had my chance in life; but I was wild. Whatever happens I will bring no more disgrace to the name. I shall stick to Elmer Moss. If it had rained and washed the tracks out—if the wind had covered them with sand—what a shape I would be in now! They are quite close. I am leaving my gun on these sheets of paper. I am going out to meet them.

"That's all," said Tom Hall.

No one answered. Every man drew a long, deep breath—almost a sigh. There was a shuffling of feet.

The dark looks that had been bent on Moss, where he sat leaning heavily on the table, were turned long since to pity and rough friendliness. A dozen stern-faced men were crowded in the kitchen —a little white and sick, some of them, from what they had seen in the corral.

Each man looked at the others. Young Broyles let his hand rest lightly on Moss' shoulder. Then Old Man Teagardner frowned into his beard and spoke:

"Your story sounds like the truth, Mr. Moss," he said. "The boot-tracks going away from here are the same tracks we found in Bluewater Pens, and these two played-out horses came from Bluewater. If you're telling the truth you've been up against it hard. Still, you must be held as a prisoner—for the present, at least, till we find your man. And we'll want you to answer a few questions. What kind of a horse did you have!"

"A blue roan, V R brand, thin, fifteen hands high, no shoe on left forefoot, seven or eight years old. Saddle nearly new," answered Moss dully.

Then he raised his head and his voice swelled to sudden anger:

"You can ask me questions any time—you got me. Why don't you go after Ellis? That's your business! He's gettin' farther away every minute. Of course you'll keep me prisoner. What do you take me for—a fool? S'pose I'd think you'd find a man in the shape I'm in an' let him go foot-loose as soon as he said: 'Please, mister, I didn't do it!' Send some of your gang after Ellis and I'll answer all the fool questions you can think up."

"Son," said Teagardner evenly, "your party won't get away. We've sent men or messages all over the country and everybody's forwarded it on. Every man not accounted for will be held on suspicion. Some of the boys will go in a little while; but ten to one, your man Ellis is caught now—or killed. Say, boys, let's get out where we can get a breath of air."

"He won't fight, I tell you!" urged Moss as he followed his questioner outdoors. "He'll be as innocent as a lamb. If he don't ooze away without bein' seen his plan is to saw it off onto me."

"All the more reason, then, why you should answer our questions."

"Questions!" cried Moss bitterly. "I wish somebody'd answer me a few. Who was that dead man? What did Ellis kill him for? Who was your gang lookin' for?"

"We don't know the dead man's name. None of us ever seen him before," said Cook. "We've followed them for two days. Robbery and murder. Now one has killed the other for his share of the stolen money."

"Then you didn't know the man you was after! But," said Moss, "this man may have got killed himself for reasons of his own. He may have nothing to do with your bank robbers. There was all sorts of shod horse-tracks leading away from the gate—I saw 'em this morning. Maybe that was the outfit you're after."

Teagardner stroked his long white beard and motioned the others to silence. Said he:

"Some of us'll follow 'em up, to be sure—but them was only saddle horses that they turned out, I judge—so us fellows couldn't get 'em. As I figure it out, that's how come your man Ellis came to be in the fix he was. He shot his pardner and his pardner set him afoot before he died. So, when you come, Ellis left you to hold the sack…Well! Cal, you and Hall pick out two other men to suit yourselves, and follow Ellis up. Watch close for any sign of him hiding out the money. He dassent keep it with him. We'll look for it here. Made your choice?"

"These two sticks'll do us, Uncle Ben."

"All right, then; get a mouthful to eat first and take something with you. I'll see you before you start. Broyles, you and Dick take the trail of that bunch of saddle horses after dinner. Bring 'em back—or see where they went to. It's just barely possible that there's been two separate gangs on the warpath here; but I judge not. I judge them's just saddle horses. Sam, you and Spike cook dinner. You other chaps make some sort of a coffin. Keep Moss with you. After while we'll all turn to and see if Ellis hid the money here."

In the kitchen Teagardner spoke aside to the four who were to follow Ellis.

"Now, whatever happens, you fellows get that man alive—*sabe?* No shooting. I ain't quite satisfied. Moss, he tells a straight-enough story and everything seems to back him up so far; but this man Ellis—where does he get off? If he comes along peaceful and unsuspicious—why, he's guilty and playin' foxy, layin' it all onto Moss. If he's scared it hangs him; if he keeps his upper lip right he's brazening it out, and we hang him for that. If he fights you he's guilty; if he hides out that proves he's guilty. If he gets clean away that's absolute proof. Any game where a man hasn't got one chance to win don't look just right."

Young Broyles burst into the room.

"See what I found! It was out in the corral, in the sand. I kicked at that ore sack layin' there by the dead horses—and I kicked up this! Nineteen five-dollar bills, done up like a pack of envelopes."

"They're all torn—see! And they're usually put up in hundred-dollar bunches, aren't they?" said Hall. "There's one gone—maybe."

"Yes," said Cal eagerly, "and that ore sack—there was two of 'em likely, and after the murder Ellis put all the stuff into one and dropped this bundle doin' it! Say! We ought to call Moss."

"I'll tell him," said Teagardner.

"But how'd them bills get torn? And where's the other one?" demanded Cal.

Hall shrugged his shoulders. "How'd I know? Come on, fellows—let's hike!"

DINNER WAS EATEN; Broyles and Dick departed on their search; the coffin was made; and the dead man was laid in it.

"Shall you bury him now?" asked Moss.

"I hope so!" said Spike with a shudder.

"Me, too," echoed Sam. "I can't stand that awful laugh on his face. Let's get him out of sight, Uncle Ben."

"No. We want Ellis to see him, for one thing. Then again the sheriff may come and he may want to take charge. Besides, I think maybe we'll bury the murderer here and take this one to San Marcial."

Moss licked his lips.

"Put them both in one grave—why not? It's deep enough," suggested Cook. "They killed old Mims—let them talk it over together."

"Only one man shot Mims," said Teagardner. "This poor fellow may not have been the one. The man that killed him—his own pardner—the man that shot him in the back from behind a 'dobe wall, and then left an innocent man to stand for it—that's the man killed Mims. I don't think we've any right to force such company on this dead man. Come on! Let's get to work."

They dragged the dead horses far out on the plain; they piled sand where the blood pools had been; roof and wall and floor, they ransacked the house, the outbuildings and the stables for the stolen money.

"You're forgetting one thing," said Moss. "As I am still your prisoner I am naturally still under some suspicion. I may be the murderer after all and Ellis may be the victim—as, of course, he'll claim to be. Somebody ought to follow my track where I walked out to the rim this morning."

Teagardner eyed him, with mild reproach.

"Set your mind at rest, Mr. Moss. We're taking all bets. We did exactly that while you were resting just before dinner. You didn't take a step that isn't accounted for. You didn't ride one of the give-out horses down in the canyon and hide it there, either. And it will be the same with Ellis. That money will be found. We need it—as evidence."

"Well, if you've done looking I'd like to rest—go to sleep if I can. I'm done!"

"Yes—you look fagged out. No wonder—you've been under a strain. It's blistering hot—we'll all go out to the grave, under that tree. It's the only cool place round here. Bring some water, you boys."

"Nice pleasant place for a sleep," suggested Sam, with a nervous giggle, at the grave side. "What's the matter with the shady side of the house?"

"No air," said Moss. "This suits me."

Teagardner sat on a stone and gazed long into the grave, smoking placidly. He was a very old man—tough and sturdy and straight and tall for all that. Long and long ago, Teagardner had been an old-timer here. Half a lifetime since—at an age when most are content to become spectators—he had fared forth to new ventures; after a quarter century in Australia and the Far East—Hong Kong last—he had come back to the land of his youth—to die.

If Napoleon, at eighty, had come back from St. Helena, some such position might have been his as was Uncle Ben's. Legend and myth had grown about his name, wild tales of the wild old days—the days when he had not been the Old Man, or everybody's Uncle Ben, but strong among the strongest. The chase had passed his way that morning and he had taken horse, despite his seven-and-seventy years, with none to say him nay.

"It is a deep grave—and the soil is tough," he said, raising his eyes at last. "You have been a miner, Mr. Moss?"

"After a fashion—yes."

"You must have worked hard digging this."

"I did. It seemed to do me good. I was nervous and excited. Shucks! I was scared—that's the kind of nervous I was."

"You say you rode across from Arizona. Where did you stay night before last?"

"In a two-room log house under San Mateo Peak, to the south; H. G. Ranch—or it has been once, for them letters are branded on the door. No one was there."

Spike nodded. "Charley Graham's. Charley, he's at the round-up."

"Well, I'm right sorry he wasn't there, as things turned out; but if you'll send a man over to-morrow he'll find the corn cans I opened—and some flour and coffee, and nothing else—only my horse's tracks and the shoe he lost somewhere on the road. That'll prove my alibi, all right—at least, as far as your bank robbery's concerned. The greenbacks you found seem to hook these two other gentlemen up with that."

"We'll send a man there, all right, if needed. And it wasn't a bank that was robbed—it was a mine—a paymaster," said Uncle Ben.

"Well, you didn't tell me."

"No; I didn't tell you. And the night before that?"

"I stayed at the Anchor X Ranch. No one there, either. If your man goes that far he'll get canned corn straight—not even coffee to go with it. And he'll find a note to the effect that the outfit has gone to ship a bunch of steers at Magdalena."

Again Teagardner's quiet eye went round the circle and again the prisoner's story was confirmed.

"That's right. They load up to-day. Aw, let the man sleep, Uncle Ben. He's giving it to you straight."

But Uncle Ben persisted.

"And before that? You must have seen some man, somewhere, sometime."

Moss shook his head impatiently.

"For nearly a week before that I camped with an old Mexican hunter, on the divide south of Chloride, letting my horse rest up and hunting deer. Leastwise he hunted and I went along for company. I didn't have any rifle and he wouldn't lend me his. His name was Delfin Something-or-Other, and he lived in Springerville, he said. Say, old man, you make me tired! Am I to blame because no one lives in this accursed country? By George! If I could have taken a long look ahead I'd have hired me a witness and carried him with me."

"If we could take a long look ahead—or a short one—we'd be greatly surprised, some of us," Teagardner answered, without heat. "There—go to sleep, all of you. I slept last night. I'll call you when it's time."

He changed his seat to a softer one on the fresh mound of earth; he twisted his long gray beard and looked down into the grave. Moss watched him through narrowed lids. Then fatigue claimed him, stronger than horror or hate or fear, and he fell asleep.

"YOU CHUCKLE-HEADED IDIOTS!" gasped Charley Ellis.

"Oh, that's all right too," said Tom Hall. "Some folks is too smart for their own good. You keep still."

Three men held Charley, one by each arm and one by the collar. His eyes were flashing; he was red with anger and considerably the worse for wear, having just made a sincere and conscientious attempt to break the neck of Mr. Moss—an almost successful attempt. It had taken more than three men to pull him off. Moss, white and smiling, mopped his bruised face beyond the coffin and the open grave; the sun setting between the clouds threw a red, angry light over all.

"Quiet having been resumed," observed Teagardner patiently, "let us pass on to unfinished business. Tom, we've been so afired busy explainin' the situation to Mr. Ellis that we haven't got your report yet. Spit it out!"

"Uncle Ben, this Ellis is the man we want," said Tom Hall. "We found where he'd tacked a shoe on the horse—of course Moss couldn't know that. We tracked him a ways toward Rosedale and then we met these three Rosedale men coming back with him.

They told him they was holdin' everybody and gathered him in. He made no objection—handed over his gun without a word. It was an automatic thirty-two. Horse and saddle just as Moss described 'em, all right—and this ore sack tied on the saddle besides."

Uncle Ben shook his head.

"It won't do, Tom. Everything is as Moss told it—but everything is just as Ellis tells it, too. So far as I can see they've got only one horse, one saddle and one interestin' past between them."

"You blithering, blistering, gibbering, fat-headed fools!" said Charley pleasantly. "If you'd told me about what Moss said I would 'a told you to cave my horse and let Moss try his hand at describin' him. He's got one white hoof; he's been cut with barbed wire; and my saddle's been sewed up with buckskin where the linin's ripped. Moss couldn't have told you that. Did you give me a fair chance for my life? No, sir; you come blunderin' in and let Moss look 'em all over—pertendin' to be petting old Vine-

garoan. I wasn't mistrustin' anything like this. They said there'd been trouble and they was makin' all strangers account for themselves. That seemed reasonable enough and I wasn't worrying."

"We've got only your word for that," sneered Sam. "I reckon Moss could have told us all about it if we had asked him."

"And maybe again he couldn't—Ellis is right," said Hall soberly. "You didn't get an even break. I'm sorry."

"What about the ore sack?"

"Boys," said Uncle Ben, "you're going at this all wrong. Mr. Ellis says he took feed in that sack—that's reasonable. And that he kept the sack by him counts in his favor, I think."

"So do I," said Cal. "And I'll swear that if he had any money in it he must 'a eat the bills and flung the coins away, one piece at a time. He never hid it after he left this house—that's sure. I know every inch of ground he's been over and my eyes is pretty near out from reading sign. I even went on, to make sure, after we met the Rosedale men, clear to where he met them and loped all the way back to catch up with 'em."

"How about this then?" cried Spike triumphantly. He was one of those who held Ellis. "I just took it out of his pocket."

It was a new five-dollar bill, and it was torn. Teagardner produced the package of bills. The tears matched exactly.

A horrible snarl burst from a dozen throats. They crowded and jostled, Moss with the rest; hands reached out to clutch at the prisoner.

"Hang him! Hang him!"

"Stand back! Stand back, you blind fools! I'll shoot the next man that touches him!" shouted Teagardner. "Stand back."

"You'll hang nobody, you howling dogs!" said Ellis coolly. "We stand just where we did before, my word against Moss'."

"Exactly!" said Uncle Ben. "Have a little sense, can't ye? Cook, if you was this man, and guilty, how would you say you got this bill?"

"I'd say Moss gave it to me, of course."

"And you, Spike, if you knew positively that Ellis was innocent—then how did he get this bill?"

"He must have got it from Moss," said Spike reluctantly.

Charley laughed. "Well, that's where I got it—when we traded boots and guns, like I was tellin' you."

"You're a damned liar!"

No one was holding Charley's foot. It now caught Moss squarely in the breast and hurled him over the mound of earth and almost into the grave.

"Old gentleman—Uncle Ben, as they call you—" said Charley then, "you seem to have charge here, and you're old enough to have a real idea once in a while. There's just as much against Moss as against me, and no more—isn't there?"

"Precisely—up to date."

"Well, then, why aren't we treated the same? Why am I held this way while he goes free?"

"That's right!" said Cal.

"Hold Moss, a couple of you," said Uncle Ben. "Now, Mr. Ellis, look here!" He pushed aside the unnailed coffin lid to show the dead man's face. "Do you know this man?"

"Hell, he's laughing! No; I never saw him before. What's he laughing at? What's the joke?"

"He is laughing at his murderer."

"Well, I know who that is," said Charley. "And that's more than the rest of you do."

Teagardner replaced the lid.

"All we know—yet—is that he is either laughing at you or laughing at Moss. Your stories exactly offset each other. What are we going to do next? Understand me—there'll be nobody hanged till he's proved guilty."

"Keep us!" said Charley. "Watch us night and day! Chain us together with every chain on the ranch. One of us is a liar. Send some of your men along the back track till you find where the liar's story don't fit with the certain truth. I can describe every little trifling thing at the ranches where I stayed; I can tell what my old Mexican hunter looks like, if you can find him. Can Moss?"

"Son," said Teagardner, "you've got the right idea, and your plan would work—if we had to do it; but we don't have to do it. You've overlooked one thing. There's two ends to every lie—and one end of this lie is on this side of the murder. If we find the money where you hid it after you left here—you swing, Ellis. If we find it here at the ranch—why, either of you may have hid it. Everything that's happened at the ranch may have been done by either of you two men—everything but one."

He turned a slow eye on Moss, who stood by the coffin, white and trembling, with a man at each arm. His voice rang—measured, stern and hard.

"Everything but one," he repeated. "Ellis had nothing to do with one thing…Moss dug the grave. And the grave is too deep. I always thought the grave was too deep. Jump into the grave, Sam, and see why Moss made it so deep!"

Moss dropped to his knees; his guards held him up; they forced him forward to the edge of the grave. A shudder ran through the crowd; they swayed forward; the last ray of the sun fell on them in a golden shaft. Sam leaped into the grave.

"Moss dug his grave too deep—because he was afraid somebody might want to make it a little deeper," said Teagardner. "Ground solid there? Try the other end."

Sam found loose earth at the other end. He shoveled furiously; he came to a package wrapped in slickers. He threw it up. They slashed the cords; they unrolled the slickers; at the grave's edge they poured the blood-bought money at the murderer's feet.

EUGENE MANLOVE RHODES *(1869–1934) is among the most favored writers by Western-story readers as he always tells a good, well-crafted tale. He is famous for his novella Pas'o Por Aqui (1927).*

AN INGENUE OF THE SIERRAS

BRET HARTE

We all held our breath as the coach rushed through the semidarkness of Galloper's Ridge. The vehicle itself was only a huge lumbering shadow; its sidelights were carefully extinguished, and Yuba Bill he'd just politely removed from the lips of an outside passenger even the cigar with which he had been ostentatiously exhibiting his coolness. For it had been rumored that the Ramon Martinez gang of road agents were laying for us on the second grade, and would time the passage of our lights across Galloper's in order to intercept us in the brush beyond. If we could cross the ridge without being seen and so get through the brush before they reached it, we were safe. If they followed, it would only be a stern chase with the odds in our favor.

The huge vehicle swayed from side to side, rolled, dipped, and plunged, but Bill kept the track as if, in the whispered words of the expressman, he could feel and smell the road he could no longer see. We knew that at times we hung perilously over the edge of slopes that eventually dropped a thousand feet sheer to the tops of the sugar pines below, but we knew that Bill knew it also. The half-visible heads of the horses, drawn wedgewise together by the tightened reins, appeared to cleave the darkness like a ploughshare, held between his rigid hands. Even the hoofbeats of the six horses had fallen into a vague monotonous distant roll. Then the ridge was crossed

and we plunged into the still blacker obscurity of the brush. Rather we no longer seemed to move—it was only the phantom night that rushed by us. The horses might have been submerged in some swift Lethean stream; nothing but the top of the coach and the rigid bulk of Yuba Bill rose above them. Yet even in that awful moment our speed was unslackened; it was as if Bill cared no longer to guide but only to drive, or as if the direction of his huge machine was determined by other hands than his. An incautious whisperer hazarded the paralyzing suggestion of our meeting another team. To our great astonishment Bill overheard it; to our greater astonishment he replied. "It 'ud be only a neck and neck race which would get to blazes first," he said quietly. But we were relieved—for he had *spoken*! Almost simultaneously the wider turnpike began to glimmer faintly as a visible track before us; the wayside trees fell out of line, opened up and dropped off one after another; we were on the broader tableland, out of danger and apparently unperceived and unpursued.

Nevertheless in the conversation that broke out again with the relighting of the lamps, and the comments, congratulations and reminiscences that were freely exchanged, Yuba Bill preserved a dissatisfied and even resentful silence. The most generous praise

N. C. Wyeth, *The Admirable Outlaw*, 1906.
Oil, 38 x 24"

of his skill and courage awoke no response. "I reckon the old man was just spilin' for a fight and is feelin' disappointed," said a passenger. But those who knew that Bill had the true fighter's scorn for any purely purposeless conflict were more or less concerned and watchful of him. He would drive steadily for four or five minutes with thoughtfully knitted brows, but eyes still keenly observant under his slouched hat and then, relaxing his strained attitude, would give way to a movement of impatience. "You ain't uneasy about anything, Bill, are you?" asked the expressman confidentially. Bill lifted his eyes with a slightly contemptuous surprise. "Not about anything ter *come*. It's what *hez* happened that I don't exactly *sabe*. I don't see no signs of Ramon's gang ever havin' been out at all, and ef they was out I don't see why they didn't go for us."

"The simple fact is that our ruse was successful," said an outside passenger. "They waited to see our lights on the ridge, and not seeing them missed us until we had passed. That's my opinion."

"You ain't puttin' any price on that opinion, air ye?" inquired Bill politely.

"No."

"Cos thar's a comic paper in Frisco pays for them things, and I've seen worse things in it."

"Come off, Bill," retorted the passenger, slightly nettled by the tittering of his companions. "Then what did you put out the lights for?"

"Well," returned Bill grimly, "it mout have been because I didn't keer to hev you chaps blazin' away at the first bush you *thought* you saw move in your skeer and bringin' down their fire on us."

The explanation, though unsatisfactory, was by no means an improbable one and we thought it better to accept it with a laugh. Bill, however, resumed his abstracted manner.

"Who got in at the Summit?" he at last asked abruptly of the expressman.

"Derrick and Simpson of Cold Spring and one of the Excelsior boys," responded the expressman.

"And that Pike County girl from Dow's Flat with her bundles. Don't forget her," added the outside passenger ironically.

"Does anybody here know her?" continued Bill, ignoring the irony.

"You'd better ask Judge Thompson; he was mighty attentive to her, gettin' her a seat by the off window and lookin' after her bundles and things."

"Gettin' her a seat by the *window*?" repeated Bill.

"Yes, she wanted to see everything and wasn't afraid of the shooting."

"Yes," broke in a third passenger, "and he was so durned civil that when she dropped her ring in the straw he struck a match agin all your rules, you know, and held it for her to find it. And it was just as we were crossin' through the brush, too. I saw the hull thing through the window, for I was hanging over the wheels with my gun ready for action. And it wasn't no fault of Judge Thompson's if his durned foolishness hadn't shown us up and got us a shot from the gang."

Bill gave a short grunt but drove steadily on without further comment or even turning his eyes to the speaker.

We were now not more than a mile from the station at the crossroads where we were to change horses. The lights already glimmered in the distance, and there was a faint suggestion of the coming dawn on the summits of the ridge to the west. We had plunged into a belt of timber, when suddenly a horseman emerged at a sharp canter from a trail that seemed to be parallel with our own. We were all slightly startled, Yuba Bill alone preserving his moody calm.

"Hullo!" he said.

The stranger wheeled to our side as Bill slackened his speed. He seemed to be a packer, or freight muleteer.

"Ye didn't get held up on the Divide?" continued Bill cheerfully.

"No," returned the packer with a laugh. "I don't carry treasure. But I see you're all right too. I saw you crossin' over Galloper's."

"*Saw us*?" said Bill sharply. "We had our lights out."

"Yes, but there was suthin' white, a handkerchief or woman's veil, I reckon, hangin' from the window. It was only a movin' spot agin the hillside, but ez I was lookin' out for ye I knew it was you by that. Good night!"

He cantered away. We tried to look at each other's faces and at Bill's expression in the darkness, but he neither spoke nor stirred until he threw down the reins when we stopped before the station. The passengers quickly descended from the roof; the expressman was about to follow, but Bill plucked his sleeve.

"I'm goin' to take a look over this yer stage and these yer passengers with ye afore we start."

"Why, what's up?"

"Well," said Bill, slowly disengaging himself from one of his enormous gloves, "when we waltzed down into the brush up there I saw a man ez plain ez I see you rise up from it. I thought our time had come and the band was goin' to play, when he sorter drew back, made a sign, and we just scooted past him."

"Well. "

"Well," said Bill, "it means that this yer coach was *passed through free tonight.*"

"You don't object to *that*—surely? I think we were deucedly lucky."

Bill slowly drew off his other glove. "I've been riskin' my everlastin' life on this durned line three times a week," he said with mock humility, "and I'm allus thankful for small mercies. *But,*" he added grimly, "when it comes down to bein' passed free by some pal of a hoss thief, and thet called a speshal Providence, *I ain't in it!* No sir, I ain't in it!"

IT WAS WITH MIXED emotions the passengers heard that a delay of fifteen minutes to tighten certain screw bolts had been ordered by the autocratic Bill. Some were anxious to get their breakfast at Sugar Pine, but others were not averse to linger for the daylight that promised greater safety on the road. The expressman, knowing the real cause of Bill's delay, was nevertheless at a loss to understand the object of it. The passengers were all well known; any idea of complicity with the road agents was wild and impossible, and even if there was a confederate of the gang among them he would have been more likely to precipitate a robbery than to check it. Again, the discovery of such a confederate—to whom they clearly owed their safety—and his arrest would have been quite against the Californian sense of justice, if not actually illegal. It seemed evident that Bill's quixotic sense of honor was leading him astray.

The station consisted of a stable, a wagon shed, and a building containing three rooms. The first was fitted up with bunks or sleeping berths for the employees; the second was the kitchen; and the third and larger apartment was dining room or sitting room, and was used as general waiting room for the passengers. It was not a refreshment station and there was no bar. But a mysterious command from the omnipotent Bill produced a demijohn of whiskey, with which he hospitably treated the company. The seductive influence of the liquor loosened the tongue of the gallant Judge Thompson. He admitted to having struck a match to enable the fair Pike Countian to find her ring which, however, proved to have fallen in her lap. She was "a fine healthy young woman—a type of the Far West, sir; in fact, quite a prairie blossom yet simple and guileless as a child." She was on her way to Marysville, he believed, "although she expected to meet friends, a friend, in fact, later on." It was her first visit to a large town—in fact to any civilized center—since she had crossed the plains three years ago. Her girlish curiosity was quite touching, and her innocence irresistible. In fact, in a country whose tendency was to produce "frivolity and forwardness in young girls" he found her "a most interesting young person." She was even then out in the stableyard watching the horses being harnessed, "preferring to indulge a pardonable healthy young curiosity than to listen to the empty compliments of the younger passengers."

The figure, which Bill saw thus engaged, without being otherwise distinguished certainly seemed to justify the judge's opinion. She appeared to be a well-matured country girl, whose frank gray eyes and large laughing mouth expressed a wholesome and abiding gratification in her life and surroundings. She was watching the replacing of luggage in the boot. A little feminine start as one of her own parcels was thrown somewhat roughly on the roof gave Bill his opportunity. "Now there, he growled to the helper, "ye ain't carting stone! Look out, will yer! Some of your things, miss?" he added with gruff courtesy, turning to her. "These yer trunks, for instance?"

She smiled a pleasant assent and Bill, pushing aside the helper, seized a large square trunk in his arms. But from excess of zeal or some other mischance, his foot slipped and he came down heavily, striking the corner of the trunk on the ground and loosening its hinges and fastenings. It was a cheap common-looking affair, but the accident discovered in its yawning lid a quantity of white lace-edged feminine apparel of an apparently superior quality. The young lady uttered another cry and came quickly forward, but Bill was profuse in his apologies, himself girded the broken box with a strap, and declared his intention of having the company "make it good" to her with a new one. Then he casually accompanied her to the door of the waiting room, entered, made a place for her before the fire by simply lifting the nearest and most youthful passenger by the coat collar from the stool that he was occupying, and installing the lady in it. He then displaced another man who was standing before the chimney and, drawing himself up to his full six feet of height in front of her, glanced down on his fair passenger as he took his waybill from his pocket.

"Your name is down here as Miss Mullins?" he said.

She looked up, became suddenly aware that she and her questioner were the center of interest to the whole circle of passengers, and with a slight rise of color, returned, "Yes."

"Well, Miss Mullins, I've got a question or two to ask ye. I ask it straight out afore this crowd. It's in my rights to take ye aside and ask it—but that ain't my style; I'm no detective. I needn't ask it at all, but act as ef I knowed the answer, or I might leave it to be asked by others. Ye needn't answer it ef ye don't like; ye've got a friend over there—Judge Thompson—who is a friend to ye, right or wrong, jest as any other man here is—as though ye'd packed your own jury.

Well, the simple question I've got to ask ye is *this*: Did you signal to anybody from the coach when we passed Galloper's an hour ago?"

We all thought that Bill's courage and audacity had reached its climax here. To openly and publicly accuse a lady before a group of chivalrous Californians, and that lady possessing the further attractions of youth, good looks and innocence, was little short of desperation. There was an evident movement of adhesion toward the fair stranger, and a slight muttering broke out on the right, but the very boldness of the act held them in stupefied surprise. Judge Thompson, with a bland propitiatory smile began, "Really, Bill, I must protest on behalf of this young lady"—when the fair accused, raising her eyes to her accuser, to the consternation of everybody answered with the slight but convincing hesitation of conscientious truthfulness, "I did."

"Ahem!" interposed the judge hastily, "er—that is—er—you allowed your handkerchief to flutter from the window—I noticed it myself—casually, one might say even playfully, but without any particular significance."

The girl, regarding her apologist with a singular mingling of pride and impatience, returned briefly, "I signaled."

"Who did you signal to?" asked Bill gravely.

"The young gentleman I'm going to marry."

A start, followed by a slight titter from the younger passengers, was instantly suppressed by a savage glance from Bill.

"What did you signal to him for?" he continued.

"To tell him I was here and that it was all right," returned the girl with a steadily rising pride and color.

"*Wot* was all right?" demanded Bill.

"That I wasn't followed and that he could meet me on the road beyond Cass's Ridge Station." She hesitated a moment and then with a still greater pride, in which a youthful defiance was still mingled, said, "I've run away from home to marry him. And I mean to! No one can stop me. Dad didn't like him just because he was poor, and Dad's got money. Dad

Frederic Remington, *Sunday Morning Spruce-up*

wanted me to marry a man I hate, and got a lot of dresses and things to bribe me."

"And you're taking them in your trunk to the other feller?" said Bill grimly.

"Yes, he's poor," returned the girl defiantly.

"Then your father's name is Mullins?" asked Bill.

"It's not Mullins. I—I—took that name," she hesitated, with her first exhibition of self-consciousness.

"Wot is his name?"

"Eli Hemmings."

A smile of relief and significance went around the circle. The fame of Eli or "Skinner" Hemmings as a notorious miser and usurer had passed even beyond Galloper's Ridge.

"The step that you're taking, Miss Mullins, I need not tell you, is one of great gravity," said Judge Thompson, with a certain paternal seriousness of manner in which, however, we were glad to detect a glaring affectation. "And I trust that you and your afianced have fully weighed it. Far be it from me to interfere with or question the natural affections of two young people, but may I ask you what you know of the—er—young gentlemen for whom you are sacrificing so much, and perhaps imperiling your whole future? For instance, have you known him long?"

The slightly troubled air of trying to understand, not unlike the vague wonderment of childhood, with which Miss Mullins had received the beginning of this exordium changed to a relieved smile of comprehension as she said quickly, "Oh yes, nearly a whole year."

"And," said the judge, smiling, "has he a vocation—is he in business?"

"Oh yes," she returned, "he's a collector."

"A collector?"

"Yes; he collects bills, you know—money," she went on with childish eagerness, "not for himself—he never has any money, poor Charley—but for his firm. It's dreadful hard work, too; keeps him out for days and nights, over bad roads and baddest weather. Sometimes when he's stole over to the ranch just to see me he's been so bad he could scarcely keep his seat in the saddle, much less stand. And he's got to take mighty big risks, too. Times the folks are cross with him and won't pay; once they shot him in the arm and he came to me and I helped do it up for him. But he don't mind. He's real brave, jest as brave as he's good." There was such a wholesome ring of truth in this pretty praise that we were touched in sympathy with the speaker.

"What firm does he collect for?" asked the judge gently.

"I don't know exactly—he won't tell me; but I think it's a Spanish firm. You see"—she took us all into her confidence with a sweeping smile of innocent yet half-mischievous artfulness—"I only know because I peeped over a letter he once got from his firm tellin' him he must rustle up and be ready for the road the next day; but I think the name was Martinez—yes, Ramon Martinez."

In the dead silence that ensued—a silence so profound that we could hear the horses in the distant stable yard rattling their harness—one of the younger Exelsior boys burst into a hysteric laugh, but the fierce eye of Yuba Bill was down upon him and seemed to instantly stiffen him into a silent grinning mask. The young girl, however, took no note of it. Following out with loverlike diffusiveness the reminiscences thus awakened, she went on:

"Yes, it's mighty hard work, but he says it's all for me, and as soon as we're married he'll quit it. He might have quit it before but he won't take no money of me, nor what I told him I could get out of Dad! That ain't his style. He's mighty proud—if he is poor—is Charley. Why thar's all ma's money which she left me in the savin's bank that I wanted to draw out, for I had the right, and give it to him, but he wouldn't hear of it! Why he wouldn't take one of the

things I've got with me, if he knew it. And so he goes on ridin' and ridin', here and there and everywhere, and gettin' more and more played out and sad and thin and pale as a spirit, and always so uneasy about his business and startin' up at times when we're meetin' out in the South Woods or in the far clearin' and sayin', 'I must be goin' now, Polly,' and yet always tryin' to be chime and chipper afore me. Why, he must have rid miles and miles to have watched for me thar in the brush at the foot of Galloper's tonight, jest to see if all was safe; and Lordy! I'd have given him the signal and showed a light if I'd died for it the next minit. There! That's what I know of Charley—that's what I'm runnin' away from home for—that's what I'm runnin' to him for, and I don't care who knows it! And I only wish I'd done it afore—and I would of—if—if—he'd only *asked* me! There now!" She stopped, panted, and choked. One of the sudden transitions of youthful emotion had overtaken the eager laughing face; it clouded up with the swift change of childhood, a lightning quiver of expression broke over it, and—then came the rain!

I think this simple act completed our utter demoralization. We smiled feebly at each other with that assumption of masculine superiority which is miserably conscious of its own helplessness at such moments. We looked out of the window, blew our noses, said, "Eh—what?" and "I say," vaguely to each other, and were greatly relieved and yet apparently astonished when Yuba Bill, who had turned his back upon the fair speaker and was kicking the logs in the fireplace, suddenly swept down upon us and bundled us all into the road, leaving Miss Mullins alone. Then he walked aside with Judge Thompson for a few moments, returned to us, autocratically demanded of the party a complete reticence toward Miss Mullins on the subject matter under discussion, reentered the station, reappeared with the young lady, suppressed a faint idiotic cheer which broke from us at the spectacle of her innocent face once more cleared and rosy, climbed the box, and in another moment we were under way.

"Then she don't know what her lover is yet?" asked the expressman gingerly.

"No."

"Are *you* certain it's one of the gang?"

"Can't say for *sure*. It mout be a young chap from Yolo who bucked agin the tiger at Sacramento, got regularly cleaned out and busted, and joined the gang for a nier. They say thar was a new hand in that job over at Keeley's, and a mighty game one, too; and ez there was some buckshot on-loaded that trip he might hev got his share, and that would tally with what the gurl said about his arm. See! Ef that's the man, I've heered he was the son of some big preacher and a college sharp to boot, who ran wild in Frisco and played himself for all he was worth. They're the wust kind to kick when they once get a foot over the traces. For stiddy comf'ble kempany," added Bill reflectively, "give *me* the son of a man that was *hanged*!"

"But what are you goin' to do about this?"

"That depends on the feller who comes to meet her."

"But you ain't going to try to take him? That would be playing it pretty low down on them both."

"Keep your hair on, Jimmy! The Judge and me are only going to rastle with the spent of that gay young galoot when he drops down for his girl—and exhort him pow'full if he allows he's convicted of sin and will find the Lord, we'll marry him and the gal off-hand at the next station, and the Judge will officiate himself for nothin'. We're goin' to have this yer elopement done on the square, and our waybill clean—you bet!"

"But you don't suppose he'll trust himself in your hands?"

"Polly will signal to him that it's all square."

"Ah!" said the expressman. Nevertheless in those few moments the men seemed to have exchanged dispositions. The expressman looked doubtfully, critically and even cynically before him. Bill's face had relaxed, and something like a bland smile beamed across it as he drove confidently and unhesitatingly forward.

Day, meantime, although full blown and radiant on the mountain summits around us, was yet nebulous and uncertain in the valleys into which we were going. Lights still glimmered in the cabins and the few ranch buildings which began to indicate the thicker settlements. The shadows were heaviest in a little copse where a note from Judge Thompson in the coach was handed up to Yuba Bill, who at once slowly began to draw up his horses. The coach stopped finally near the junction of a small crossroad. At the same moment Miss Mullins slipped down from the vehicle, and with a parting wave of her hand to the jube, who had assisted her from the steps, tripped down the crossroad and disappeared in its semiobscurity. To our surprise the stage waited, Bill holding the reins listlessly in his hands. Five minutes passed—an eternity of expectation, and as there was that in Yuba Bill's face which forbade idle questioning, an aching void of silence also. This was at last broken by a strange voice from the road:

"Go on—we'll follow."

The coach started forward. Presently we heard the sound of other wheels behind us. We all craned our necks backward to get a view of the unknown, but by the growing light we could only see that we were followed at a distance by a buggy with two figures in it. Evidently Polly Mullins and her lover! We hoped that they would pass us. But the vehicle, although drawn by a fast horse, preserved its distance always, and it was plain that its driver had no desire to satisfy our curiosity. The expressman had recourse to Bill.

"Is it the man you thought of?" he asked eagerly.

"I reckon," said Bill briefly.

"But," continued the expressman, returning to his former skepticism, "what's to keep them both from levanting together now?"

Bill jerked his hand toward the boot with a grim smile.

"Their baggage."

"Oh!" said the expressman.

"Yes," continued Bill. "We'll hang on to that gal's little frills and fixin's until this here job's settled and the ceremony's over, jest as ef we was her own father. And what's more, young man," he added, suddenly turning to the expressman, "*you'll* express them

trunks of hers through to Sacramento with your kembany's labels and hand her the receipts and checks for them, so she can get 'em there. That'll keep n'um outer temptation and the reach o' the gang until they get away among white men and civilization again. When your hoary-headed ole grandfather, or to speak plainer, that partikler old whiskey-soaker known as Yuba Bill wot sits on this box," he continued with a diabolical wink at the expressman, "waltzes in to pervide for a young couple jest startin' in life, thar's nothin' mean about his style, you bet. He fills the bill every time! Speshul Providences take a back seat when he's around."

When the station hotel and straggling settlement of Sugar Pine, now distinct and clear in the growing light, at last rose within rifleshot on the plateau the buggy suddenly darted swiftly by us, so swiftly that the faces of the two occupants were barely distinguishable as they passed, and keeping the lead by a dozen lengths, reached the door of the hotel. The young girl and her companion leaped down and vanished within as we drew up. They had evidently determined to elude our curiosity, and were successful.

But the material appetites of the passengers, sharpened by the keen mountain air, were more potent than their curiosity and as the breakfast bell rang out at the moment the stage stopped, a majority of them rushed into the dining room and scrambled for places without giving much heed to the vanished couple or to the judge and Yuba Bill, who had disappeared also. The through coach to Marysville and Sacramento was likewise waiting, for Sugar Pine was the limit of Bill's ministration and the coach which we had just left went no farther. In the course of twenty minutes, however, there was a slight and somewhat ceremonious bustling in the hall and on the veranda, and Yuba Bill and the Judge reappeared. The latter was leading with some elaboration of manner and detail the shapely figure of Miss Mullins, and Yuba Bill was accompanying her companion to the buggy.

Charles Schreyvogel, *Saving the Mail*, 1900.
Oil, 48 x 35½"

We all rushed to the windows to get a good view of the mysterious stranger and probable ax-brigand whose life was now linked with our fair fellow passenger. I am afraid, however, that we all participated in a certain impression of disappointment and doubt. Handsome and even cultivated-looking he assuredly was—young and vigorous in appearance. But there was a certain half-shamed, half-defiant suggestion in his expression, yet coupled with a watchful lurking uneasiness which was not pleasant and hardly becoming in a bridegroom, and the possessor of such a bride. But the frank joyous innocent face of Polly Mullins, resplendent with a simple happy confidence, melted our hearts again and condoned the fellow's shortcomings. We waved our hands; I think we would have given three rousing cheers as they drove away if the omnipotent eye of Yuba Bill had not been upon us. It was well, for the next moment we were summoned to the presence of that softhearted autocrat.

We found him alone with the Judge in a private sitting room standing before a table on which there were a decanter and glasses. As we filed expectantly into the room and the door closed behind us, he cast a glance of hesitating tolerance over the ground.

"Gentlemen," he said slowly, "you was all present at the beginnin' of a little game this mornin', and the Judge thar thinks that you oughter be let in at the finish. *I* don't see that it's any of *your* durned business—so to speak; but ez the Judge here allows you're all in the secret, I've called you in to take a partin' drink to the health of Mr. and Mrs. Charley Byng—ez is now comf'ably off on their bridal tower. What *you* know or what *you* suspects of the young galoot that's married the gal ain't worth shucks to anybody and I wouldn't give it to a yaller pup to play with, but the Judge thinks you ought all to promise right here that you'll keep it dark. That's his opinion. Ez far as my opinion goes, gen'l'men," continued Bill with greater blandness and apparent cordiality, "I wanter simply remark in a keerless offhand gin'ral way, that ef I ketch any God-forsaken lop-eared chuckle-headed blatherin' idjet airin' *his* opinion—"

"One moment, Bill," interposed Judge Thompson with a grave smile. "Let me explain. You understand, gentlemen," he said turning to us, "the singular and I may say affecting situation which our goodhearted friend here has done so much to bring to what we hope will be a happy termination. I want to give here as my professional opinion, that there is nothing in his request which in your capacity as good citizens and law-abiding men you may not grant! I want to tell you also that you are condoning no offense against the statutes. There is not one particle of legal evidence before us of the criminal antecedents of Mr. Charles Byng except that which has been told you by the innocent lips of his betrothed, which the law of the land has now sealed forever in the mouth of his wife; and our own actual experience of his acts has been in the main exulpatory of any previous irregularity—if not incompatible with it. Briefly, no judge would charge, no jury convict on such evidence. When I add that the young girl is of legal age, that there is no evidence of any previous undue influence, but rather of the reverse on the part of the bridegroom, and that I was content as a magistrate to perform the ceremony, I think you will be satisfied to give your promise for the sake of the bride, and drink a happy life to them both."

I need not say that we did this cheerfully, and even extorted from Bill a grunt of satisfaction. The majority of the company, however, who were going with the through coach to Sacramento, then took their leave and as we accompanied them to the veranda we could see that Miss Polly Mullins' trunks were already transferred to the other vehicle under the protecting seals and labels of the all-potent express company. Then the whip cracked, the coach rolled away, and the last traces of the adventurous young couple disappeared in the hanging red dust of its wheels.

But Yuba Bill's grim satisfaction at the happy issue of the episode seemed to suffer no abatement. He even exceeded his usual deliberately regulated potations, and standing comfortably with his back to the center of the now deserted barroom, was more than usually loquacious with the expressman. "You see," he said, in bland reminiscence, "when your old Uncle Bill takes hold of a job like this he puts it straight through without changin' hosses. Yet thar was a moment, young feller, when I thought I was stompt! It was when we'd made up our mind to make that chap tell the gal fust all what he was! Ef she'd rared or kicked in the traces, or hung back only ez much ez that, we'd hev given him jest five minits' law to get up and get and leave her, and we'd hev toted that gal and her fixin's back to her dad again! But she jest gave a little scream and start and then went off inter hysterics, right on his buzzum, laughin' and cryin' and sayin' that nothin' should part 'em. Gosh! if I didn't think *he* was more cut up than she about it; a minit it looked as ef *he* didn't allow to marry her arter all, but that passed and they was married hard and fast—you bet! I reckon he's had enough of stayin' out o' nights to last him, and ef the valley settlements hevn't got hold of a very shinin' member at least the foothills hev got shut of one more of the Ramon Martinez gang."

"What's that about the Ramon Martinez gang?" said a quiet yet powerful voice.

Bill turned quickly. It was the voice of the divisional superintendent of the express company, a man of eccentric determination of character and one of the few whom the autocratic Bill recognized as an equal, who had just entered the barroom. His dusty pongee cloak and soft hat indicated that he had that morning arrived on a route of inspection.

"Don't care if I do, Bill," he continued in response to Bill's invitatory gesture, walking to the bar. "It's a little raw out on the road. Well, what were you sayin' about Ramon Martinez gang? You haven't come across one of 'em, have you?"

"No," said Bill with a slight blinking of his eye as he ostentatiously lifted his glass to the light.

"And you *won't*," added the superintendent, leisurely sipping his liquor. "For the fact is, the gang is about played out. Not from want of a job now and then, but from the difficulty of disposing of the results of their work. Since the new instructions to the agents to identify and trace all dust and bullion offered to them went into force, you see, they can't get rid of their swag. All the gang are spotted at the offices and it costs too much for them to pay a fence or a middle-man of any standing. Why, all that flaky river gold they took from the Excelsior Company can be identi-fied as easy as if it was stamped with the company's mark. They can't melt it down themselves; they can't get others to do it for them; they can't ship it to the mint or assay offices in Marysville and Frisco, for they won't take it without our certificate and seals; and *we* don't take any undeclared freight within the lines that we've drawn around their boat, except from people and agents known. Why, *you* know that well enough, Jim," he said, suddenly appealing to the expressman, "don't you?"

Possibly the suddenness of the appeal caused the expressman to swallow his liquor the wrong way, for he was overtaken with a fit of coughing and stam-mered hastily as he laid down his glass, "Yes, er—certainly."

"No sir," resumed the superintendent cheerfully, "they're pretty well played out. And the best proof of it is that they've lately been robbing ordinary passen-gers' trunks. There was a freight wagon held up near Dow's Flat the other day and a lot of baggage gone through. I had to go down there to look into it. Darned if they hadn't lifted a lot o' woman's wed-ding things from that rich couple who got married the other day out at Marysville. Looks as if they were playing it rather low down, don't it? Coming down to hardpan and the bedrock—eh?

The expressman's face was turned anxiously toward Bill, who after a hurried gulp of his remaining liquor still stood staring at the window. Then he slowly drew on one of his large gloves. "Ye didn't," he said, with a slow drawling but perfectly distinct articulation, "happen to know old Skinner Hem-mings when you were over there?"

"Yes."

"And his daughter?"

"He hasn't got any."

"A sort o' mild innocent guileless child of nature?" persisted Bill with a yellow face, a deadly calm and Satanic deliberation.

"No. I tell you he hasn't any daughter. Old man Hemmings is a confirmed old bachelor. He's too mean to support more than one."

"And you didn't happen to know any o' that gang, did ye?" continued Bill with infinite protraction.

"Yes. Knew 'em all. There was French Pete, Cherokee Bob, Kanaka Joe, One-eyed Stinson, Softy Brown, Spanish Jack and two or three Mexicans."

"And ye didn't know a man by the name of Charley Byng?"

'No," returned the superintendent, with a slight suggestion of weariness and a distraught glance toward the door.

"A dark stylish chap with shifty black eyes and a curled-up merstache?" continued Bill, with dry col-orless persistence.

"No. Look here, Bill, I'm in a little bit of a hurry—but I suppose you must have your little joke before we part. Now, what is your little game?"

"Wot you mean?" demanded Bill with sudden brusqueness.

"Mean? Well, old man, you know as well as I do. You're giving me the very description of Ramon Martinez himself, ha! ha! No, Bill! You didn't play me this time. You're mighty spry and clever but you didn't catch on just then."

He nodded and moved away with a light laugh. Bill turned a stony face to the expressman. Suddenly a gleam of mirth came into his gloomy eyes. He bent over the young man and said in a hoarse chuckling whisper:

"But I got even after all!"

"How?"

"He's tied up to that lying little she-devil, hard and fast!"

BRET HARTE *(1836–1902) was once the highest-paid short story writer in America. Born in Albany, New York, at age nineteen he left for California, where he began his writing career. Later he became United States consul in Germany and Scotland.*

SHOOT-OUTS

THE BLUE HOTEL

STEPHEN CRANE

The Palace Hotel at Fort Romper was painted a light blue, a shade that is on the legs of a kind of heron, causing the bird to declare its position against any background. The Palace Hotel, then, was always screaming and howling in a way that made the dazzling winter landscape of Nebraska seem only a gray swampish hush. It stood alone on the prairie, and when the snow was falling, the town two hundred yards away was not visible. But when the traveler alighted at the railway station, he was obliged to pass the Palace Hotel before he could come upon the company of low clapboard houses which composed Fort Romper, and it was not to be thought that any traveler could pass the Palace Hotel without looking at it. Pat Scully, the proprietor, had proved himself a master of strategy when he chose his paints. It is true that on clear days, when the great transcontinental expresses, long lines of swaying Pullmans, swept through Fort Romper, passengers were overcome at the sight, and the cult that knows the brown reds and the subdivisions of the dark greens of the East expressed shame, pity, horror, in a laugh. But to the citizens of this prairie town and to the people who would naturally stop there, Pat Scully had performed a feat. With this opulence and splendor, these creeds, classes, egotisms, that streamed through Romper on the rails day after day, they had no color in common.

As if the displayed delights of such a blue hotel were not sufficiently enticing, it was Scully's habit to go every morning and evening to meet the leisurely trains that stopped at Romper and work his seductions upon any man that he might see wavering, gripsack in hand.

One morning, when a snow-crusted engine dragged its long string of freight cars and its one passenger coach to the station, Scully performed the marvel of catching three men. One was a shaky and quick-eyed Swede, with a great shining cheap valise; one was a tall bronzed cowboy, who was on his way to a ranch near the Dakota line; one was a little silent man from the East, who didn't look it and didn't announce it. Scully practically made them prisoners. He was so nimble and merry and kindly that each probably felt it would be the height of brutality to try to escape. They trudged off over the creaking board sidewalks in the wake of the eager little Irishman. He wore a heavy fur cap squeezed tightly down on his head. It caused his two red ears to stick out stiffly, as if they were made of tin.

At last, Scully, elaborately, with boisterous hospitality, conducted them through the portals of the blue hotel. The room which they entered was small. It seemed to be merely a proper temple for an enormous stove, which, in the center, was humming with godlike violence. At various points on its surface, the iron had become luminous and glowed yellow from the heat. Beside the stove Scully's son Johnnie was playing high-five with an old farmer who had whiskers both gray and sandy. They were quarreling. Frequently the old

Previous pages: Donald Teague, *Waiting for Trouble*, 1972. Watercolor, 20 x 30"

farmer turned his face toward a box of sawdust—colored brown from tobacco juice—that was behind the stove and spat with an air of great impatience and irritation. With a loud flourish of words, Scully destroyed the game of cards and bustled his son upstairs with part of the baggage of the new guests. He himself conducted them to three basins of the coldest water in the world. The cowboy and the Easterner burnished themselves fiery red with this water, until it seemed to be some kind of metal polish. The Swede, however, merely dipped his fingers gingerly and with trepidation. It was notable that throughout this series of small ceremonies, the three travelers were made to feel that Scully was very benevolent. He was conferring great favors upon them. He handed the towel from one to another with an air of philanthropic impulse.

Afterward they went to the first room, and, sitting about the stove, listened to Scully's officious clamor at his daughters, who were preparing the midday meal. They reflected in the silence of experienced men who tread carefully amid new people. Nevertheless, the old farmer, stationary, invincible in his chair near the warmest part of the stove, turned his face from the sawdust box frequently and addressed a glowing commonplace to the strangers. Usually he was answered in short but adequate sentences by either the cowboy or the Easterner. The Swede said nothing. He seemed to be occupied in making furtive estimates of each man in the room. One might have thought that he had the sense of silly suspicion which comes to guilt. He resembled a badly frightened man.

Later, at dinner, he spoke a little, addressing his conversation entirely to Scully. He volunteered that he had come from New York where for ten years he had worked as a tailor. These facts seemed to strike Scully as fascinating, and afterward he volunteered that he had lived at Romper for fourteen years. The Swede asked about the crops and the price of labor. He seemed barely to listen to Scully's extended replies. His eyes continued to rove from man to man.

Finally, with a laugh and a wink, he said that some of these Western communities were very dangerous; and

after his statement he straightened his legs under the table, tilted his head and laughed again, loudly. It was plain that the demonstration had no meaning to the others. They looked at him wondering and in silence.

AS THE MEN TROOPED heavily back into the front room, the two little windows presented views of a turmoiling sea of snow. The huge arms of the wind were making attempts—mighty, circular, futile—to embrace the flakes as they sped. A gatepost like a still man with a blanched face stood aghast amid this profligate fury. In a hearty voice Scully announced the presence of a blizzard. The guests of the blue hotel, lighting their pipes, assented with grunts of lazy masculine contentment. No island of the sea could be exempt in the degree of this little room with its humming stove. Johnnie, son of Scully, in a tone which defined his opinion of his ability as a cardplayer, challenged the old farmer of both gray and sandy whiskers to a game of high-five. The farmer agreed with a contemptuous and bitter scoff. They sat close to the stove, and squared their knees under a wide board. The cowboy and the Easterner watched the game with interest. The Swede remained near the window, aloof, but with a countenance that showed signs of an inexplicable excitement.

The play of Johnnie and the graybeard was suddenly ended by another quarrel. The old man arose while casting a look of heated scorn at his adversary. He slowly buttoned his coat, and then stalked with fabulous dignity from the room. In the discreet silence of all the other men, the Swede laughed. His laughter rang somehow childish. Men by this time had begun to look at him askance, as if they wished to inquire what ailed him.

A new game was formed jocosely. The cowboy volunteered to become the partner of Johnnie, and they all then turned to ask the Swede to throw in his lot with the little Easterner. He asked some questions about the game, and, learning that it wore many names, and that he had played it when it was under an alias, he accepted the invitation. He strode toward the

men nervously, as if he expected to be assaulted. Finally, seated, he gazed from face to face and laughed shrilly. This laugh was so strange that the Easterner looked up quickly, the cowboy sat intent and with his mouth open, and Johnnie paused, holding the cards with still fingers.

Afterward there was a short silence. Then Johnnie said, "Well, let's get at it. Come on, now!" They pulled their chairs forward until their knees were bunched under the board. They began to play, and their interest in the game caused the others to forget the manner of the Swede.

The cowboy was a board-whacker. Each time that he held superior cards he whanged them, one by one, with exceeding force, down upon the improvised table, and took the tricks with a glowing air of prowess and pride that sent thrills of indignation into the hearts of his opponents. A game with a board-whacker in it is sure to become intense. The countenances of the Easterner and the Swede were miserable whenever the cowboy thundered down his aces and kings, while Johnnie, his eyes gleaming with joy, chuckled and chuckled.

Because of the absorbing play none considered the strange ways of the Swede. They paid strict heed to the game. Finally, during a lull caused by a new deal, the Swede suddenly addressed Johnnie. "I suppose there have been a good many men killed in this room." The jaws of the others dropped and they looked at him.

"What in hell are you talking about?" said Johnnie.

The Swede laughed again his blatant laugh, full of a kind of false courage and defiance. "Oh, you know what I mean all right," he answered.

"I'm a liar if I do!" Johnnie protested. The card was halted, and the men stared at the Swede. Johnny evidently felt that as the son of the proprietor he should make a direct inquiry. "Now, what might you be drivin' at, mister?" he asked. The Swede winked at him. It was a wink full of cunning. His fingers shook on the edge of the board. "Oh, maybe you think I have been to nowheres. Maybe you think I'm a tenderfoot?"

"I don't know nothin' about you," answered Johnnie, "and I don't give a damn where you've been. All I got to say is that I don't know what you're driving at. There hain't never been nobody killed in this room."

The cowboy, who had been steadily gazing at the Swede, then spoke. "What's wrong with you, mister?"

Apparently it seemed to the Swede that he was formidably menaced. He shivered and turned white near the corners of his mouth. He sent an appealing glance in the direction of the little Easterner. During these moments he did not forget to wear his air of advanced pot-valor. "They say they don't know what I mean," he remarked mockingly to the Easterner.

The latter answered after prolonged and cautious reflection. "I don't understand you," he said impassively.

The Swede made a movement then which announced that he thought he had encountered treachery from the only quarter where he had expected sympathy, if not help. "Oh, I see you are all against me. I see—"

The cowboy was in a state of deep stupefaction. "Say," he cried, as he tumbled the deck violently down upon the board, "say, what are you gittin' at, hey?"

The Swede sprang up with the celerity of a man escaping from a snake on the floor. "I don't want to fight!" he shouted. "I don't want to fight!"

The cowboy stretched his long legs indolently and deliberately. His hands were in his pockets. He spat into the sawdust box. "Well, who the hell thought you did?" he inquired.

The Swede backed rapidly toward a corner of the room. His hands were out protectingly in front of his chest, but he was making an obvious struggle to control his fright. "Gentlemen," he quavered, "I suppose I am going to be killed before I can leave this house!" In his eyes was the dying-swan look. Through the windows could be seen the snow turning blue in the shadow of dusk. The wind tore at the house, and some loose thing beat regularly against the clapboards like a spirit tapping.

A door opened, and Scully himself entered. He

Previous pages: Oscar E. Berninghaus, *Forgotten*, 1916. Oil, 22 x 30" paused in surprise as he noted the tragic attitude of the Swede. Then he said, "What's the matter here?"

The Swede answered him swiftly and eagerly, "These men are going to kill me."

"Kill you!" ejaculated Scully. "Kill you! What are you talkin'?"

The Swede made the gesture of a martyr.

Scully wheeled sternly upon his son. "What is this, Johnnie?"

The lad had grown sullen. "Damned if I know," he answered. "I can't make no sense to it." He began to shuffle the cards, fluttering them together with an angry snap. "He says a good many men have been killed in this room, or something like that. And he says he's goin' to be killed here too. I don't know what ails him. He's crazy, I shouldn't wonder."

Scully then looked for explanation to the cowboy, but the cowboy simply shrugged his shoulders.

"Kill you?" said Scully again to the Swede. "Kill you? Man, you're off your nut."

"Oh, I know," burst out the Swede. "I know what will happen. Yes, I'm crazy—yes. Yes, of course, I'm crazy—yes. But I know one thing—" There was a sort of sweat of misery and terror upon his face. "I know I won't get out of here alive."

The cowboy drew a deep breath, as if his mind was passing into the last stages of dissolution. "Well, I'm doggoned," he whispered to himself.

Scully wheeled suddenly and faced his son. "You've been troublin' this man!"

Johnnie's voice was loud with its burden of grievance. "Why, good Gawd, I ain't done nothin' to 'im."

The Swede broke in. "Gentlemen, do not disturb yourselves. I will leave this house. I will go away, because"—he accused them dramatically with his glance—"because I do not want to be killed."

Scully was furious with his son. "Will you tell me what is the matter, you young devil? What's the matter, anyhow? Speak out!"

"Blame it!" cried Johnnie in despair, "don't I tell you I don't know? He—he says we want to kill him, and that's all I know. I can't tell what ails him."

The Swede continued to repeat, "Never mind, Mr. Scully; never mind. I will leave this house. I will

go away, because I do not wish to be killed. Yes, of course, I am crazy—yes. But I know one thing! I will go away. I will leave this house. Never mind, Mr. Scully; never mind. I will go away."

"You will not go 'way," said Scully. "You will not go 'way until I hear the reason of this business. If anybody has troubled you, I will take care of him. This is my house. You are under my roof, and I will not allow any peaceable man to be troubled here." He cast a terrible eye upon Johnnie, the cowboy and the Easterner.

"Never mind, Mr. Scully; never mind. I will go away. I do not wish to be killed." The Swede moved toward the door which opened upon the stairs. It was evidently his intention to go at once for his baggage.

"No, no," shouted Scully peremptorily; but the white-faced man slid by him and disappeared. "Now," said Scully severely, "what does this mean?"

Johnnie and the cowboy cried together, "Why, we didn't do nothin' to 'im!"

Scully's eyes were cold. "No," he said, "you didn't?"

Johnnie swore a deep oath. "Why, this is the wildest loon I ever see. We didn't do nothin' at all. We were just sittin' here playin' cards, and he—"

The father suddenly spoke to the Easterner. "Mr. Blanc," he asked, "what has these boys been doin'?"

The Easterner reflected again. "I didn't see anything wrong at all," he said at last slowly.

Scully began to howl. "But what does it mane?" He stared ferociously at his son. "I have a mind to lather you for this, me boy."

Johnnie was frantic. "Well, what have I done?" he bawled at his father.

"I THINK YOU ARE tongue-tied," said Scully finally to his son, the cowboy and the Easterner; and at the end of this scornful sentence, he left the room.

Upstairs the Swede was swiftly fastening the straps of his great valise. Once his back happened to be half turned toward the door, and, hearing a noise there, he wheeled and sprang up, uttering a loud cry. Scully's wrinkled visage showed grimly in the light of the small lamp he carried. This yellow effulgence, streaming upward, colored only his prominent features, and left his eyes, for instance, in mysterious shadow. He resembled a murderer.

"Man! man!" he exclaimed, "have you gone daffy?"

"Oh, no! Oh, no!" rejoined the other. "There are people in this world who know pretty nearly as much as you do—understand?"

For a moment they stood gazing at each other. Upon the Swede's deathly pale cheeks were two spots brightly crimson and sharply edged, as if they had been carefully painted. Scully placed the light on the table and sat himself on the edge of the bed. He spoke ruminatively. "By cracky, I never heard of such a thing in my life. It's a complete muddle. I can't, for the soul of me, think how you ever got this idea into your head." Presently he lifted his eyes and asked, "And did you sure think they were going to kill you?"

The Swede scanned the old man as if he wished to see into his mind. "I did," he said at last. He obviously suspected that this answer might precipitate an outbreak. As he pulled on a strap his whole arm shook, the elbow wavering like a bit of paper.

Scully banged his hand impressively on the footboard of the bed. "Why, man, we're goin' to have a line of ilictric streetcars in this town next spring."

" 'A line of electric streetcars,' " repeated the Swede stupidly.

"And," said Scully, "there's a new railroad goin' to be built down from Broken Arm to here. Not to mention the four churches and the smashin' big brick schoolhouse. Then there's the big factory, too. Why, in two years Romper'll be a met-tro-*pol*-is."

Having finished the preparation of his baggage, the Swede straightened himself. "Mr. Scully," he said, with sudden hardihood, "how much do I owe you?"

"You don't owe me anythin'," said the old man, angrily.

"Yes, I do," retorted the Swede. He took seventy-five cents from his pocket and tendered it to Scully; but the latter snapped his fingers in disdainful refusal. However, it happened that they both stood gazing in a strange fashion at three silver pieces on the Swede's open palm.

"I'll not take your money," said Scully at last. "Not after what's been goin' on here." Then a plan seemed to strike him. "Here," he cried, picking up his lamp and moving toward the door. "Here! Come with me a minute."

"No," said the Swede, in overwhelming alarm.

"Yes," urged the old man. "Come on! I want you to come and see a picter—just across the hall—in my room."

The Swede must have concluded that his hour was come. His jaw dropped and his teeth showed like a dead man's. He ultimately followed Scully across the corridor, but he had the step of one hung in chains.

Scully flashed the light high on the wall of his own chamber. There was revealed a ridiculous photograph of a little girl. She was leaning against a balustrade of gorgeous decoration, and the formidable bang to her hair was prominent. The figure was as graceful as an upright sled-stake, and, withal, it was of the hue of lead. "There," said Scully, tenderly, "that's the picter of my little girl that died. Her name was Carrie. She had the purtiest hair you ever saw. I was that fond of her, she—"

Turning then, he saw that the Swede was not contemplating the picture at all, but, instead, was keeping keen watch on the gloom in the rear.

"Look, man!" cried Scully, heartily. "That's the picter of my little gal that died. Her name was Carrie. And then here's the picter of my oldest boy, Michael. He's a lawyer in Lincoln, an' doin' well. I gave that boy a grand eddication, and I'm glad for it now. He's a fine boy. Look at 'im now. Ain't he bold as blazes, him there in Lincoln, an honored an' respicted gintelman! An honored and respected gintleman," concluded Scully with a flourish. And, so saying, he smote the Swede jovially on the back.

The Swede faintly smiled.

"Now," said the old man, "there's only one more thing." He dropped suddenly to the floor and thrust his hand beneath the bed. The Swede could hear his muffled voice. "I'd keep it under me piller if it wasn't for that boy Johnnie. Then there's the old woman—Where is it now? I never put it twice in the same place. Ah, now come out with you!"

Presently he backed clumsily from under the bed, dragging with him an old coat rolled into a bundle. "I've fetched him," he muttered. Kneeling on the floor, he unrolled the coat and extracted from its heart a large yellow brown whisky bottle.

His first maneuver was to hold the bottle up to the light. Reassured, apparently, that nobody had been tampering with it, he thrust it with a generous movement toward the Swede.

The weak-kneed Swede was about to eagerly clutch this element of strength, but he suddenly jerked his hand away and cast a look of horror upon Scully.

"Drink," said the old man affectionately. He had risen to his feet, and now stood facing the Swede.

There was a silence. Then again Scully said, "Drink!"

The Swede laughed wildly. He grabbed the bottle, put it to his mouth; and as his lips curled absurdly around the opening and his throat worked, he kept his glance, burning with hatred, upon the old man's face.

AFTER THE DEPARTURE OF Scully the three men, with the cardboard still upon their knees, preserved for a long time an astounded silence. Then Johnnie said, "That's the daddangedest Swede I ever see."

"He ain't no Swede," said the cowboy scornfully.

"Well, what is he then?" cried Johnnie. "What is he then?"

"It's my opinion," replied the cowboy deliberately, "he's some kind of a Dutchman." It was a venerable custom of the country to entitle as Swedes all light-haired men who spoke with a heavy tongue. In consequence the idea of the cowboy was not without its daring. "Yes, sir," he repeated. "It's my opinion this feller is some kind of a Dutchman."

"Well, he says he's a Swede, anyhow," muttered Johnnie, sulkily. He turned to the Easterner. "What do you think, Mr. Blanc?"

"Oh, I don't know," replied the Easterner.

"Well, what do you think makes him act that way?" asked the cowboy.

"Why, he's frightened." The Easterner knocked his pipe against a rim of the stove. "He's clear frightened out of his boots."

"What at?" cried Johnnie and the cowboy together.

The Easterner reflected over his answer.

"What at?" cried the others again.

"Oh, I don't know, but it seems to me this man has been reading dime novels, and he thinks he's right out in the middle of it—the shootin' and stabbin' and all."

"But," said the cowboy, deeply scandalized, "this ain't Wyoming, ner none of them places. This is Nebrasker."

"Yes," added Johnnie, "an' why don't he wait till he gits out West?"

The traveled Easterner laughed. "It isn't different there even—not in these days. But he thinks he's right in the middle of hell."

Johnnie and the cowboy mused long.

"It's awful funny," remarked Johnnie at last.

"Yes," said the cowboy. "This is a queer game. I hope we don't git snowed in, because then we'd have to stand this here man bein' around with us all the time. That wouldn't be no good."

"I wish Pop would throw him out," said Johnnie.

Presently they heard a loud stamping on the stairs, accompanied by ringing jokes in the voice of old Scully, and laughter, evidently from the Swede. The men around the stove stared vacantly at each other. "Gosh!" said the cowboy. The door flew open, and old Scully, flushed and anecdotal, came into the room. He was jabbering at the Swede, who followed him, laughing bravely. It was the entry of two roisterers from a banquet hall.

"Come now," said Scully sharply to the three seated men, "move up and give us a chance at the stove." The cowboy and the Easterner obediently sidled their chairs to make room for the newcomers. Johnnie, however, simply arranged himself in a more indolent attitude, and then remained motionless.

"Come! Sit over there," said Scully.

"Plenty of room on the other side of the stove," said Johnnie.

"Do you think we want to sit in the draught?" roared the father.

But the Swede here interposed with a grandeur of confidence. "No, no. Let the boy sit where he likes," he cried in a bullying voice to the father.

"All right! All right!" said Scully, deferentially. The cowboy and the Easterner exchanged glances of wonder.

The five chairs were formed in a crescent about one side of the stove. The Swede began to talk; he talked arrogantly, profanely, angrily. Johnnie, the cowboy and the Easterner maintained a morose silence, while old Scully appeared to be receptive and eager, breaking in constantly with sympathetic ejaculations.

Finally the Swede announced that he was thirsty. He moved in his chair, and said that he would go for a drink of water.

"I'll git it for you," cried Scully at once.

"No," said the Swede, contemptuously. "I'll get it for myself." He arose and stalked with the air of an owner off into the executive parts of the hotel.

As soon as the Swede was out of hearing, Scully sprang to his feet and whispered intensely to the others, "Upstairs he thought I was tryin' to poison 'im."

"Say," said Johnnie, "this makes me sick. Why don't you throw 'im out in the snow?"

"Why, he's all right now," declared Scully. "It was only that he was from the East, and he thought this was a tough place. That's all. He's all right now."

The cowboy looked with admiration upon the Easterner. "You were straight," he said. "You were on to that there Dutchman."

"Well," said Johnnie to his father, "he may be all right now, but I don't see it. Other time he was scared, but now he's too fresh."

Scully's speech was always a combination of Irish brogue and idiom, Western twang and idiom, and scraps of curiously formal diction taken from the storybooks and newspapers. He now hurled a strange mass of language at the head of his son. "What do I keep? What do I keep? What do I keep?" he demanded, in a voice of thunder. He slapped his knee impressively, to indicate that he himself was going to make reply, and that all should heed. "I keep a hotel," he shouted. "A hotel, do you mind? A guest under my roof has sacred privileges. He is to be intimidated by none. Not one

word shall he hear that would prijudice him in favor of goin' away. I'll not have it. There's no place in this here town where they can say they iver took in a guest of mine because he was afraid to stay here." He wheeled suddenly upon the cowboy and the Easterner. "Am I right?"

"Yes, Mr. Scully," said the cowboy, "I think you're right."

"Yes, Mr. Scully," said the Easterner, "I think you're right."

AT SIX O'CLOCK SUPPER, the Swede fizzed like a fire wheel. He sometimes seemed on the point of bursting into riotous song, and in all his madness he was encouraged by old Scully. The Easterner was encased in reserve; the cowboy sat in wide-mouthed amazement, forgetting to eat, while Johnnie wrathily demolished great plates of food. The daughters of the house, when they were obliged to replenish the biscuits, approached as warily as Indians, and, having succeeded in their purpose, fled with ill concealed trepidation. The Swede domineered the whole feast, and he gave it the appearance of a cruel bacchanal. He seemed to have grown suddenly taller; he gazed, brutally disdainful, into every face. His voice rang through the room. Once when he jabbed out harpoon-fashion with his fork to pinion a biscuit, the weapon nearly impaled the hand of the Easterner, which had been stretched quietly out for the same biscuit.

After supper, as the men filed toward the other room, the Swede smote Scully ruthlessly on the shoulder. "Well, old boy, that was a good, square meal." Johnnie looked hopefully at his father; he knew that shoulder was tender from an old fall; and, indeed, it appeared for a moment as if Scully was going to flame out over the matter, but in the end he smiled a sickly smile and remained silent. The others understood from his manner that he was admitting his responsibility for the Swede's new viewpoint.

Johnnie, however, addressed his parent in an aside. "Why don't you license somebody to kick you downstairs?" Scully scowled darkly by way of reply.

When they were gathered about the stove, the

Swede insisted on another game of high-five. Scully gently deprecated the plan at first, but the Swede turned a wolfish glare upon him. The old man subsided, and the Swede canvased the others. In his tone there was always a great threat. The cowboy and the Easterner both remarked indifferently that they would play. Scully said that he would presently have to go to meet the 6:58 train, and so the Swede turned menacingly upon Johnnie. For a moment their glances crossed like blades, and then Johnnie smiled and said, "Yes, I'll play."

They formed a square, with the little board on their knees. The Easterner and the Swede were again partners. As the play went on, it was noticeable that the cowboy was not board-whacking as usual. Meanwhile, Scully, near the lamp, had put on his spectacles and, with an appearance curiously like an old priest, was reading a newspaper. In time he went out to meet the 6:58 train, and, despite his precautions, a gust of polar wind whirled into the room as he opened the door. Besides scattering the cards, it chilled the players to the marrow. The Swede cursed frightfully. When Scully returned, his entrance disturbed a cozy and friendly scene. The Swede again cursed. But presently they were once more intent, their heads bent forward and their hands moving swiftly. The Swede had adopted the fashion of board-whacking.

Scully took up his paper and for a long time remained immersed in matters which were extraordinarily remote from him. The lamp burned badly, and once he stopped to adjust the wick. The newspaper, as he turned from page to page, rustled with a slow and comfortable sound. Then suddenly he heard three terrible words. "You are cheatin'!"

Such scenes often prove that there can be little of dramatic import in environment. Any room can present a tragic front; any room can be comic. This little den was now hideous as a torture chamber. The new faces of the men themselves had changed it upon the instant the Swede held a huge fist in front of Johnnie's face, while the latter looked steadily over it into the blazing orbs of his accuser. The Easterner had grown pallid; the cowboy's jaw had dropped in that expression of bovine amazement which was one of

his important mannerisms. After the three words, the first sound in the room was made by Scully's paper as it floated forgotten to his feet. His spectacles had also fallen from his nose, but by a clutch he had saved them in air. His hand, grasping the spectacles, now remained poised awkwardly and near his shoulder. He stared at the cardplayers.

Probably the silence was while a second elapsed. Then, if the floor had been suddenly twitched out from under the men, they could not have moved quicker. The five had projected themselves headlong toward a common point. It happened that Johnnie, in rising to hurl himself upon the Swede, had stumbled slightly because of his curiously instinctive care for the cards and the board. The loss of the moment allowed time for the arrival of Scully, and also allowed the cowboy time to give the Swede a great push which sent him staggering back. The men found tongue together, and hoarse shouts of rage, appeal or fear burst from every throat. The cowboy pushed and jostled feverishly at the Swede, and the Easterner and Scully clung wildly to Johnnie; but through the smoky air, above the swaying bodies of the peace-compellers, the eyes of the two warriors ever sought each other in glances of challenge that were at once hot and steely.

Of course the board had been overturned, and now the whole company of cards was scattered over the floor, where the boots of the men trampled the fat and painted kings and queens as they gazed with their silly eyes at the war that was waging above them.

Scully's voice was dominating the yells. "Stop now! Stop, I say! Stop, now—"

Johnnie, as he struggled to burst through the rank formed by Scully and the Easterner, was crying, "Well, he says I cheated! He says I cheated! I won't allow no man to say I cheated! If he says I cheated, he's a —!"

The cowboy was telling the Swede, "Quit, now! Quit, d'ye hear—"

The screams of the Swede never ceased. "He did cheat! I saw him! I saw him—"

As for the Easterner, he was importuning in a voice that was not heeded, "Wait a moment, can't you? Oh, wait a moment. What's the good of a fight over a game of cards? Wait a moment—"

In this tumult no complete sentences were clear. "Cheat"—"quit"— "he says"—these fragments pierced the uproar and rang out sharply. It was remarkable that, whereas Scully undoubtedly made the most noise, he was the least heard of any of the riotous band.

Then suddenly there was a great cessation. It was as if each man had paused for breath; and although the room was still lighted with the anger of men, it could be seen that there was no danger of immediate conflict, and at once Johnnie, shouldering his way forward, almost succeeded in confronting the Swede. "What did you say I cheated for? What did you say I cheated for? I don't cheat, and I won't let no man say I do!"

The Swede said, "I saw you! I saw you!"

"Well," cried Johnnie, "I'll fight any man what says I cheat!"

"No, you won't," said the cowboy. "Not here."

"Ah, be still, can't you?" said Scully, coming between them.

The quiet was sufficient to allow the Easterner's voice to be heard. He was repeating, "Oh, wait a moment, can't you? What's the good of a fight over a game of cards? Wait a moment!"

Johnnie, his red face appearing above his father's shoulder, hailed the Swede again. "Did you say I cheated?"

The Swede showed his teeth. "Yes."

"Then," said Johnnie, "we must fight."

"Yes, fight," roared the Swede. He was like a demoniac. "Yes, fight! I'll show you what kind of a man I am! I'll show you who you want to fight! Maybe you think I can't fight! Maybe you think I can't! I'll show you, you skin, you cardsharp. Yes, you cheated! You cheated! You cheated!"

"Well, let's go at it, then, mister," said Johnnie coolly.

The cowboy's brow was beaded with sweat from his efforts in intercepting all sorts of raids. He turned in despair to Scully. "What are you goin' to do now?"

A change had come over the Celtic visage of the old man. He now seemed all eagerness; his eyes glowed.

"We'll let them fight," he answered, stalwartly. "I can't put up with it any longer. I've stood this damned Swede till I'm sick. We'll let them fight."

THE MEN PREPARED to go out of doors. The Easterner was so nervous that he had great difficulty in getting his arms into the sleeves of his new leather coat. As the cowboy drew his fur cap down over his ears, his hands trembled. In fact, Johnnie and old Scully were the only ones who displayed no agitation. These preliminaries were conducted without words.

Scully threw open the door. "Well, come on," he said. Instantly a terrific wind caused the flame of the lamp to struggle at its wick, while a puff of black smoke sprang from the chimney top. The stove was in mid-current of the blast, and its voice swelled to equal the roar of the storm. Some of the scarred and bedab-bled cards were caught up from the floor and dashed helplessly against the farther wall. The men lowered their heads and plunged into the tempest as into a sea.

No snow was falling, but great whirls and clouds of flakes, swept up from the ground by the frantic winds, were streaming southward with the speed of bullets. The covered land was blue with the sheen of an unearthly satin, and there was no other hue save where, at the low black railway station—which seemed incredibly distant—one light gleamed like a tiny jewel. As the men floundered into a thigh-deep drift, it was known that the Swede was bawling out something. Scully went to him, put a hand on his shoulder and projected an ear. "What's that you say?" he shouted.

"I say," bawled the Swede again, "I won't stand much show against this gang. I know you'll all pitch on me."

Scully smote him reproachfully on the arm. "Tut, man!" he yelled. The wind tore the words from Scully's lips and scattered them far alee.

"You are all a gang of—" boomed the Swede, but the storm also seized the remainder of this sentence.

Immediately turning their backs upon the wind, the men had swung around a corner to the sheltered side of the hotel. It was the function of the little house to preserve here, amid this great devastation of snow, an irregular V-shape of heavily encrusted grass, which crackled beneath the feet. One could imagine the great drifts piled against the windward side. When the party reached the comparative peace of this spot, it was found that the Swede was still bellowing.

"Oh, I know what kind of a thing this is! I know you'll all pitch on me. I can't lick you all!"

Scully turned upon him panther-fashion. "You'll not have to whip all of us. You'll have to whip my son Johnnie. An' the man what troubles you durin' that time will have me to deal with."

The arrangements were swiftly made. The two men faced each other, obedient to the harsh commands of Scully, whose face, in the subtly luminous gloom, could be seen set in the austere impersonal lines that are pictured on the countenances of the Roman veterans. The Easterner's teeth were chattering, and he was hopping up and down like a mechanical toy. The cowboy stood rocklike.

The contestants had not stripped off any clothing. Each was in his ordinary attire. Their fists were up, and they eyed each other in a calm that had the elements of leonine cruelty in it.

During this pause, the Easterner's mind, like a film, took lasting impressions of three men—the iron-nerved master of the ceremony; the Swede, pale, motionless, terrible; and Johnnie, serene yet ferocious, brutish yet heroic. The entire prelude had in it a tragedy greater than the tragedy of action, and this aspect was accentuated by the long, mellow cry of the blizzard as it sped the tumbling and wailing flakes into the black abyss of the south.

"Now!" said Scully.

The two combatants leaped forward and crashed together like bullocks. There was heard the cushioned sound of blows, and of a curse squeezing out from between the tight teeth of one.

As for the spectators, the Easterner's pent-up breath exploded from him with a pop of relief, absolute relief from the tension of the preliminaries. The cowboy bounded into the air with a yowl.

Scully was immovable as from supreme amazement and fear at the fury of the fight which he himself had permitted and arranged.

For a time the encounter in the darkness was such a perplexity of flying arms that it presented no more detail than would a swiftly revolving wheel. Occasionally, a face, as if illumined by a flash of light, would shine out, ghastly and marked with pink spots. A moment later, the men might have been known as shadows if it were not for the involuntary utterance of oaths that came from them in whispers.

Suddenly a holocaust of warlike desire caught the cowboy, and he bolted forward with the speed of a bronco. "Go it, Johnnie! Go it! Kill him! Kill him!"

Scully confronted him. "Kape back," he said; and by his glance the cowboy could tell that this man was Johnnie's father.

To the Easterner there was a monotony of unchangeable fighting that was an abomination. This confused mingling was eternal to his sense, which was concentrated in a longing for the end, the priceless end. Once the fighters lurched near him, and as he scrambled hastily backward he heard them breathe like men on the rack.

"Kill him, Johnnie! Kill him! Kill him! Kill him!" The cowboy's face was contorted like one of those agony masks in museums.

"Keep still," said Scully icily.

Then there was a sudden loud grunt, incomplete, cut short, and Johnnie's body swung away from the Swede and fell with sickening heaviness to the grass. The cowboy was barely in time to prevent the mad Swede from flinging himself upon his prone adversary. "No, you don't," said the cowboy, interposing an arm. "Wait a second."

Scully was at his son's side. "Johnnie! Johnnie, me boy!" His voice had a quality of melancholy tenderness. "Johnnie! Can you go on with it?" He looked anxiously down into the bloody, pulpy face of his son.

There was a moment of silence, and then Johnnie answered in his ordinary voice. "Yes, I—it—yes."

Assisted by his father he struggled to his feet. "Wait a bit now till you git your wind," said the old man.

A few paces away the cowboy was lecturing the Swede. "No, you don't. Wait a second!"

The Easterner was plucking at Scully's sleeve. "Oh, this is enough," he pleaded. "This is enough! Let it go as it stands. This is enough!"

"Bill," said Scully, "git out of the road." The cowboy stepped aside. "Now." The combatants were actuated by a new caution as they advanced toward collision. They glared at each other, and then the Swede aimed a lightning blow that carried with it his entire weight. Johnnie was evidently half stupid from weakness, but he miraculously dodged, and his fist sent the overbalanced Swede sprawling.

The cowboy, Scully and the Easterner burst into a cheer that was like a chorus of triumphant soldiery, but before its conclusion the Swede had scuffed agilely to his feet and come in berserk abandon at his foe. There was another perplexity of flying arms, and Johnnie's body again swung away and fell, even as a bundle might fall from a roof. The Swede instantly staggered to a little wind-waved tree and leaned upon it, breathing like an engine, while his savage and flame-lit eyes roamed from face to face as the men bent over Johnnie. There was a splendor of isolation in his situation at this time which the Easterner felt once when, lifting his eyes from the man on the ground, he beheld that mysterious and lonely figure, waiting.

"Are you any good yet, Johnnie?" asked Scully in a broken voice.

The son gasped and opened his eyes languidly. After a moment he answered, "No—I ain't—any good—any—more." Then from shame and bodily ill, he began to weep, the tears furrowing down through the bloodstains on his face. "He was too—too—heavy for me."

Scully straightened and addressed the waiting figure. "Stranger," he said, evenly, "it's all up with our side." Then his voice changed into that vibrant huskiness which is commonly the tone of the most simple and deadly announcements. "Johnnie is whipped."

Without replying, the victor moved off on the route to the front door of the hotel.

The cowboy was formulating new and unspellable blasphemies. The Easterner was startled to find that

they were out in a wind that seemed to come direct from the shadowed arctic floes. He heard again the wail of the snow as it was flung to its grave in the south. He knew now that all this time the cold had been sinking into him deeper and deeper, and he wondered that he had not perished. He felt indifferent to the condition of the vanquished man.

"Johnnie, can you walk?" asked Scully.

"Did I hurt—hurt him any?" asked the son.

"Can you walk, boy? Can you walk?"

Johnnie's voice was suddenly strong. There was a robust impatience in it. "I asked you whether I hurt him any!"

"Yes, yes, Johnnie," answered the cowboy, consolingly, "he's hurt a good deal."

They raised him from the ground, and as soon as he was on his feet, he went tottering off, rebuffing all attempts at assistance. When the party rounded the corner, they were fairly blinded by the pelting of the snow. It burned their faces like fire. The cowboy carried Johnnie through the drift to the door. As they entered, some cards rose from the floor and beat against the wall.

The Easterner rushed to the stove. He was so profoundly chilled that he almost dared to embrace the glowing iron. The Swede was not in the room. Johnnie sank into a chair and, folding his arms on his knees, buried his face in them. Scully, warming one foot and then the other at the rim of the stove, muttered to himself with Celtic mournfulness. The cowboy had removed his fur cap, and with a dazed and rueful air he was running one hand through his tousled locks. From overhead they could hear the creaking of boards as the Swede tramped here and there in his room.

The sad quiet was broken by the sudden flinging open of a door that led toward the kitchen. It was instantly followed by an onrush of women. They precipitated themselves upon Johnnie amid a chorus of lamentation. Before they carried their prey off to the kitchen, there to be bathed and harangued with that mixture of sympathy and abuse which is a feat of their sex, the mother straightened herself and fixed old Scully with an eye of stern reproach. "Shame be upon you, Patrick Scully!" she cried. "Your own son, too. Shame be upon you!"

"There, now! Be quiet, now!" said the old man weakly to this slogan, sniffed disdainfully in the direction of those trembling accomplices, the cowboy and the Easterner. Presently they bore Johnnie away, and left the three men to dismal reflection.

"I'D LIKE TO FIGHT this here Dutchman myself," said the cowboy, breaking a long silence.

Scully wagged his head sadly. "No, that wouldn't do. It wouldn't be right. It wouldn't be right."

"Well, why wouldn't it?" argued the cowboy. "I don't see no harm in it."

"No," answered Scully, with mournful heroism. "It wouldn't be right. It was Johnnie's fight, and now we mustn't whip the man just because he whipped Johnnie."

"Yes, that's true enough," said the cowboy, "but— he better not get fresh with me, because I couldn't stand no more of it."

"You'll not say a word to him," commanded Scully, and even then they heard the tread of the Swede on the stairs. His entrance was made theatric. He swept the door back with a bang and swaggered to the middle of the room. No one looked at him. "Well," he cried, insolently, at Scully, "I s'pose you'll tell me now how much I owe you?"

The old man remained stolid. "You don't owe me nothin'."

"Huh!" said the Swede, "huh! Don't owe 'im nothin'."

The cowboy addressed the Swede. "Stranger, I don't see how you come to be so gay around here."

Old Scully was instantly alert. "Stop!" he shouted, holding his hand forth, fingers upward. "Bill, you shut up!"

The cowboy spat carelessly into the sawdust box. "l didn't say a word, did I?" he asked.

"Mr. Scully," called the Swede, "how much do I owe you?" It was seen that he was attired for departure, and that he had his valise in his hand.

"You don't owe me nothin'," repeated Scully in the same imperturbable way.

"Huh!" said the Swede. "I guess you're right. I guess if it was any way at all, you'd owe me somethin'. That's what I guess." He turned to the cowboy. " 'Kill him! Kill him! Kill him!' " he mimicked, and then guffawed victoriously. " 'Kill him!' " He was convulsed with ironical humor.

But he might have been jeering the dead. The three men were immovable and silent, staring with glassy eyes at the stove.

The Swede opened the door and passed into the storm, giving one derisive glance backward at the still group.

As soon as the door was closed, Scully and the cowboy leaped to their feet and began to curse. They trampled to and fro, waving their arms and smashing into the air with their fists. "Oh, but that was a hard minute!" wailed Scully. "That was a hard minute! Him there leerin' and scoffin'! One bang at his nose was worth forty dollars to me that minute! How did you stand it, Bill?"

"How did I stand it?" cried the cowboy in a quivering voice. "How did I stand it? Oh!"

The old man burst into sudden brogue. "I'd loike to take that Swade," he wailed, "and hould 'im down on a shtone flure and bate 'im to a jelly wid a shtick!"

The cowboy groaned in sympathy. "I'd like to git him by the neck and ha-ammer him"—he brought his hand down on a chair with a noise like a pistol shot—"hammer that there Dutchman until he couldn't tell himself from a dead coyote!"

"I'd bate 'im until he—"

"I'd show him some things—"

And then together they raised a yearning, fantastic cry—"Oh-o-oh! if we only could—"

"Yes!"

"Yes!"

"And then I'd—"

"Ooh!"

THE SWEDE, TIGHTLY GRIPPING his valise, tacked across the face of the storm as if he carried sails. He was following a line of little naked, grasping trees which, he knew, must mark the way of the road. His face, fresh from the pounding of Johnnie's fists, felt more pleasure than pain in the wind and the driving snow. A number of square shapes loomed upon him finally, and he knew them as the houses of the main body of the town. He found a street and made travel along it, leaning heavily upon the wind whenever, at a corner, a terrific blast caught him.

He might have been in a deserted village. We picture the world as thick with conquering and elate humanity, but here, with the bugles of the tempest pealing, it was hard to imagine a peopled earth. One viewed the existence of man then as a marvel, and conceded a glamour of wonder to these lice which were caused to cling to a whirling, fire-smitten, ice-locked, disease-stricken, space-lost bulb. The conceit of man was explained by this storm to be the very engine of life. One was a coxcomb not to die in it. However, the Swede found a saloon.

In front of it an indomitable red light was burning, and the snowflakes were made blood color as they flew through the circumscribed territory of the lamp's shining. The Swede pushed open the door of the saloon and entered. A sanded expanse was before him, and at the end of it four men sat about a table drinking. Down one side of the room extended a radiant bar, and its guardian was leaning upon his elbows listening to the talk of the men at the table. The Swede dropped his valise upon the floor and, smiling fraternally upon the barkeeper, said, "Gimme some whisky, will you?" The man placed a bottle, a whisky glass, and a glass of ice-thick water upon the bar. The Swede poured himself an abnormal portion of whisky and drank it in three gulps. "Pretty bad night," remarked the bartender indifferently. He was making the pretension of blindness which is usually a distinction of his class; but it could have been seen that he was furtively studying the half-erased bloodstains on the face of the Swede. "Bad night," he said again.

"Oh, it's good enough for me," replied the Swede hardily as he poured himself some more whisky. The barkeeper took his coin and maneuvered it through its reception by a highly nickeled cash-machine. A bell rang, a card labeled "20 cts." had appeared.

"No," continued the Swede, "this isn't too bad weather. It's good enough for me."

"So?" murmured the barkeeper languidly.

The copious drams made the Swede's eyes swim, and he breathed a trifle heavier. "Yes, I like this weather. I like it. It suits me." It was apparently his design to impart a deep significance to these words.

"So?" murmured the bartender again. He turned to gaze dreamily at the scroll-like birds and birdlike scrolls which had been drawn with soap upon the mirrors in back of the bar.

"Well, I guess I'll take another drink," said the Swede presently. "Have something?"

"No, thanks; I'm not drinkin'," answered the bartender. Afterward he asked, "How did you hurt your face?"

The Swede immediately began to boast loudly. "Why, in a fight. I thumped the soul out of a man down here at Scully's hotel."

The interest of the four men at the table was at last aroused.

"Who was it?" said one.

"Johnnie Scully," blustered the Swede. "Son of the man what runs it. He will be pretty near dead for some weeks, I can tell you. I made a nice thing of him, I did. He couldn't get up. They carried him in the house. Have a drink?"

Instantly the men in some subtle way encased themselves in reserve. "No, thanks," said one. The group was of curious formation. Two were prominent local businessmen; one was the district attorney; and one was a professional gambler of the kind known as "square." But a scrutiny of the group would not have enabled an observer to pick the gambler from the men of more reputable pursuits. He was, in fact, a man so delicate in manner when among people of fair class, and so judicious in his choice of victims, that in the strictly masculine part of the town's life he had come to be explicitly trusted and admired. People called him a thoroughbred. The fear and contempt with which his craft was regarded were undoubtedly the reason why his quiet dignity shone conspicuous above the quiet dignity of men who might be merely hatters, billiard markers or grocery clerks. Beyond an occasionally unwary traveler who came by rail, this gambler was supposed to prey solely upon reckless and senile farmers, who, when flush with good crops, drove into town in all the pride and confidence of an absolutely invulnerable stupidity. Hearing at times in circuitous fashion of the despoilment of such a farmer, the important men of Romper invariably laughed in contempt of the victim, and if they thought of the wolf at all, it was with a kind of pride at the knowledge that he would never dare think of attacking their wisdom and courage. Besides, it was popular that this gambler had a real wife and two real children in a neat cottage in a suburb, where he led an exemplary home life; and when any one even suggested a discrepancy in his character, the crowd immediately vociferated descriptions of this virtuous family circle. Then men who led exemplary home lives, and men who did not lead exemplary home lives, all subsided in a bunch, remarking that there was nothing more to be said.

However, when a restriction was placed upon him—as, for instance, when a strong clique of members of the new Polywog Club refused to permit him, even as a spectator, to appear in the rooms of the organization—the candor and gentleness with which he accepted the judgment disarmed many of his foes and made his friends more desperately partisan. He invariably distinguished between himself and a respectable Romper man so quickly and frankly that his manner actually appeared to be a continual broadcast compliment.

And one must not forget to declare the fundamental fact of his entire position in Romper. It is irrefutable that in all affairs outside his business, in all matters that occur eternally and commonly between man and man, this thieving cardplayer was so generous, so just, so moral, that in a contest he could have put to flight the consciences of nine-tenths of the citizens of Romper.

And so it happened that he was seated in this saloon with the two prominent local merchants and the district attorney.

The Swede continued to drink raw whisky, meanwhile babbling at the barkeeper and trying to induce him to indulge in potations. "Come on. Have a drink. Come on. What—no? Well, have a little one, then.

By Gawd, I've whipped a man tonight, and I want to celebrate. I whipped him good, too. Gentlemen," the Swede cried to the men at the table. "Have a drink?"

"Ssh!" said the barkeeper.

The group at the table, although furtively attentive, had been pretending to be deep in talk, but now a man lifted his eyes toward the Swede and said shortly, "Thanks. We don't want any more."

At this reply the Swede ruffled out his chest like a rooster. "Well," he exploded, "it seems I can't get anybody to drink with me in this town. Seems so, don't it? Well!"

"Ssh!" said the barkeeper.

"Say," snarled the Swede, "don't you try to shut me up. I won't have it. I'm a gentleman, and I want people to drink with me. And I want 'em to drink with me now. Now—do you understand?" He rapped the bar with his knuckles.

Years of experience had calloused the bartender. He merely grew sulky. "I hear you," he answered.

"Well," cried the Swede, "listen hard then. See those men over there? Well, they're going to drink with me, and don't you forget it. Now you watch."

"Hi!" yelled the barkeeper, "this won't do!"

"Why won't it?" demanded the Swede. He stalked over to the table, and by chance laid his hand upon the shoulder of the gambler. "How about this?" he asked wrathfully. "I asked you to drink with me."

The gambler simply twisted his head and spoke over his shoulder. "My friend, I don't know you."

"Oh, hell!" answered the Swede, "come and have a drink."

"Now, my boy," advised the gambler kindly, "take your hand off my shoulder and go 'way and mind your own business." He was a little, slim man, and it seemed strange to hear him use this tone of heroic patronage to the burly Swede. The other men at the table said nothing.

"What! You won't drink with me, you little dude? I'll make you, then! I'll make you!" The Swede had grasped the gambler frenziedly at the throat, and was dragging him from his chair. The other men sprang up. The barkeeper dashed around the corner of his bar. There was a great tumult, and then was seen a long blade in the hand of the gambler. It shot forward, and a human body, this citadel of virtue, wisdom, power, was pierced as easily as if it had been a melon. The Swede fell with a cry of supreme astonishment.

The prominent merchants and the district attorney must have at once tumbled out of the place backward. The bartender found himself hanging limply to the arm of a chair and gazing into the eyes of a murderer.

"Henry," said the latter as he wiped his knife on one of the towels that hung beneath the bar rail, "you tell 'em where to find me. I'll be home, waiting for 'em." Then he vanished. A moment afterward the barkeeper was in the street, dinning through the storm for help and, moreover, companionship.

The corpse of the Swede, alone in the saloon, had its eyes fixed upon a dreadful legend that dwelt atop of the cash-machine: "This registers the amount of your purchase."

Months later the cowboy was frying pork over the stove of a little ranch near the Dakota line when there was a quick thud of hoofs outside, and presently the Easterner entered with the letters and the papers.

"Well," said the Easterner at once, "the chap that killed the Swede has got three years. Wasn't much, was it?"

"He has? Three years?" The cowboy poised his pan of pork while he ruminated upon the news. "Three years. That ain't much."

"No. It was a light sentence," replied the Easterner as he unbuckled his spurs. "Seems there was a good deal of sympathy for him in Romper."

"If the bartender had been any good," observed the cowboy thoughtfully, "he would have gone in and cracked that there Dutchman on the head with a bottle in the beginnin' of it and stopped all this here murderin'."

"Yes, a thousand things might have happened," said the Easterner tartly.

The cowboy returned his pan of pork to the fire, but his philosophy continued. "It's funny, ain't it? If he hadn't said Johnnie was cheatin', he'd be alive this minute. He was an awful fool. Game played for fun,

too. Not for money. I believe he was crazy."

"I feel sorry for that gambler," said the Easterner.

"Oh, so do I," said the cowboy. "He don't deserve none of it for killin' who he did."

"The Swede might not have been killed if everything had been square."

"Might not have been killed?" exclaimed the cowboy. "Everythin' square? Why, when he said that Johnnie was cheatin' and acted like such a jackass? And then in the saloon he fairly walked up to git hurt?" With these arguments the cowboy browbeat the Easterner and reduced him to rage.

"You're a fool!" cried the Easterner, viciously. "You're a bigger jackass than the Swede by a million majority. Now let me tell you one thing. Let me tell you something. Listen! Johnnie was cheating!"

" 'Johnnie,' said the cowboy, blankly. There was a minute of silence, and then he said, robustly, "Why, no. The game was only for fun."

"Fun or not," said the Easterner, "Johnnie was cheating. I saw him, I know it. I saw him. And I refused to stand up and be a man. I let the Swede fight it out alone. And you—you were simply puffing around the place and wanting to fight. And then old Scully himself! We are all in it! This poor gambler isn't even a noun. He is kind of an adverb. Every sin is the result of a collaboration. We, five of us, have collaborated in the murder of this Swede. Usually there are from a dozen to forty women really involved in every murder, but in this case it seems to be only men—you, I, Johnnie, old Scully and that fool of an unfortunate gambler came merely as a culmination, the apex of a human movement, and gets all the punishment."

The cowboy, injured and rebellious, cried out blindly into this fog of mysterious theory, "Well, I didn't do anythin', did I?"

Stephen Crane *(1871–1900), one of the best American short story writers, was among the first to use a realistic approach in fiction. He worked for his brother's news service in Ashbury, New Jersey, and later became famous for* The Red Badge of Courage *(1895).*

THE REFORMATION OF CALLIOPE

O. HENRY

Calliope Catesby was in his humors again. Ennui was upon him. This goodly promontory, the earth—particularly that portion of it known as Quicksand—was to him no more than a pestilent congregation of vapors. Overtaken by the megrims, the philosopher may seek relief in soliloquy; my lady find solace in tears; the flaccid Easterner scold at the millinery bills of his women folk. Such recourse was insufficient to the denizens of Quicksand. Calliope, especially, was wont to express his ennui according to his lights.

Overnight Calliope had hung out signals of approaching low spirits. He had kicked his own dog on the porch of the Occidental Hotel, and refused to apologize. He had become capricious and fault-finding in conversation. While strolling about he reached often for twigs of mesquite and chewed the leaves fiercely. That was always an ominous act. Another symptom alarming to those who were familiar with the different stages of his doldrums was his increasing politeness and a tendency to use formal phrases. A husky softness succeeded the usual penetrating drawl in his tones. A dangerous courtesy marked his manners. Later his smile became crooked, the left side of his mouth slanting upward, and Quicksand got ready to stand from under.

At this stage Calliope generally began to drink. Finally, about midnight, he was seen going homeward, saluting those whom he met with exaggerated but inoffensive courtesy. Not yet was Calliope's melancholy at the danger point. He would seat himself at the window of the room he occupied over Silvester's tonsorial parlors and there chant lugubrious and tuneless ballads until morning, accompanying the noises by appropriate maltreatment of a jingling guitar. More magnanimous than Nero, he would thus give musical warning of the forthcoming municipal upheaval that Quicksand was scheduled to endure.

A quiet, amiable man was Calliope Catesby at other times—quiet to indolence, and amiable to worthlessness. At best he was a loafer and a nuisance; at worst he was the terror of Quicksand. His ostensible occupation was something subordinate in the real-estate line; he drove the beguiled Easterner in buckboards out to look over lots and ranch property. Originally he came from one of the Gulf states, his lank six feet, slurring rhythm of speech, and sectional idioms giving evidence of his birthplace.

And yet, after taking on Western adjustments, this languid pine-box whittler, cracker-barrel hugger, shady-corner lounger of the cotton fields and sumac hills of the South, became famed as a bad man among men who had made a lifelong study of the art of truculence.

At nine the next morning Calliope was fit. Inspired by his own barbarous melodies and the contents of his jug, he was ready-primed to gather fresh laurels from the diffident brow of Quicksand. Encircled and crisscrossed with cartridge belts, abundantly garnished with revolvers and copiously drunk, he poured forth into Quicksand's main street. Too chivalrous to surprise and capture a town by silent sortie, he paused at the nearest corner and emitted his slogan—that fearful, brassy yell, so reminiscent of the steam piano, that had gained for him the classic appellation that had superseded his own baptismal name. Following close upon his vociferation came three shots from his .45 by way of limbering up the guns and testing his aim. A yellow dog, the personal property of Colonel Swazey, the proprietor of the Occidental, fell feet upward in the dust with one farewell yelp. A Mexican, who was crossing the street from the Blue Front grocery carrying in his hand a bottle of kerosene, was stimulated to a sudden and admirable burst of speed, still grasping the neck of the shattered bottle. The new gilt weathercock on Judge Riley's lemon and ultramarine two-story residence shivered, flapped, and hung by a splinter, the sport of the wanton breezes.

The artillery was in trim. Calliope's hand was steady. The high, calm ecstasy of habitual battle was upon him, though slightly embittered by the sadness of Alexander in that his conquests were limited to the small world of Quicksand.

Down the street went Calliope, shooting right and left. Glass fell like hail; dogs vamoosed, chickens flew, squawking; feminine voices shrieked concernedly to youngsters at large. The din was perforated at intervals by the staccato of the Terror's guns, and was drowned periodically by the brazen screech that Quicksand knew so well. The occasions of Calliope's low spirits were legal holidays in Quicksand. All along the main street, in advance of his coming, clerks were putting up shutters and closing doors. Business would languish for a space. The right of way was Calliope's, and as he advanced, observing the dearth of opposition and the few opportunities for distraction, his ennui perceptibly increased.

But some four squares farther down, lively preparations were being made to minister to Mr. Catesby's love for interchange of compliments and repartee. On the previous night numerous messengers had

hastened to advise Buck Patterson, the city marshal, of Calliope's impending eruption. The patience of that official, often strained in extending leniency toward the disturber's misdeeds, had been overtaxed. In Quicksand some indulgence was accorded the natural ebullition of human nature. Providing that the lives of the more useful citizens were not recklessly squandered or too much property needlessly laid waste, the community sentiment was against a too strict enforcement of the law. But Calliope had raised the limit. His outbursts had been too frequent and too violent to come within the classification of a normal and sanitary relaxation of spirit.

Buck Patterson had been expecting and awaiting in his little ten-by-twelve frame office that preliminary yell announcing that Calliope was feeling blue. When the signal came the city marshal rose to his feet and buckled on his guns. Two deputy sheriffs and three citizens who had proven the edible qualities of fire also stood up, ready to bandy with Calliope's leaden jocularities.

"Gather that fellow in," said Buck Patterson, setting for the lines of the campaign. "Don't have no talk, but shoot as soon as you can get a show. Keep behind cover and bring him down. He's a no-good 'un. It's up to Calliope to turn up his toes this time, I reckon. Go to him all spraddled out, boys. And don't git too reckless, for what Calliope shoots at he hits."

Buck Patterson, tall, muscular and solemn-faced, with his bright City Marshal badge shining on the breast of his blue flannel shirt, gave his posse directions for the onslaught upon Calliope. The plan was to accomplish the downfall of the Quicksand Terror without loss to the attacking party, if possible.

The splenetic Calliope, unconscious of retributive plots, was steaming down the channel, cannonading on either side, when he suddenly became aware of breakers ahead. The city marshal and one of the deputies rose up behind some dry-goods boxes half a square to the front and opened fire. At the same time the rest of the posse, divided, shelled him from two side streets up which they were cautiously maneuvering from a well-executed detour.

The first volley broke the lock of one of Calliope's guns, cut a neat underbite in his right ear and exploded a cartridge in his crossbelt, scorching his ribs as it burst. Feeling braced up by this unexpected tonic to his spiritual depression, Calliope executed a fortissimo note from his upper register, and returned the fire like an echo. The upholders of the law dodged at his flash, but a trifle too late to save one of the deputies a bullet just above the elbow, and the marshal a bleeding cheek from a splinter that a ball tore from the box he had ducked behind.

And now Calliope met the enemy's tactics in kind. Choosing with a rapid eye the street from which the weakest and least accurate fire had come, he invaded it at a double-quick, abandoning the unprotected middle of the street. With rare cunning the opposing force in that direction—one of the deputies and two of the valorous volunteers—waited, concealed by beer barrels, until Calliope had passed their retreat, and then peppered him from the rear. In another moment they were reinforced by the marshal and his other men, and then Calliope felt that in order to successfully prolong the delights of the controversy, he must find some means of reducing the great odds against him. His eye fell upon a structure that seemed to hold out this promise, providing he could reach it.

Not far away was the little railroad station, its building a strong box house, ten by twenty feet, resting upon a platform four feet above ground. Windows were in each of its walls. Something like a fort it might become to a man thus sorely pressed by superior numbers.

Calliope made a bold and rapid spurt for it, the marshal's crowd "smoking" him as he ran. He reached the haven in safety, the station agent leaving the building by a window, like a flying squirrel, as the garrison entered the door.

Patterson and his supporters halted under protection of a pile of lumber and held consultations. In the station was an unterrified desperado who was an excellent shot and carried an abundance of ammunition. For thirty yards on each side of the besieged was a stretch of bare, open ground. It was a sure thing that the man who attempted to enter that unprotected area would be stopped by one of Calliope's bullets.

The city marshal was resolved. He had decided that Calliope Catesby should no more wake the echoes of Quicksand with his strident whoop. He had so announced. Officially and personally he felt imperatively bound to put the soft pedal on that instrument of discord. It played bad tunes.

Standing near was a hand truck used in the manipulation of small freight. It stood by a shed full of sacked wool, a consignment from one of the sheep ranches. On this truck the marshal and his men piled three heavy sacks of wool. Stooping low, Buck Patterson started for Calliope's fort, slowly pushing this loaded truck before him for protection. The posse, scattering broadly, stood ready to nip the besieged in case he should show himself in an effort to repel the juggernaut of justice that was creeping upon him. Only once did Calliope make demonstration. He fired from a window, and some tufts of wool spurted from the marshal's trustworthy bulwark. The return shots from the posse pattered against the window frame of the fort. No loss resulted on either side.

The marshal was too deeply engrossed in steering his protected battleship to be aware of the approach of the morning train until he was within a few feet of the platform. The train was coming up on the other side of it. It stopped only one minute at Quicksand. What an opportunity it would offer to Calliope! He had only to step out the other door, mount the train, and away.

Abandoning his breastworks, Buck, with his gun ready, dashed up the steps and into the room, driving open the closed door with one heave of his weighty shoulder. The members of the posse heard one shot fired inside, and then there was silence.

AT LENGTH THE WOUNDED man opened his eyes. After a blank space he again could see and hear and feel and think. Turning his eyes about, he found himself lying on a wooden bench. A tall man with a perplexed countenance, wearing a big badge with

City Marshal engraved upon it, stood over him. A little old woman in black, with a wrinkled face and sparkling black eyes, was holding a wet handkerchief against one of his temples. He was trying to get these facts fixed in his mind and connected with past events, when the old woman began to talk.

"There now, great, big, strong man! That bullet never tetched ye! Jest skeeted along the side of your head and sort of paralyzed ye for a spell. I've heard of sech things afore; cun-cussion is what they names it. Abel Wadkins used to kill squirrels that way—barkin' em, he called it. You jest been barked. sir, and you'll be all right in a little bit. Feel lots better already, don't ye! You just lay still a while longer and let me bathe your head. You don't know me, I reckon, and 'tain't surprisin' that you shouldn't. I come in on that train from Alabama to see my son. Big son, ain't he? Lands! you wouldn't hardly think he'd ever been a baby, would ye? This is my son, sir."

Half turning, the old woman looked up at the standing man, her worn face lighting with a proud and wonderful smile. She reached out one veined and callused hand and took one of her son's. Then smiling cheerily down at the prostrate man, she continued to dip the handkerchief in the waiting-room washbasin and gently apply it to his temple. She had the benevolent garrulity of old age.

"I ain't seen my son before," she continued, "in eight years. One of my nephews, Elkanah Price, he's a conductor on one of them railroads and he got me a pass to come out here. I can stay a whole week on it, and then it'll take me back again. Jest think, now, that little boy of mine has got to be a officer—a city marshal of a whole town! That's somethin' like a constable, ain't it? I never knowed he was a officer; he didn't say nothin' about it in his letters. I reckon he thought his old mother'd be skeered about the danger he was in. But, laws! I never was much of a hand to git skeered. 'Tain't no use. I heard them guns a-shootin' while I was gittin' off them cars, and I see smoke a-comin' out of the depot, but I jest walked right along. Then I see son's face lookin' out through the window. I knowed him at onct. He met me at the door and squeezed me

'most to death. And there you was, sir, a-lyin' there jest like you was dead, and I 'lowed we'd see what might be done to help sot you up."

"I think I'll sit up now," said the concussion patient. "I'm feeling pretty fair by this time."

He sat, somewhat weakly yet, leaning against the wall. He was a rugged man, big-boned and straight. His eyes, steady and keen, seemed to linger upon the face of the man standing so still above him. His look wandered often from the face he studied to the marshal's badge upon the other's breast.

"Yes, yes, you'll be all right," said the old woman, patting his arm, "if you don't get to cuttin' up agin, and havin' folks shootin' at you. Son told me about you, sir, while you was layin' senseless on the floor. Don't you take it as meddlesome fer an old woman with a son as big as you to talk about it. And you mustn't hold no grudge agin' my son for havin' to shoot at ye. A officer has got to take up for the law— it's his duty—and them that acts bad and lives wrong has to suffer. Don't blame my son any, sir —'tain't his fault. He's always been a good boy—good when he was growin' up, and kind and 'bedient and well behaved. Won't you let me advise you, sir, not to do so no more? Be a good man and leave liquor alone and live peaceably and godly. Keep away from bad company and work honest and sleep sweet."

The black-mittened hand of the old pleader gently touched the breast of the man she addressed. Very earnest and candid her old, worn face looked. In her rusty black dress and antique bonnet she sat, near the close of a long life, and epitomized the experience of the world. Still the man to whom she spoke gazed above her head, contemplating the silent son of the old mother.

"What does the marshal say?" he asked. "Does he believe the advice is good? Suppose the marshal speaks up and says if the talk's all right?"

The tall man moved uneasily. He fingered the badge on his breast for a moment, and then he put an arm around the old woman and drew her close to him. She smiled the unchanging mother smile of three-score years, and patted his big brown hand with her crooked, mittened fingers while her son spoke.

"I says this," he said, looking squarely into the eyes of the other man, "that if I was in your place I'd follow it. If I was a drunken, desp'rate character, without shame or hope, I'd follow it. If I was in your place and you was in mine, I'd say, 'Marshal, I'm willin' to swear if you'll give me the chance, I'll quit the racket. I'll drop the tanglefoot and the gun play, and won't play hoss no more. I'll be a good citizen and go to work and quit my foolishness. So help me, God! That's what I'd say to you if you was marshal and I was in your place."

"Hear my son talkin'," said the old woman softly. "Hear him, sir. You promise to be good and he won't do you no harm. Forty-one year ago his heart first beat agin' mine, and it's beat true ever since."

The other man rose to his feet, trying his limbs and stretching his muscles.

"Then," said he, "if you was in my place and said that, and I was marshal, I'd say, 'Go free, and do your best to keep your promise.'"

"Lawsy!" exclaimed the old woman, in a sudden flutter, "ef I didn't clear forget that trunk of mine! I see a man settin' it on the platform jest as I seen son's face in the window, and it went plum out of my head. There's eight jars of homemade quince jam in that trunk that I made myself. I wouldn't have nothin' happen to them jars for a red apple."

Away to the door she trotted, spry and anxious. And then Calliope Catesby spoke out to Buck Patterson:

"I just couldn't help it, Buck. I seen her through the window a-comin' in. She never had heard a word 'bout my tough ways. I didn't have the nerve to let her know I was a worthless cuss bein' hunted down by the community. There you was lyin' where my shot laid you, like you was dead. The idea struck me sudden, and I just took your badge off and fastened it onto myself, and I fastened my reputation onto you. I told her I was the marshal and you was a holy terror. You can take your badge back now, Buck."

With shaking fingers Calliope began to unfasten the disk of metal from his shirt.

"Easy there!" said Buck Patterson. "You keep that badge right where it is, Calliope Catesby. Don't you dare to take it off till the day your mother leaves this town. You'll be city marshal of Quicksand as long as she's here to know it. After I stir around town a bit and put 'em on, I'll guarantee that nobody won't give the thing away to her. And say, you leather-headed, rip-roarin', low-down son of a locoed cyclone, you follow that advice she give me! I'm goin' to take some of it myself, too."

"Buck," said Calliope feelingly, "ef I don't, I hope I may—"

"Shut up," said Buck. "She's a-comin' back."

O. HENRY *(1862–1910), born in Greensboro, North Carolina, was convicted of embezzlement and jailed for three years. Later he won fame and success as a writer of stories known for their surprise endings, including "The Gift of the Magi."*